# JACOB'S DESTINY

## LANCE B WILKINS

This is a work of fiction. The events described here are imaginary: the major characters, the town of Blackham, MA, and certain structures mentioned in the text are fictitious.

Copyright © 2021 Lance B Wilkins
All rights reserved. This book, or parts thereof, may not be reproduced in any form without permission.

Dedicated to:

To Scott for teaching me how to write. I look back at some of that work and know it must have been really painful at times. But you hung in there.


To the young people I have worked with over the years. You don't know it, but my life has been incredibly changed for the better because of my interactions with you, no matter how brief some of those interactions might have been. My grandsons Jacob and Jackson, youth (12 – 18) and young adults (18 – 25ish). In different capacities I have been thrown together with you and have come away a much better person.


My Mom, Jewel Alberta Wilkins, who, had she been allowed to, would have supported me in this endeavor more than any other.

March 1775

Blackham Massachusetts

# Chapter 1

The sharp ringing of iron on iron tells me that Talbott the blacksmith is hard at work. It's late March and a small patch of snow hides in perpetual shade against the north side of the building. Still, the double doors gape open, exposing the interior of the shop. Talbott sweats as he beats a piece of red-hot iron on the monstrous anvil that sits only a couple of steps from the blistering forge.

He stops swinging the hammer and lifts the tongs, bringing the metal, now a dull dissipating orange, closer to his face and scrutinizes it. He must catch a glimpse of me standing in the open door. He turns.

"Sorry, Jacob. Not a lot going on this week."

I keep my face a mask and allow no change of expression.

"I understand, Mr. Talbott. You'll let me know if something changes?"

"You'll be the first to know." He smiles and moves the tongs as though saying goodbye. He turns back to his work, shoving the iron into glowing coals in the forge.

No work. Again.

The Boston Post Road, splits the little village of Blackham, Massachusetts. I barely notice the other shops and buildings as I retrace my steps towards the church. White clapboard siding. A tall white steeple that stabs into a clear blue sky.

The building doubles as the school during the week and Mr. Potts will be waiting. I'm past the normal age for school here, but Mother is committed to me continuing my studies. So am I.

The light snow that lined the road and survived in shady places only a couple of weeks ago is mostly gone now. I skirt the low, muddy area just left of the church where people park wagons and carriages in drier seasons.

At seventeen, I should be starting some kind of profession already. I imagine myself practicing law, an office filled with books. John Adams in Boston - Braintree if you count his family's farm - has already made quite a name for himself.

Politics. That's not really a profession. Teaching. Maybe a professor at Harvard. I bet people listen close when someone that educated speaks.

But who am I kidding? I'm poor Jacob Greyson, living on the family farm with my parents and brother. I do chores every day. I can't even afford to be a student at Harvard. The idea of being a professor is so laughable I wouldn't dare suggest it to anyone.

Stopping for a moment, I adjust the well-worn end of my breeches, just below the knee, so the tops of my stockings are neatly tucked underneath. I scowl at the missing button on the left leg. A tug on my waistcoat and I convince myself I have the appearance of a young scholar that actually has a future.

When I mount the first step at the front of the church, Destiny appears from around the far corner. Her large blue eyes catch mine. Her blonde hair is roughly tied at the back of her head. She's dressed as she normally is in a soft doeskin shirt. Destiny wears doeskin trousers as well.

The opposite end of the social scale from Destiny is the Waterford family, the closest thing to aristocracy in this part of the colony. Mrs. Waterford views Destiny's habit of wearing trousers as positively scandalous. If Mrs. Waterford ever gets her way, Destiny will not be allowed in public. Not in those clothes.

"Hi Destiny," I stutter a little, surprised at running into her like this.

"Hi Jake!" she enthusiastically replies. She smiles and peers into my eyes for a moment.

She has pretty eyes. Not a light blue like the sky is now. A darker hue. Like the sky shortly before the sun gives up and slips below the horizon.

I consider what to say for a second or two then, unable to find the right words, I mount the remaining step and open the door. I let her go in first.

Destiny's an intriguing girl, young woman, actually. Her father was a sailor. Lost at sea as one more casualty of a dangerous profession.

Destiny and her mother came to Blackham. Something about meeting relatives that never materialized. Now they live in abject poverty just outside the village in a log cabin with a dirt floor.

As I follow her inside, I'm trying to guess why she's here. Did I forget something? This is supposed to be *my* time with Mr. Potts.

The door swings silently behind me as I pause. Across the rows of pews, way in the front, Destiny takes a seat at a small table directly across from Potts. My teacher looks up, finds my gaze, and motions me inside.

"I've a bit of a conflict this week and thought the two of you could meet with me together."

I take deliberate steps down the center aisle between the pews. Destiny's nice, interesting even. I just don't want any misunderstanding to develop between us. She's such a frontier kind of person.

I don't look down on her like Mrs. Waterford. Not at all. I'm not sure how more education applies to her life though. She lives off the game she can shoot and she's already better at that than anyone else in the area. Maybe the whole colony.

I slide the empty chair a little farther from her and sit down, feet straddling the table leg. Potts watches me then opens the book in front of him.

"I've had both of you reading material from John Locke, one of England's premier philosophers of the last century…"

I listen. Potts' voice drones on. Questions will come, but I think I know the material.

Destiny, on the other hand, appears to pay strict attention. She seems riveted to the teacher, but that could just be the natural —.

"So Jacob, what do you make of that?"

I draw myself together, bringing my hands to my lap. Potts and Destiny both watch me.

As I sort out my thoughts, the silence in the great building seems to dare me to conjure up an astute answer.

Potts doesn't wait. "Let me read the last line again. 'This is to think that men are so foolish that they take care to avoid what mischiefs may be done them by polecats or foxes, but are content, nay, think it safety, to be devoured by lions.'"

The intent gaze of an expectant lecturer drills into me. Potts stares with an inspired look on his face, the words of John Locke alone enough to send him into intellectual rhapsody.

I've been working on this. Always the conflict is between the ideal and the real. Trying to strike a balance I stumble with weak attempts at an answer.

Men could fail to see the dangers of some— sometimes thinking evil men could be safety— men should be wise and have wise leaders. I'm almost sweating in the chilly air of the unheated chapel.

"Alright. Good thinking, Jacob. Destiny?"

Words flow from her like honey. According to Destiny the passage refers to rulers of absolute authority. Would men wisely create laws to protect them from each other yet leave a ruler without law who could do them far greater harm?

I'm gaping, too shocked to think and close my mouth. I squirm in my seat.

"Excellent Destiny! You have a complete grasp of Locke's treatise!" Potts fairly jumps in his chair.

The girl casts a glance at me but I refuse to meet her gaze. Inside I churn with frustration.

Life is not so simple. Half our family farm is rented from the Waterford's. We don't own enough land to provide for a family. And I have a brother.

So where exactly am I going to find a living in this world if I insist on pretending it's something far different than what it actually is?

It's not that I want things to be that way, it's just that they *are* that way.

Waterford, our landlord, many people's landlord, did not acquire his numerous farms by tearing down existing rules of society. He became successful because of the people he knows for one thing. Knowing the right people, being in the right social circles... Do that and opportunities appear. Passed from one well-intentioned gentleman to another.

Waterford has connections, even stretching across the Atlantic.

The idea of all men being equal is nice, but it's an impossible dream. Those that try to live it are doomed to a low and mean station in life. I'm not so starry-eyed, not so willing to live out my life in near-poverty.

Destiny mutters something softly. I miss the words as Mr. Potts speaks at the same time.

"Maybe. Philosophers are generally not describing the world as it is as much as how it could be better," he says with little enthusiasm.

Wrenching us all from our discussion, Destiny's stomach growls so loudly it echoes through the hall. She grips her middle, face turning a flaming red as she looks at the floor.

It jolts me back to the present world. A world in which Destiny may not have eaten this morning. Maybe hadn't eaten yesterday.

Mother sent a wrapped apple turnover in my book bag. I'm supposed to give it to my teacher. Mother's even more excited about my lessons than Mr. Potts.

Now, suddenly, the food seems mysteriously hidden in there.

Heavy. Secret. Unmentionable.

Potts dismisses us. I glance down the street as Destiny and I exit the building.

"Destiny." I call her just as she begins to turn the opposite way from me.

She looks back at me instantly, hopeful, her face an inquiry.

I reach into my bag, pull out the wrapped pastry and hand it to her.

"My mother asked me to give you this," I lie.

Destiny's eyes brighten and I can almost see her salivate over the food. She doesn't even know what it is since it's still wrapped.

"Thank you, Jake," she exclaims, eyes now lighting to a fiery blue sparkle and her mouth broadening into a grin. "Maybe we'll meet for class next time too."

"Maybe."

Destiny's glances at me communicate again her wish to be more than mere acquaintances. I feel a pang of compassion for her.

It does seem unfair that a mere accident of birth requires she be an outcast, go hungry, and live so poorly.

And what about me? Why wasn't I born a Waterford instead of a Greyson?

# Chapter 2

Destiny watches Jake dash down the Boston Road. Daydreaming, she imagines what it would mean if he were not in such a hurry.

They could talk; walk leisurely through the woods to her house. Maybe he would find out who she really is.

Jake disappears over a swell in the road. She is now safe from any backward glances, however unlikely that may be.

Leaving the church building behind, she runs the fifty yards to the woods. She hides herself inside. The paper covering on the pastry rips easily.

She stares at the apple turnover inside, then devours it greedily.

Crumbs fall through her fingers though she grasps at every morsel. A piece of flaky crust tumbles to the leaves lying wet and musty from surviving winter's assault of rain and snow. She snatches it up.

She pushes it into her mouth, getting her fingers out of the way of her chewing teeth just in time.

Manna from heaven.

Surely the Israelites, who received food from God, never tasted anything as delicious as this.

She should have saved some for her mother, but once she started eating…

From frequent trips to the village, a discernible path leads straight to Destiny's home. Belly filled, she's able to appreciate her surroundings. Despite passing this way three or four times a week, the sights and smells of her forest never grow old.

The canopy overhead waits for a nod from Mother nature to again leaf out under the bright spring sunshine. Destiny takes a deep breath of the damp air and the forest reveals all its secrets. She picks up her pace. Jackson, Jake's brother, will be waiting for her.

She'll make it up to her mother. She won't tell her of the turnover of course, but she and Jackson will shoot something edible and Mother will be thrilled.

The great oak, surely the largest tree in the colony, comes into view. The halfway point.

The tree must be the choicest of home sites for squirrels. Two of them run along branches, then freeze and watch her as she passes.

They're large squirrels and would make fine eating. She almost relented a couple of months ago, she was so hungry. This last winter had been particularly bleak.

But she'd been watching this pair for two years now. Had even watched two of their babies grow up last summer. She would have to be near starvation before she could shoot them as game.

Eating after such a long fast sends a jolt of energy through her. Destiny runs the rest of the distance, bursting into the cabin door.

"Destiny!" Mother calls. "Look what Jackson brought us. Apple turnovers." She smiles broadly, eyes unable to disguise the almost greedy response to the pastries.

Mother is short, like Destiny. Thin too, as anyone would have to be on this family's diet. Her hair, long over her shoulders and nearly to her waist is gray from years and worry and fatigue.

And heartache.

Bent a little in her back, she extends a hand with the turnover.

Jackson sits in one of the two straight back chairs near the fireplace. Coals still glow like malicious varmints staring through a black night.

Destiny hesitantly accepts the pastry from Mother as she peers at Jackson. "Your mother sent one with you too?"

Jackson scrunches his face in confusion as he tries to form an answer to a question he doesn't understand.

"Jake gave me one at class." Destiny throws her hand to her mouth and looks back at her mother.

The truth is out. The guilt floods her so swiftly her eyes sting and she can feel the tears dancing on her lower lids.

"I'm so sorry! I started eating— It was gone before I realized— I just —."

Mother smiles and reaches for Destiny's hand. "I'm glad," is all she says.

Jackson rises, face still a mask of confusion. Another minute of conversation and the mystery is deciphered. Jake's turnover had been meant for Mr. Potts.

For Mr. Potts. Not her.

Destiny breaks from her surroundings for a moment, eyes losing focus. Jake decided to give it to her.

The tutoring at the little table plays out in her mind. The growl of her stomach. Jake knew she was hungry. He gave the food to her despite the fact it should have belonged to another.

One of his better moments for sure. Inside, Destiny smiles. She knows Jake. Knows him better than he knows himself.

Jackson's still speaking and Destiny turns to see his inquisitive expression.

"Let's go hunting," she says.

He grins in response. Destiny makes a promise to bring enough savory ingredients for two or three meals at least.

She glances about the cabin, rock fireplace on one wall, rough wood counter making a kitchen, tree limb legs supporting wood beds fastened into the walls, and the primitive dirt floor.

With all this lack, could they not just have enough food to eat? In her mind, a figure resembling the grim reaper, but in a cloudy, mystical gray, lingers perpetually about the door, watching them.

# Chapter 3

Just before I reach Thornby's apple orchard, I stop running and slow to a more dignified walk. Allowing my breathing to slow, I extend my arms to each side letting my jacket hang open in front. The brisk air cools me. I'm not going to enter my secret meeting with Amelia still sweating from the run

Blackham is out of sight behind me as the road snakes through the countryside. A patchwork of family farms lies on my right. Much of the forest that must have covered this land before it was cleared by early settlers, on my left.

Up a slight grade and around the last curve, and I find my destination. I hop the short piled-rock fence.

Industrious songbirds call to each other incessantly as they organize their work. Somewhere far distant, a farmer shouts at his horses or mules.

I plunge into the middle of the orchard and crane my neck for a better view. Too early for leaves yet, the branches and twigs of the trees are still dense enough to hide the route that brings Amelia Waterford through fields and farms from her back door.

I start to wonder if she's here when a flash of movement catches my eye. Breathlessly Amelia dashes towards me. She doesn't slow, but keeps running until she throws herself into my arms.

I let the soft collision send us both tumbling. Amelia laughs as, lying on my back, I grin at her. Her auburn hair hangs down, reaching my face.

I study her shining eyes, flecked with green, and staring back into mine. Amelia, never shy with me, lowers her head and presses her warm lips to mine. Her eyes are closed.

Once again, I'm left to wonder why. Amelia Waterford, the most beautiful girl for miles, can have her pick of suitors. Not only can she choose one that loves her, she can choose one that will keep her financially wealthy as well.

And that's what will happen eventually. Her mother will see to it.

"I love you, Jacob Greyson." Amelia's eyes reflect her words as her fingers trace a line along my cheek.

"I'm going to Boston," I tell her.

She keeps that radiant smile on her face as she looks at me. As though she breathlessly hangs on my every word.

We both pull ourselves to our feet. We drift aimlessly through the orchard. Sunlight falls through tree branches, speckling Amelia's face with shifting shadows as we walk.

"You're going with William," she guesses.

In a twist of fate that strains credulity, my best friend William is also a Waterford, Amelia's brother. I would never see Amelia without William's help in arranging these clandestine meetings.

I nod. "With any luck, we'll both come back to visit Blackham as British officers."

That's not something I would admit to just anyone. Neither British officers nor soldiers are very popular in the colony right now. That is, unless you are one of those whose fortune is inseparable from the current British ruling classes. Like the Waterford's.

Amelia's arm clings to me around my waist. She stops, presses into my side and places an open hand on my chest. She searches my face.

"I don't care what your profession is. I just want you to be with me." Her words are so tender. I marvel that I mean so much to her.

There's an aching part of me that wants to say, Yes! Let's just go off together and leave the rest of this complicated, dysfunctional world behind. But, I understand things that Amelia doesn't.

"I know you don't care. But, your mother does," I say, trying to bring us back to reality.

Amelia's face loses its glimmer. "My mother," she mutters. She looks darkly at the ground.

Fearing I've shattered the moment, I touch her arm, to calm her.

"It will be alright."

Discord between Amelia and her parents can have disastrous consequences. Becoming closer and more accepted by the Waterford's is the goal.

Amelia looks at me questioningly, as if not understanding how I can say everything is alright.

"It will be better for all of us if your parents accept me."

Amelia kicks at the debris left from last autumn as we walk. She watches her feet.

"Jacob?" she pauses for my assurance that I'm listening. "I would go with you, you know. Anywhere you wanted to go. We could just leave Blackham, as long as I was with you."

A deep stir expands in my chest. Almost. Almost I could do it.

I love it when she expresses these things to me. But I come from a different world. One Amelia doesn't really comprehend. Her mother will never accept me as her daughter's husband unless I'm something more than I am now.

I don't want to seem crass, but an Amelia that's been rejected by her family will open no doors. For either of us.

"Where would we go?" I ask just to humor her.

"Buy a house in Boston!" Amelia's face lights up at the prospect.

"Well— we wouldn't have money to buy a house."

"What if we saved up? You could work on the docks. You hate farming, but maybe you'd like the docks better?"

She stabs a finger playfully into my chest.

"Just don't be a sailor. I don't want you gone from me more than one day at a time." She clutches my arm tighter in an affectionate squeeze.

A dock worker. I make some quick calculations and estimate that a dock worker may never be able to buy a house. At least, not one that Amelia would ever recognize as a real home. I exaggerate a little as I explain the hopeless poverty that ensnares such common laborers.

"I've seen the neighborhoods," Amelia assures me. "I'm willing to make some sacrifices."

She stares off through the trees as if still scheming.

"Could we get a farm in the west?"

Farming? We can eke out a subsistence in a log cabin with a dirt floor? I describe the conditions to Amelia.

"The army is the only way," I assure her. "Besides, I like the idea of being an officer. And there's another thing."

Amelia turns her face up to me expectantly.

"You don't deserve to lose your family. I love you enough to make this happen. I will return in the uniform of a British officer. Surely, that will change your mother's impression of me."

The frustrated look on Amelia's face vanishes as though purposely swept away.

"I'm sure it will." she smiles broadly as she jumps out ahead and stares at me head to foot.

"We'll get you a tailored scarlet coat," she gushes. "White breeches, riding boots you could use as a mirror!"

I laugh.

"And a really fine sword! What are those gold things?" Amelia is touching her shoulders as she wiggles her fingers. "Epaulettes! Gold epaulettes on both shoulders."

I watch her, amused.

"I'll call you Major Greyson!"

Again, I laugh. "My dreams are pretty grand already. Let's not push them into the impossible."

"It's not impossible for you to be a major."

"In time. I hope to be married to you long before then."

Amelia grins broadly, leaps into my arms, and meets my lips with a passionate kiss.

# Chapter 4

Destiny's world turns to a new dimension. She slides through hardwood forest, leaving domesticity behind. One of the animals. A predator.

Instinctively, she creeps to the northwest, towards the rocky higher elevations where game is likely to be on the move.

Clad in soft deerskin moccasins, her feet silently negotiate the refuse of the forest floor. Her breathing slows. Tension leaches from her. She's home.

She and Jackson are silent. Jackson, so different from his brother, wears the same style clothing as Destiny. Deerskin shirt and trousers. Enamored of the few Wampanoag Indians still in the area, and one of their occasional companions, he does it by choice. With Destiny, it's necessity.

Shafts of sunlight pierce through the overhead cover, slanting in now as afternoon progresses. She halts and examines the ground before her. High and low. Side to side.

Every twitch of a twig communicates life, movement.

Jackson's hand steals over her shoulder. His whisper sounds near to her ear.

"Squirrels are out."

Destiny nods. She's seen them. But she hopes for something bigger. Impress her mother. Make the precious apple turnover she selfishly inhaled seem trivial.

She whispers back to Jackson then begins a slow, long stalk through the woods.

The throaty call of a wild turkey cuts the silence as though a knife came slicing through the air from her right. A turkey. It's the male calling. He must have company.

A glance at Jackson and Destiny throws a hand to her mouth to silence her laugh. With wide eyes and a beckoning of his head he urges her in the direction of the calls.

The characteristic gobbling of the bird echoes through the forest and the two friends follow. It fades then strengthens. The bird is moving away from them. The hunter's slow pace makes it difficult to catch up yet, more speed means more noise and that savory meal will disappear.

Destiny feels the twist of her stomach, still hungry after the two pastries.

Tension returns to her muscles. The pursuit. Pursuit always does this to her. As the prey begins to move away, anxiety forces her to press on, demanding she not lose her quarry.

There's another sound, but her ears are attuned to the turkeys. They're getting away, the call of the male now sounding even more distant.

Destiny steps just a bit quicker, rounding trees and thickets, looking for cover in case she suddenly stumbles on the birds.

The other sound again. She brushes it off and skirts the edge of another patch of the forest undergrowth.

A cluster of oak trees grows up ahead past the maples and chestnuts about her now. Acorns left from last fall will still litter the ground beneath them.

A perfect place. The turkeys will surely search the space under the trees carefully, knowing the chances of finding food are high.

Adrenaline mounts. Destiny pauses to check on Jackson.

The noise again. He points.

The sound is of someone scratching or digging off to their left. Destiny stares hard in the direction from which it comes. Nothing.

But, now that she's more attuned to it, it continues, quieter, then louder.

Like a revelation her mind solves the mystery. She looks back at Jackson who, still excited, mouths the word with exaggerated movements, but making no sound.

Bear.

A bear is tearing apart a rotting log finding grubs and eating them. Hibernation is ending. The bear must be starving. Destiny can visualize the chinks of rotten wood flying as the bear scratches the log apart, desperate for food.

Does she dare?

Taking on a bear is no small feat, but one that Destiny is sure she can manage.

There are other reasons. Reasons she hasn't shared with Jackson, and she should.

But it's too late. And it's worth the risk. She and her mother will eat for days. If it isn't already, the apple turnover will surely be forgotten if Destiny returns home with a prize like this.

The two hunters don't share a word.

They know each other's minds perfectly anyway. Their direction shifts. The wind is right. They creep toward the ravenous bear.

He must be close. The sounds reveal him.

Slinking through what cover they can find, Destiny and Jackson close the distance.

Just as she'd pictured. But not for long.

The tree fell over long ago and all but the trunk has been pulverized into forest litter. What remains is riddled with the tunneling of insects.

The bear searches for them. The long claws on his paws rip the rotten wood as if it were paper and the pieces hurtle through the air.

It's an easy shot. He has no idea they're here.

He can't smell them and is too starving to think of anything but the last remaining scraps of food before him. Like Destiny devouring the turnover.

Destiny nods to Jackson. He would love to tell his family of shooting a bear.

At first he shakes his head then capitulates when Destiny insists. Kneeling in the clump of bushes, Jackson levels his musket.

It takes a moment. He draws a deep breath, lines up his shot, and fires.

The implosion of a tuft of hair marks where the bullet hits. Right inside the animals left front leg. It buries itself in the bear's chest. An instantly fatal shot.

Destiny stands, congratulating her friend. Jackson fumbles with his musket as he fiddles with the chore of re-arming the muzzle-loading piece.

The blast of Jackson's gun hushes every animal within earshot. Destiny can even hear the break of twigs as he drops the butt of his musket to the earth to ram home a new load of powder.

A roar shatters the silence.

Destiny snaps her head back toward the bear. It lives.

The animal jumps to its hind legs. Its head turns, searching for its new enemy.

What happened? Destiny saw the bullet hit. It was a fatal shot.

The bear should be dead. It's big, but still—.

She'd been careless. She gave away their position when she stood. That and Jackson's animated re-loading routine make a spectacle that can't be missed.

The bear finds Destiny's stare.

Black glimmering and accusing eyes drill into her. The enraged animal becomes a bundle of fury. Its roar is deep, loud. It chills her.

Destiny's shoulders shake with a terrified shiver.

Shiny black lips peel back revealing long, pointed teeth. Still staring at her, the beast swats at an imaginary Destiny as though practicing. Its claws slice at the air.

Destiny takes a ragged breath. A mad bear. A charging bear.

The animal roars another threat and launches itself.

Jackson gapes and stares at Destiny. He's empty, his gun useless.

On instinct, she raises her weapon. She *has* to shoot the bear. She *has* to put it on the ground. There is no time for error.

Her breath rattles as she draws it into her lungs. Trembling arms fight to steady her musket.

The top of the barrel looks long and straight. The tip of it aligns right into the target. Another deep breath jiggles the gun away from the closing bear.

Even as it charges, it bellows another threatening roar. Curled back lips, expose those razor-like incisors.

Tip of the musket barrel back on target.

Destiny's finger pulls steady on the trigger.

Gunpowder in the pan flashes.

The load in the barrel ignites and throws the weapon into her shoulder.

A blast echoes through the woods.

Staring intently through the smoke, Destiny sees the implosion of animal fur where her bullet hits.

Into its head, almost between the eyes.

The bear drops like a stone.

Destiny has never seen Jackson's eyes so large.

#

"I should tell you." Destiny peers at Jackson as he works vigorously with his knife, preparing the bear for transport. He stops and stares expectantly.

Jackson looks so much like his brother, same light-brown hair, same gray eyes. The deerskin he wears most of the time he made himself, learning from the few Wampanoag Indians that venture around Blackham from time to time.

Destiny loves Jackson as a friend. But she loves Jacob as a man.

"We're not supposed to hunt out here," she says.

Jackson opens his mouth as though to reply, but says nothing. His face contorts in surprise and disbelief.

He glances quickly about them, then returns his stare to Destiny. "Why? Who? That's ridiculous!"

"You know we rent from the great Earl of Ledenberry, right?" Destiny allows some sarcasm into her voice.

Jackson just nods. Destiny spreads her arms wide.

"All this belongs to him. His own hunting preserve."

"But he's in England," Jackson sputters.

Destiny nods. "He might visit."

"We've killed plenty of animals in these woods."

"Squirrels and turkeys. I've never worried about those. I hesitated with the bear, but…"

They both watch each other for a moment.

"You think his agent will find out? What's his name?"

"Jasper." Destiny spits the name with disdain. "No. The bear's too big to carry home but whatever we leave'll be gone in a couple of days."

Jackson stops cutting, but he stares at the bear meat for a few moments. When he speaks, it's quiet.

"How're you supposed to eat, Destiny?" He raises his gaze to catch hers.

She shrugs. "Don't cut any trees. No hunting. No anything. It all belongs to his lordship."

Jackson starts cutting again. "Well, he won't find this bear. If he visits—."

"Comes calling for the rent," Destiny corrects.

"If he comes calling for the rent and sees it in your house, tell him it came from Jacob and me."

Destiny smiles. "Thanks."

Jacob and Jackson.

Jacob.

"Too bad Jake couldn't have joined us."

Jackson continues to cut, talking into the carcass. "Oh, no. He's off with Amelia today. Big plans for a big future—."

Too late. Destiny tries to turn away, but Jackson looks up and catches her. He must see the tears in her eyes, the disappointment on her face. After the turnover, she just—

"I'm sorry Destiny."

She shakes her head and chokes out an attempt at a little laugh, mocking herself.

# Chapter 5

A line of infantry should extend this far. I reverse and try to see the marker I placed at the other end.

It's too dark. No matter how fast I labor, there's never time to work on my own advancement before the sun leaves me. It's true I attend sessions with Mr. Potts. Sneak away for stolen moments with Amelia.

Are those not reasonable diversions? Shouldn't I be able to do those things, complete my work on the farm, and still have time to advance myself?

It's just never enough. Never.

Orange flames from a small fire lick at the cold, night air. Our home sits at the end of a lane about a hundred yards from the post road. There's a packed dirt area where we drive in and out, access the barn another ten yards past the house.

At the edge of that, the fields start, or what will be the fields. We haven't started spring plowing yet.

At the border where the field begins, the dirt's softer from being worked. I can punch the stubs of branches into the ground and they stay upright. The fire flickers towards my fingers as I extend my hands for a moment of warmth. Then I start to pace again.

If the left end of an infantry company's line was here, the other end would extend to…

I pace off the distance and find the stick I had already put into the ground. I had it measured right after all.

So, if this were the line of a company of infantry, they would extend back... two deep right? Yes, I'm sure that's right. That is far too elementary a thing to forget.

Then if that line were given the command to change into a column formation.... I make more calculations and draw patterns in the dirt.

"Jacob?"

Startled I whirl about to face my mother who must have left the house to find me.

"This is really important to you, isn't it?" she asks.

She has to ask?

"I really have to be thinking about a future, don't I? At my age?"

She sighs. "I know, Jacob. I— I wish we could have provided more..."

I shake my head. I know she would do anything to be able to send me to Cambridge to attend Harvard. She doesn't really understand what that means though. I don't know Greek. I can't translate Latin. They'd never let me in even if I had the money. And there's not a prayer that anywhere in this colony I'd find that kind of money. It would take a lifetime of saving.

She stares off across the fields as though searching, but it's too dark to see anything. Whatever she's searching is pictured in her mind, not in the brushy creek bed that lies at the far end of the empty fields in front of us.

"Son. The army—. I, just—."

"What else can I do? It's not your fault, it's not anyone's fault. It's the world we live in."

Her face scrunches into an expression that seems to indicate disagreement, or disappointment, I don't know.

"All the problems will blow over. Besides," I say. "I like the idea of being an army officer. It's an honorable profession and an exciting one too."

She smiles at me and touches my arm. "I have one last apple turnover. If you don't tell your brother, I'll let you have it. Come on inside."

I release the mental preparing of arguments that would defend my decisions. As we walk to the house together, I glance back at my imaginary company of infantry.

This will work. It has to. If it doesn't…

Well, there isn't anything if it doesn't. It has to work.

# Chapter 6

Jackson pauses and looks at me. A quick nod and solemn wave, and my brother disappears into the barn.

I hear the smaller doors at the rear open, the ones that lead out to the pasture. After a moment Jackson leads Lily, the plow horse all harnessed up and ready to work, away towards the back of the meadow.

He must be dragging out the last of those stumps. With me gone, chores will fall more heavily on him.

I continue to watch. Just in case Jackson turns to see me again.

The farm doesn't seem to confine my brother the way it does me. He fairly leaps into the fray when it comes time to harvest corn and other crops.

He grins with boundless enthusiasm at wagonloads of harvested grains. Then escapes to the creek beds in brush-choked gullies for 'fun' after the work is done.

The farm, what part of it we own, should go to him when that time comes.

Another look at the house and nostalgic, hazy emotions try to ensnare me. My mind drifts away into the past.

Mother dishing out fresh biscuits and fried ham on those harvest mornings. Mornings I dreaded. As I look back, I think my negative feelings must have shown even though I tried to hide it.

The table was always laden with my favorite foods on trying days - the ones that drew long and hard. Spring plowing and planting. Fall harvest.

Always desserts. I could count on treats in abundance during those times.

I recall following my brother and father out into fields shrouded with a drifting mist. A mist that rolled by and soon dissipated.

The celebration when the job was through.

Only with great difficulty do I pull my attention away from the past and tell myself to look to the future. The sound of trotting horses draws near.

William Waterford drives the matched gray geldings that the Waterford's prize so highly. The two horses, dappled markings beautifully setting off their color, seem almost in step with each other.

The open-air, two-seat coach has the top pulled back. Black enamel paint gleams on its sides and traces. The spokes are painted red and race in a blur of color as the wheels speed down the drive.

William pulls the horses to a halt. In the back of the coach, a maple-wood trunk carries the baggage he is taking to Boston. I throw my haversack next to it and climb into the seat.

The pair of gray horses breaks into a brisk trot.

"So, you'll be an officer?"

William nods. "I hope so. My father has promised enough to get me commissioned as a lieutenant."

What a system. In order to get commissioned as an officer, you pay.

I think wistfully about the different career path my friend's life seems destined to take. I might not enter the army as an officer at all. I still reach for hope, but where would I get the money?

"Well, let's be sure we're in the same unit. You be my officer and give me a chance to do something really heroic." I force a smile and peer at the road ahead.

Thornby's apple orchard whisks by as the carriage seems to race down the road.

Beautiful Amelia. Beautiful Amelia who is in love with me.

I'll accept being assigned position based on the economic and social station of my family if I must. But I'll prove myself to deserve better. And I'll earn a position that will allow me to marry Amelia in a dignified manner. Even if reluctantly, eventually her family will approve.

Everything in life is subordinate to that.

Conversation with my friend becomes intermittent. The growing divergence in our career paths sits between us on the carriage seat like some noble bastion of aristocracy.

Will the English officers see my capability right off? What if they doubt my ability and are reluctant to take a chance on me?

A couple of hours into the trip, dark lines appear on the horses as they sweat under the straps of the harness. Another couple of hours and William allows them to slow as they pull the carriage up the last long incline before Boston.

On my right the sea stretches off into infinity. Silver sparks all across the expanse as a low sun glints off its uneven surface.

Boston appears. Tightly packed buildings huddle together on a little peninsula that slumbers in the afternoon sun surrounded by water.

Little land masses venture into the ocean, some complete islands, others peninsulas jutting from the mainland. The grass that covers them contrasts with channels of the sea infiltrating the solid earth like fingers.

Tiny toy figures of animals graze on some of them. The sight of the city causes some of my initial excitement to return.

"Stay at my sister Patty's house with me." I stare hopefully at my friend.

William studies the road carefully. He flicks the reins and urges the horses into a faster gait as the road begins a slow descent to the city.

"I— I'd love to. But my father already arranged for me to stay at Traveler's Inn. He thinks I should be entertaining some of the other officers, you know."

He gives a shrug like *what else can I do*.

Only weeks ago had I made the same suggestion, William would have jumped at the opportunity. Now. Now careers and futures are on the line.

The horses clatter down the paved streets of Boston. I point and give instructions. William directs the carriage to the home of my only sister, Patty.

The matched grays pull to a halt in front of a shipper's storefront, a closed storefront.

Silent, I stare at the windows.

They're covered with accumulating dust and grime. The door hasn't been opened in weeks. Leaves and debris are blown against it and left on the walkway, unswept.

Once the door stood open and inviting. The clean windows welcomed the daylight. They illuminated the room, crammed with crates and barrels. Boston merchants brought their goods for my brother-in-law, Meacham, to freight out on the next sailing ship.

The unhappy shop now peers out at a lonely street as though abandoned. I can almost imagine the windows as mournful eyes, weeping.

Of course, the closure of Boston's port has closed Meacham's business. But—.

*Seeing* it. It's like traveling to a family member's home and finding it boarded up.

The home Patty and Meacham live in is in back and a second story to the shop. The door on the side of the building flies open. She must have seen me.

Haversack clutched under one arm, I step out of the carriage just as Patty reaches me and throws her arms about my neck. She hugs me tearfully.

From the embrace, I glance up and give a small wave to William who orders his horses forward.

Patty can barely reach me with her hugs. Her round face always betrays her every emotion. Always sympathetic. She's always loved me.

"You look quite the gentleman," she says, smoothing the lapels of my coat.

"William gave it to me," I admit. "The boots too."

"I guessed as much." Patty looks up into my face with a warm smile.

Inside, Meacham, Patty's husband, pumps my hand and welcomes me with enthusiasm. There's no parlor. The kitchen though is overly large, sitting behind the storefront.

Besides the stove and chests for kitchen goods, a table with several chairs sits near the wall that adjoins the business. One of them chatters across the wood floor as I pull and lower myself into it.

"Jacob," Meacham starts in an upbeat tone. "You should move to Boston. Word is, even though the port is closed, a fair trade can be had by moving freight wagons overland to Philadelphia."

Philadelphia? The roads close every time it rains. I watch him for a moment. He's not kidding.

Patty smiles indulgently at her husband. She sets plates of apple cobbler for each of us.

I compliment her on the treat, which is delicious. Immediately, she begins to question me about my plans. Why am I in Boston?

Drawing a deep breath, I fiddle with my spoon.

The gloomy face of Patty and Meacham's once thriving business can't be erased from my mind. The sad and grimy windows. The door that never opens. A storefront that now stands perpetually empty.

I stumble as I reluctantly make my confession. I want to become a British officer.

Patty stares at me, stunned. Meacham looks blankly at my face.

"Jacob. They've been killing us for years. You want to join that side?"

The hurt on her face. It's almost too much. I stare at the table.

It's one thing to take an opposing view to Mr. Potts. Even somewhat to my parents, Jackson, my friends.

But Patty. Patty has suffered. Really suffered.

She and Meacham are withering, losing everything they worked for. It's like watching the last hope for life being strangled from someone I love.

Inside I implore her to understand.

"I wouldn't be making policy," I lecture. "It's the politicians that do that. This is Parliament's fault, not the army's."

It's true. No British soldier in the colony created this mess.

It still seems a pathetic excuse. But what choice do I have? It's the only army. We belong to England.

Patty thinks for a moment.

"Seems like I remember a very pretty Waterford girl who was somewhat smitten with you."

I shift in my chair. *Only partly*, I insist, is my plan designed to make myself a palatable suitor to Amelia's parents.

Seemingly satisfied, at least for the moment, Patty steers the conversation to the farm and family.

Darkness creeps into Boston. I find the spare room waiting for me upstairs. My one extra set of clothes I place neatly in the chest.

My books. I flip though some of my favorite chapters about the British army.

There are drawings of the battle of Blenheim. Thousands of French Grenadiers cast their weapons into a pile as they march past a triumphant Duke of Marlborough.

The Duke sits proud upon his horse.

I peer about the room. All has an efficient, military appearance.

I repeat my arguments: how I'm not hurting my family, or anyone else - how order will be restored, politicians and hotheads will eventually come together, and everything will go back to the way it was.

And Amanda will become Mrs. Amanda Greyson.

# Chapter 7

Boots. Coat. I place my hat on my head as I exit through Patty's side door.

On the street I thread my way past a smattering of pedestrians. No one I know. I search them as if I could recognize someone like John Adams if I saw him.

No one familiar. Only a few minutes and I circle the last corner.

William stands about a block away. There's no denying it. My friend looks positively elegant in a suit of black velvet. His hand flies into the air, waving to get my attention.

Traveler's Inn is on my left. I just cannot resist. I glance that direction.

British officers, sun blinking from the gold braid and buttons attached to their bright red coats, spill onto the street. Sunlight mirrors off the polished brass and sparkling glass doors of the inn as they swing shut.

Animated conversation passes between the officious men. They laugh at some humorous, shared anecdote - their hair all neatly pulled back and tied or covered with a white wig.

They place their hats on their heads, still jesting with each other. Presumably they enjoyed a leisurely breakfast.

I look at William. A shadow of concern flits across his face.

A look back at the spirited cadre of army leaders.

"Have you had breakfast?" I ask William as he nears.

"Yes," William admits. "You?"

"Couldn't eat a bite," I admit. "Where do we go?"

William beckons and we proceed down Hanover Street. The air smells of sea salt. Everywhere is covered with paved cobblestone ways. So different from the muddy lanes we endure in Blackham.

I shoot glances down some of the side streets where the two-story houses are so close it would give one claustrophobia to venture in. Not the street we walk though. The broad avenue moves boldly up an incline to a higher portion of the city.

I'm reasoning with myself this morning. Trying to overcome the guilt of Patty's life, now made so difficult by our British cousins across the sea.

Who will be the greater blessing to my family? The Jacob that stays on the farm he dislikes? Or the Jacob that is recognized, British officer, married into the Waterford clan? I'm not leaving my family. I'm about to bless their lives far greater than they can imagine.

William leads through several blocks and two turns into other neighborhoods.

"Nervous?"

"Very," William admits. "Surely, battle will be less stressful than this."

We approach a great white, three-story house. Multiple chimneys thrust through the roof far above my head.

Sunlight gleams off the painted walls. Trimmed, green gardens surround the building. With the brilliant white walls as contrast, red-coated soldiers, ramrod straight, muskets held vertically before them, stand on either side of the double doors.

We both stand staring.

I can't get comfortable with my own weight. First leaning on my left foot then shifting to my right. My insides, growing confident only moments before, now fill with a restlessness I can't seem to control.

I clear my throat. "We don't have to do this today."

I can't believe I said that. The rest of my life depends on this interview and here I am, so unnerved by it I'm ready to abandon the entire plan.

"I know. But it will just face us again tomorrow."

Easy for William to say. He'll be walking in to purchase an officer's commission with a fistful of British pound notes. And a recognizable family name.

I kick at the gravel covering the approach to the doors.

My palms are sweaty. How can I avoid shaking hands? Or how will I keep my hands dry? I thrust them into pockets, pressing against the fabric.

William flashes a quick, but brave smile and strides toward the entrance.

We're allowed through the guarded entryway. The latch clicks softly as the perfectly fitting door swings closed behind us.

What a large sitting room. Fine upholstered furniture fills the space. How many people could be seated comfortably in this one room?

An officer stands beside a desk. He possesses the unique ability to peer down at us, even though he stands at eye-level. William communicates why we're here.

The officer, a lieutenant I see, scrutinizes me then orders us to wait as he disappears down a long hall.

Slow, anxious moments pass in silence. The dark wood floors echo the approach of the officer. His boots are so similar to mine, the ones William gave me.

He gestures toward me with an order to wait. William though, is asked to follow.

I glance back and forth between Lieutenant and friend. William gives a little nod and proceeds to follow the British soldier.

Quiet closes in again. I lower slowly into a chair.

The silence grows heavy. I search the room, re-examining the furnishings. I would give anything for a clock, but there is none.

What will they ask William? It doesn't matter. William has all the right answers, the right credentials.

I think ahead to my own interview. What can I say to convince these professional soldiers I have what's necessary to be an officer? I'm educated, well-read. I've studied many volumes regarding history, military formations, and the like.

I own a copy of a British infantry drill manual. I have it memorized and can issue every command.

Rising from my seat, I touch some of the furnishings, the rich fabrics smooth under my fingertips. The mar-free, luminous finish of the wood is glass under my touch.

Everything has been arranged with complete order. I nearly turn an entire circle. I can't find one thing out of place. I return to my seat, then rise and take another tour of the room, then sit again.

The sound of boots tramping up the hall brings me to my feet. I step slightly to the side so that the lieutenant can see my riding boots, so similar to his. I tug on my coat, making sure it shows to best advantage.

I'm a gentleman. Just like William.

My friend appears. The officer though, turns and retreats.

I start to call out then think better of it. What about my meeting? I turn a quizzical look towards William.

"We've got an assignment," William says. He smiles but his eyes don't quite match the rest of his expression. "They've got an all-provincial unit across town. That's where we're posted."

"They— they don't want to talk to me?"

William glances at the floor then to the front entry. He shakes his head. "We're both in the provincial unit, but we need to go directly there."

"You're a lieutenant, aren't you?"

William nods.

"And I'm enlisted into the ranks."

William nods more slowly. "Jacob…" My friend seems to search for words. "We knew that's what would happen." His gaze locks onto the front entrance.

The weight of the disappointment. The finality.

I've been kicked breathless, the wind gone out of me.

The officers in charge don't even want to see me, talk to me. Just, "where's your money? Here's your commission."

I had let that hope flicker. But, no. I'm a Greyson. William is a Waterford.

My face grows hot, my eyes moist.

But I'm not a little boy. I'm not going to cry, or pout, or run home which is what everyone expects to happen.

I'll bear it. Surely, a bright career can still be salvaged. *It has to.* No other door is open to me. If I can't make this work, I'm finished.

"You okay Jacob?"

"Yep. Where's our unit, Lieutenant?" I can't meet the gaze of my friend.

Traffic has waned on the city streets. William would stop for a meal, but I have no money. My friend drops the matter instantly.

Conversation becomes more difficult than I can ever remember. In Mr. Potts' school, we had found each other's interest in marching, shooting, volley fire, line, column…. The list is endless.

All these years.

I had been an officer, William's equal in play.

The play world is gone. Real life now encroaches upon my dreams. It pulls things mercilessly from me. Things I grasped so easily as a little boy.

The docks of the city's east side come into view. The associated warehouses, empty of goods now, line the side of the street. The buildings look so like my sister's place. Tired, starving, abandoned, and left empty.

The wharves reach like fingers into the sea on our left, asleep. No teetering piles of crates and barrels. No flurry of activity wheeling tottering stacks of merchandise down the quay.

No seamen crawling over rigging on ships, yelling indecipherable phrases to the decks below.

William approaches an unpainted building that looks like it needs help to remain standing. Some letters and numbers are scrawled on the front in paint.

"This is it," William declares in a voice filled with false cheeriness.

My friend grasps the handle on a large wooden door. The hinge groans tiredly as it swings.

Inside the dark and gloomy structure, a uniformed guard stops us and asks our business. William hands him a scrolled paper he pulls from his shirt. The soldier opens it and squints in the low light.

"New recruits. Yeah, find yourself a uniform down there." He points to the back corner, encased in darkness. "We ain't got no muskets yet."

William sighs. "Read the entire order soldier."

The boy's face, mottled with the scars of small pox, twists in annoyance. He peers hard at the paper, holding it almost against the tip of his nose.

"Oh. Yes sir." The note flutters to the floor as the soldier bolts to attention and salutes. "Sorry Lieutenant."

"No problem." William's hand flits to his head in a quick response. He looks at me and indicates the back corner of the warehouse.

"Shall we?"

I pause in a moment of indecision, picture Amelia's face in my mind, and stride into the darkness, looking for a uniform.

# Chapter 8

With a gentle push, the door to Patty's home inches open. I tilt my head and peek inside.

There's no avoiding her. She hums some merry tune as she works about the kitchen. Her back is to me. Still, I'll never manage to sneak up the stairs without her hearing.

A low fire smolders in the stove. A lidless kettle bubbles with something savory.

Patty lifts a wooden spoon from the boiling pot and turns to the door.

"I thought I heard something." She smiles, eyes a flurry of unspoken questions.

Discovered, I step the rest of the way into the house. The bundled uniform seems bigger, refusing to be hidden as I clutch it under one arm.

"How did it go?" Still, her eyes don't quite match the questions she asks.

"Fine."

"Is that your uniform?"

I nod.

"Come Jake. Sit with me for a while." Patty drops into a chair and entices me with a sweet muffin she begins to slice.

Resigned, I take a place at the table, exactly where I don't want to be.

"What's wrong?" Patty asks, handing me a portion of the muffin with just a drop of butter on it.

With small gestures I try to communicate nothing is wrong. It's so much of a lie I can't utter the words.

"I'm not an officer," I finally admit.

Patty watches. Quiet. Letting me take all the time needed to tell a story I don't want to tell.

She knows.

Resigned, I swallow and give a brief account of the day.

"They wouldn't even talk to me!" I warm to the subject and emotions begin to flow.

I admit the inequities, the injustice. The humiliation. The rejection. I want to flail out at something, pound the table.

But this is Patty. She has her own problems with the existing powers that control her life. I'm supposed to be defending that system. At least the army.

And yet, how?

"William's a lieutenant," I say. I give up on trying to secret the wad of clothing by my side. I plop it on the table, buckles clattering on the wood top. In all its humility. The vaunted uniform of a British soldier.

"Did William get one of these too?" Patty gestures at the great ball of fabric.

No, I admit. Officer's uniforms are kept in a locked chest. The assistant had carefully selected just the right pieces for William.

"You expected different?"

I feel... so weary.

"I know every bit as much about officering as William, probably more."

"Why did they make William a lieutenant then?" Patty has a ready question each time I answer her last one. Her face though, round, sincere, her eyes piercing me, not with accusations but with empathy.

"He's a Waterford." I shrug again. "And he has money."

"It's an arrogant system, isn't it?"

I nod.

"Then why defend it? Why risk your life in defense of it?" Patty grabs my forearm and clutches it tightly.

It's not just the army, she says. For years Massachusetts has fought the unlawful meddling of Parliament. A legislative body, thousands of miles away, it just assumes it can take control of whatever, whenever. Take over colonial legislatures anytime they wish. Decide this. Decide that. Close Boston's port.

The weight of the arguments presses upon me heavier than ever before.

"It's Amelia, isn't it?"

I start to protest. It's more complicated than that. Complicated and impossible to explain.

"Jake. If she insists you go through this…"

"She doesn't insist I do." I meet me sister's eyes, now defending someone I love. "Amelia would leave with me tonight, marry me and live wherever I want to live. I won't do that to her."

Patty stares at me, eyebrows arched, mouth open. Now she's the one without ready answers.

She composes herself. Her grip on my arm softens. Her other hand reaches over and envelopes mine.

"I have misjudged you. You are a noble young man."

#

Upstairs, I pull the bundle of clothing apart.

I'm not noble. I want Amelia in a proper way, of course. But position. Do I really want that as a way to help others, like my family? Or do I just want it for myself?

It's my own passions that burn within me. I think so, anyway. They pull me from the farm and search relentlessly for a life that will bring me comfort and notoriety.

Even Amelia. I love her terribly. But, while it's painful to admit, I have much to gain from marrying her.

The bundle now in pieces, I lay the parts of the uniform out on the bed. The shoes had been in the middle, surrounded by the other garments.

The belts that cross my chest I set to the side. Those will go on last.

I balance on one foot pulling the breeches over my leg.

Is it wrong to want advancement? To matter? To be among the classes that decide things?

Logically thinking through the alternatives, where would I be without that ambition? Where would the world be if men of ability did not seek for the opportunity to use that ability?

The shirt goes on large and blousy. The waistcoat stretches tightly and I wonder how a soldier can breathe in battle. I fiddle with the bottom buttons, unfastening them.

The problem with my life is that I was born into the wrong family. That's it. As much as I love them, their station in life smothers me. It keeps me from realizing my potential.

I should have been a Waterford.

How do I explain that? *Well, I have no future because of my family so I have to find that future on my own?*

There is no part of that anyone will understand. Every part of me knows it cannot be uttered. No one will comprehend it. The rest of the world will either laugh or condemn.

I'm racked with guilt. Do *I* really believe it? If not, then what?

I pull the bright red coat into place. The uniform adds twenty pounds to my weight. I lift my arms, feeling the heaviness of the wool garment.

It doesn't fit right. The breeches are rumpled from being bound in the tight bundle. The coat is wrinkled and it sags. I don't look at all like the smart officers who exited Traveler's Inn.

I sit on the bed and stare.

# Chapter 9

Early dawn creates a black and white world out my window. It provides a welcome end to a sleepless night.

Making sure Patty and Meacham still slumber, I creep down the stairs in my uniform.

Patty's right. It's an arrogant system. But it's the world we live in.

The walk to the warehouse crosses much of the city. The barracks will be home now. No coming back to sleep in Patty's house. I march out with a quick step.

Birds endlessly circle the city and the bay. They call from overhead, searching for their breakfast. I reach into my haversack and pull out a muffin. Patty had insisted they were for me.

Arriving at the wharves I find the great double doors of the warehouse gaping open, looking at the harbor. Other men in uniform meander about the street. Since they all slept in the barracks last night, it's no wonder they want to escape that dreary place.

The sun drives off the morning mist and opens the landscape about the city. I gaze out at the sea. A magnificent British warship silently rocks against its anchor. Its gun ports are all closed of course, but easily identifiable, each one the promise of withering firepower.

"Form a line!" A sergeant barks.

New recruits mix with the more experienced men.

William stands silently near the front of the barracks. The only officer in sight, his attention seems glued to the sergeant's bellowing commands.

Shafts of sunlight streak through the remnants of the morning's fog. They catch the metallic loops and buttons of William's uniform. Gold decoration flashes whenever William adjusts his stance.

Lieutenant Waterford catches my eye and gives a slight nod. We can't be friends here. We belong to two very different classes.

The sergeant stands back appraising his work. The lines are straight. The men stand at attention. And just in time, as another officer comes riding up on a beautiful gray mare that dances down the street.

The sergeant jumps to attention and gives a rigid salute.

"Men," the sergeant calls. "This here be's Lieutenant Helmsley of the regular British Army."

Lieutenant Helmsley. I examine him and see my future and my goals exhibited in real life. The officer's uniform, the dancing gray mare. Complete confidence. The center of attention.

If I were that officer, the Waterford's would absolutely be impressed. They would see me differently than they do now. I can visualize Amelia running to me, her parents looking on with approval.

Long lines of men salute and the Lieutenant throws a riding crop to his forehead in acknowledgement. He peers at William.

"You the new lieutenant?" Helmsley asks.

"Yes sir."

"Well, get on with it then. I've got other things to do."

The mare dances a circle. Lieutenant Helmsey is a fine horseman. The prancing animal cannot stand still and yet always seems to be under his complete control.

With a clatter of shod hooves on the cobblestone street, the lieutenant and his mount proceed back the way they came.

William salutes again then holds it as he watches the officer ride away. He lowers his hand slowly, turns and stares at me.

He wears an expression of bewilderment. Then, as though awakening, he squares his shoulders and re-creates his officer's face.

"Sergeant, let's drill the men in the street. Marches, change of face, line, column. You get the idea."

"Yes *sir*," the sergeant barks.

We, the enlisted men, march up and down the road, turning this way and that. It could seem monotonous, and there are annoyed expressions on the faces of my fellow soldiers.

But here it is in real life. All the little diagrams, carefully drawn out in ink on paper from the drill manual.

Just as I imagined. I know when to turn, when to stop.

With the exception of missteps by some of the others, the block of soldiers follows the directions the drawings had said they should.

There's a certain satisfaction in that.

The sun approaches midday and a wagon lumbers up the street. Another mounted British officer accompanies it.

The sergeant brings the drills to a halt and orders us all to attention. We stare, hoping the wagon brings our noon meal.

The officer approaches and William salutes first, the new British officer giving a curt reply.

The new man is an Ensign. The lowest rank in the British army.

So, it's true. Any officer in the British regulars outranks any officer in a provincial unit. The insult warms my face.

"Your muskets will arrive this afternoon," the Ensign informs William. "See that they are stored properly. You are responsible for them."

"Yes sir," William replies to the lower ranking officer.

Food is served. I find a way to angle my movements up close to William.

"Even that Ensign outranks you?"

"That's the lay of the land here."

I snort in disgust.

"We're having a bit of a party at our home in Blackham this Saturday. Several men from the army will attend. Of course, so will Amelia. Want to come?"

I examine the thoughtful and loyal look in Williams' eyes and picture Amelia being entertained by a number of elegant British officers.

"You bet I do."

William gives a small smile and winks.

# Chapter 10

After hours of drilling in the street, shadows from the row of warehouses conceal the sun from us. The air turns to mist again as the temperature drops.

William turns and disappears down the street. His home is the Traveler's Inn. Mine is the barracks.

Lines form. Cooks ladle something into tin cups and hand each man a biscuit. I take a sip of the thin gray soup. Lukewarm at best.

The meal, if it can be called that, is eaten quickly as soldiers gather in small groups up and down the way. Darkness closes on us quickly and I follow the others shuffling into the manmade cavern.

Rows of bunks line the walls. A half-dozen smoky lamps cast a dim glow about the interior.

"Why don't we get more light?" I ask no one in particular.

"Cuz then you'd see the vermin in yer bunk," someone answers to the great delight of the other soldiers. Their guffaws echo throughout the hollow space.

I examine my bed, sure now that I can see movement. With a sigh I fall onto the blanket and try to sleep.

But sleep proves elusive. Instead, dreams come roiling through my mind.

A vision opens before me. I stand in a rank of hundreds of red-coated soldiers.

To the left and right march other formations just like the one that encompasses me. A great green field lies before us, forests sprouting from the ground on either side.

Officers shout orders from the backs of their magnificent mounts. At first, I can't find the enemy we're supposedly marching towards. The far end of the field is empty.

It's hard to discern, the view hazy and elusive. But I find them.

Mr. Potts, Jackson, Destiny, Patty. About a dozen of the people I know best, stand in line at the far end of the field. Why are we marching against my friends and family?

Frantically I peer right then left. I try to ask for an explanation, but no one will answer.

It's as though all my fellow soldiers are wooden, unable to act. We're only capable of responding to the orders we're given.

On we march and I again examine the far end of the field. I see Amelia. All alone. She's in the white dress she wore when I saw her in the apple orchard just days ago.

She stands there, watching, waiting. I stumble. I turn to the rank of soldiers behind me, demanding answers.

Why are we marching towards her? Why are we at war with Amelia?

Stoically, the officers command the soldiers to keep going. They must close with the enemy.

I can go no farther.

I'll be on Amelia's side. I can never be against her. I break from the formation. Carrying my musket, I begin to run down the field towards her.

Then the officer on the dancing gray mare raises his pistol, and shoots her.

# Chapter 11

"You two have a good time!" Mrs. Greyson calls.

Destiny and Jackson walk down the lane that leads from the Greyson farm to the Boston Road. Destiny waves an acknowledgement. Jackson does the same.

"This is all yours?" Destiny spreads an arm wide, gazing at the cultivated fields all along the left side of the road.

"Half is rented from the Waterford's."

"Half." Destiny mentally measures how much the Greyson's must own. She gazes across the land as though it were already alive with corn, wheat. So much food. So different from subsisting on what the woods can provide.

Jackson positively beams.

"I'm lucky to get out of more chores. My mother must really want fresh meat for dinner."

"She was trying to be nice to you."

Destiny smiles at Jackson's quizzical expression. The tilted head. The pursed lips.

"No. I told her I'd bring something for dinner."

"She was trying to be nice to you."

Destiny giggles at the doubt that lingers on Jackson's face. Even she knows how much Jackson has been working with Jake away.

The thought transports her momentarily to Boston. She can see Jake marching in his vaunted military formations, all in uniform. Gloating over fancy ribbons and gold buttons.

"How long do you think Jake will be in Boston?" Sobered, Destiny watches the ground in front of her, not wanting Jackson to read the intensity of her expression.

Even from the corner of her eye she can see Jackson scowl.

"Who knows? Maybe forever."

"Oh, surely not—!"

She had done it. Had let out more emotion than she intended.

She risks a glance at Jake's brother. His face is sympathetic, but still annoyed at Jake.

Surely the experience will open Jake's eyes. The one thing Destiny refuses to believe is that he will never come back.

Rounding the last curve in the road before the cutoff, Destiny draws a sharp breath.

A shiny black coach and two matched black horses loaf in shade. The parked carriage sits wedged in that narrow strip of ground between the road and the forest edge.

The slickly varnished wood glistens in the morning sun. The great wheels sit motionless, spokes painted a contrasting yellow.

The horses, twins as far as the human eye can tell, stand still, heads low, gazing at their surroundings. The driver, in full livery, has found a grassy bed under a chestnut tree. He lounges at the base of it, napping.

"Jasper's?" Jackson asks, staring at the coach.

Destiny nods in answer. She scrutinizes the scene.

Jasper— she stops and corrects herself. Mr. Ellingham. It will not do to slip and show a sign of such disrespect as blurting out his first name.

Mr. Ellingham has clearly left the coach. He must have proceeded to the cabin.

He always has a driver bring him this far. Always, a prize bay mare, saddled and ready, trails behind.

Jasper can't walk the last few hundred yards of course, and the coach can't navigate the path, so…

"He's early. He comes about every three months."

"He can't have found the bear," Jackson says with a decided question in his voice.

No. Surely not. "Doubt he ever ventures into the woods." Destiny gazes off at the treetops.

That should be right. But what if…?

It's been several days since she and Jackson killed the bear. They cut up all they could carry. The woods are full of hungry animals. Normally they would relish the gift of a half a bear carcass just lying on the ground, waiting to be consumed.

So…

Destiny breaks into a trot. Jackson follows as they rush towards her home.

Mother can certainly see Mr. Ellingham alone. She usually does. But the world changed when Destiny spotted the coach.

A jolt, as if there were a frame about the world at large. It had instantly shrunk. Minimized to show only her tiny part of it. The shock forcing her back to a reality that didn't venture out past her home and mother.

The two friends lope down the well-trodden trail. Breathing heavy, they reach the clearing.

There's Ellingham's finely groomed mount standing near the door. It jerks its head up and cranes its neck to see the two friends approaching from behind.

The door isn't latched. It swings easily under Destiny's touch.

She tilts her head to peer inside as she enters.

Mother stands across the one room, hands clasped in front of her. Jackson follows Destiny inside.

Mother stops the wringing of her hands as she stares at Destiny. Her eyes fill with questions Destiny can't decipher yet.

Ellingham appears on Destiny's side of the room. He'd been blocked from her view by the door. Now, as it swings shut, he notices her.

He glances at her then turns back to face Mother.

"Well, that's it then," he says as he lifts his hat. It seems a conversation is over. He readies himself to leave.

"But—." Mother's voice has an imploring ring to it.

"What's going on?" Destiny asks.

Mother's gaze turns and she parts her lips as though to speak. No sound comes out though. Like she tries, but doesn't know what to say.

Ellingham watches her, then as though exasperated he has to explain himself, turns to Destiny.

"Your mother's short on the rent. Just as well. His lordship has been considering hiring a caretaker for his lands— a man—." Ellingham emphasizes with upraised hand when Destiny starts to speak.

"A caretaker responsible for a number of things and I will no longer have to drive out here every three months." He looks as though a great burden is being lifted from his overly encumbered shoulders.

The temperature seems to drop in the little cabin. As though time turns back months in one instant.

A caretaker? For what? And where are she and Mother supposed to live?

"You're early," Destiny says softly, unable to look at him directly. "You have to give us two more weeks. We'll have money by then."

She tries to keep the imploring ring from her own voice. Jasper's not one to be moved easily by feelings of compassion.

The look on Mother's face confirms it. Indeed, she will be paid for washing before the rent actually comes due.

"His Lordship is not required to do anything. He wants the cabin."

While she hates Jasper and everything he stands for, it's difficult standing up to him. He's taller than Destiny, much older. He wears fine midnight blue breeches with white stockings. Silk she notices.

His fashionable cutaway coat of the same blue, parts to show a matching waistcoat with gilt buttons. Ruffles spring about his neck from the spotless white shirt.

He looks like a painting of some famous lord that should be hanging in the Governor's hall.

But life is on the line. There's no other place Destiny and her mother can live. Anyone would know that.

Dirt floor cabins just don't exist anymore in Blackham. And the cost of anything finer...

Destiny's mind scrambles. She searches to recall every lesson she can remember from Mr. Potts that might help her.

"Under English law—" she blurts, calling to memory one specific lesson on the rights of tenants.

"My dear, this is not England, it is a subject colony." Ellingham enunciates the words slowly as though Destiny is dim or something. His voice drips with condescension.

Mother fairly droops in despair.

"We know someone in the General Court," Destiny lies. "He can help us."

Ellingham sighs.

"Your colonial legislature is powerless and will soon be dissolved. You pretentious provincials! You are not British citizens, you are colonists!"

Jasper snorts in disgust and stalks out the door.

Mother shakes with small sobs that she labors to conceal. Her eyes try to be in control, but they implore Destiny for a solution. "I don't know where we'll go."

"It's alright. We'll think of something." Destiny paces across the dirt floor, turns and starts back. Jackson still stands near the door watching her.

"How much do you have?" he asks. "If you don't mind—."

"I gave him all we had." Mother wails and Destiny stops in mid-stride and stares at her.

"Jasper has everything? And he's still throwing us out?"

Mother just nods.

"Destiny, I have an idea—"

"Me too." Destiny swoops up two empty flour sacks from a scrap pile next to the wall, and flies out the door.

# Chapter 12

The soil gives way under her toes. Destiny springs into a run almost due east. She dodges trees, branches, and feels the residue of last year's leaves flinging out behind her racing feet.

Shafts of sunlight pierce the treetops here and there. They cause her eyes to adjust wildly from bright light to dense shade as she races.

Sprinting, Jackson pulls even with her. She glances at him, then back to her front to avoid the snag that is sure to send her tumbling.

Ahead, a struggling mass of hobblebush clusters together, forming a dense thicket.

Destiny angles right. Jackson runs left.

As they near the tangled mass, panicked songbirds explode from their hiding places. Frantically they wing their way into the sky above.

Destiny jumps, but keeps her feet. Jackson regains his position beside her, the thicket passed. She can hear his hard breathing even over the pounding blood in her ears.

Their course takes them up a small knoll. Destiny's feet dig in to push her up as well as forward. They crest the rise and begin the descent on the other side.

"What are you doing?" Jackson pants.

"I'm going — to steal the money — back." Her lungs burn inside her chest. Destiny's gasps for air make words almost impossible to form.

## Jacob's Destiny

The declaration startles her. She's going to steal. Break the law. Become a common thief.

The admission pains her. Life has offered Destiny so few options. Her only defense against a world that judges Destiny to be of little value, is to find a new scale. A new way of assessing her own importance.

Character is her answer. She will judge herself not like a Mrs. Waterford or a Jasper Ellingham, but by who she is inside. Each new test of her integrity she greets with enthusiasm. Another opportunity to prove her value to herself, even in a world that measures by a lesser standard.

How will she measure the effect of this on her character?

They reach the bottom of the knoll and begin a long pull up the next incline in the ground.

Destiny's legs won't support her weight anymore. Each step she fears will be her last before collapsing in a helpless heap on the ground.

The race to get ahead of Jasper easily consumes every ounce of physical energy she has. But her mind is still willing and able to work.

Uncontrolled, her thoughts question her wisdom. Is she trading away her measurement of herself to get her mother's rent money back?

No, not rent money.

Jasper is collecting the money then forcing them out. It's stolen money.

Still.

Jackson catches her attention and tries to gasp out his plan.

"I think— —the bridge —." is all he can manage.

Destiny waves a small hand gesture. Jackson seems able to interpret it as agreement.

Shadows still streak by in misshapen clusters. Her eyes strain to adjust and catch the snags. One false step and she will trip and fall down the hill.

Jasper won't be in a hurry. His ride back to the carriage will have been leisurely. The trail is small and requires a rider's attention. Jasper will take his time.

But she needs a good head start. Once he's in the coach, progress will be much swifter. Measure that against Destiny's shortcut through the woods.

She shakes her head. Stop worrying. She's picked her plan. She's doing her best. It will have to be enough.

Water. She hears gurgling. Ahead the stream plunges over rocks in the little washed-out ravine. Destiny rejoices. She's near collapse.

Jackson takes the lead as they near the stream-torn gulch. He bounces down the rocks toward the road. Destiny marvels at the energy he still possesses. She's underestimated him.

Near the road, the two fall into haphazard sitting positions just at the forest's edge. Jackson reaches. With shaky hands, Destiny gives him the flour sacks. With trembling fingers, he whips out his knife and begins cutting the cloth.

"Can you — stop the coach — if I get the money from Jasper?" Destiny still pants as she stumbles over the words. She blows out a long breath and inhales great gasps of air.

Jackson shakes his head. "You stand at the far side of the bridge — gun leveled at 'em. Don't say a word." She catches Jackson's gaze. He's staring at her for emphasis. Commanding.

He's right though. A girl's voice, even with face unseen, is too distinctive.

Of course, Jasper will know who it is. But he has to prove it. Or to catch them. She and Mother might be leaving anyway.

The thought opens the door to a host of questions. Destiny thrusts them away. One step at a time.

For now, she just needs to get the money back. Later she'll worry about what to do next.

Jackson hands her a flour sack with two holes. Destiny limps across the bridge.

Both sides, right and left, look about the same. She chooses right.

She kneels beside the rock abutment that hedges in the way. Lowering herself, she can just see over the top.

Jackson continues to fiddle with his mask. Straightening, he peers at Destiny, measuring their preparations.

Thank heaven for Jackson. A true friend. Without his support, her nerve might not be sufficient.

Icy rivulets of fear begin to force their way into her. Now she's still. The sweat on her body begins to make her cold.

Nothing forces her mind into a decision now. There's only waiting and watching. Her actions seem more preposterous.

Forcibly take the money from Ellingham? At gun point?

It may be deserving but—. Can she really do this?

The rattling of trace chains sounds. Her attention springs back to what's necessary. What needs to be done. Survival.

The musket barrel sticks up too high. Lowering it, Destiny grips the familiar stock, slippery in her sweating hands.

Her left foot slips. It teeters on a slope where the ground falls off from the bridge to the stream below. She pulls it a little closer and huddles on the tiny piece of ground that allows her to hide.

One-handed, she struggles to pull the flour sack over her head. She's blind.

She fidgets, hanging on to her musket with one hand. The other pulls and tugs at the supposed disguise.

Jackson cut the holes too far apart. Twisting her head against the direction her hand pulls, she manages to arrange it. One eye matches one eyehole. It will have to suffice.

Again, the enormity of what she's about to do tries to flood her thoughts. She shoves caution and warning away.

The coach rounds the curve.

It comes right towards the bridge.

It nears the far side and Destiny springs from cover.

She levels her musket directly at the driver. The hammer pulls back with a distinctive metallic snap.

The driver's jaw drops nearly to his chest. His eyes grow so large Destiny can see the whites all around the dark centers. He leans far back and pulls the reins in an exaggerated pose.

Inside she can hear Jasper yell out in exasperation and chastise the driver.

Until he sees Jackson.

Jackson leaps from cover just as the coach slows. His musket under one arm, he seizes the door of the coach and yanks it open.

Destiny shivers.

The sack over his head. The musket in hand. Accosting the coach's passenger.

Jackson appears every bit the roadside thief.

She must look the same.

A desperate desire to move and look behind her seizes Destiny. Search the adjoining fields. Inspect every place potential witnesses might have become spectators.

But if she moves, the flour sack over her head will shift and she'll be blind. Exposed to the world, she stands, watching her friend rob a traveler on the post road.

Jackson's voice doesn't carry as his head is inside the coach and the coach is on the far side of the bridge. But he emerges after only seconds.

He holds up his hand for Destiny to see the paper notes Mother must have given Jasper. All the money they had. Every penny earned by Mother scrubbing her fingers raw on a washboard, trying to clean other people's clothes.

Jackson waves. Destiny watches.

"Go on!" he yells.

The driver glances at him and then back at Destiny, bewildered. She still blocks his path.

The eyeholes in Jackson's flour sack stare at her. Destiny pulls the pieces of her fractured thinking back together, lowers her musket, and steps to the side of the road.

The driver slaps the long reins and shouts at the horses. The team throws up their heads and bolts towards Boston.

It's done.

Destiny has robbed Jasper Ellingham and Lord Ledenberry.

# Chapter 13

I tilt my head as though somehow; this will help me hear better. It's definitely music.

The lane leading to the Waterford home seems to shrink at a ridiculous rate. I tighten the reins and slow Spencer, our family's one saddle horse.

William dropped me at home last night. I bathed and combed and cleaned this morning. All in preparation for the great Waterford party.

When I pulled on my 'British reds', an emotional knife seared through my chest. Mother had washed, dried, and pressed the ill-fitting, enlisted man's uniform. Every ounce of elegance possible had been brought to the surface of it.

The concern on her face when she looked at me was so eloquent, I almost teared up. She said nothing. Why is everyone so sure I'm on a fool's errand?

The lane sweeps into an expanse overlaid with gravel to keep the dust down. Several horses stand, heads lowered, tails swishing. They're tied to a long rail across from the home's front entryway. A few carriages clutter the far end of the open space.

Coming from inside, the music is muffled by the tall white house with elegant windows. Framed by still leafless maple and chestnut trees, the towering edifice scowls at me.

Spencer skips sideways as one of the other horses swings its head to take an annoyed nip at him. I tie him several feet from the irritable animal. Extra tugs on the knot make sure it's secure.

Imagine coming out after the party and finding Spencer gone. Admitting to everyone it appears my horse has gotten loose and run away.

A few steps and I pause to search the front of the house. The gardens. The drive. Even the windows to the inside.

I'm alone.

Grasping the lapels, I pull my coat tighter over my shoulders. Bending down I tug on the breeches. How much of the crisp uniform look that Mother found still remains?

The clearing of a throat startles me and I spring upright. An African man appears from the front door.

The man is dressed in breeches and stockings, a white shirt with a dark blue coat. I stare. I've heard that African servants are prevalent in the southern colonies, but I've never seen one. Certainly not in Massachusetts.

The man bows slightly from the waist. "Party be this way, sir." He indicates the interior of the Waterford's home.

With a deep breath, I approach him and hold out a hand. "Jacob Greyson."

The man hesitates then extends a hand of his own. His teeth shine in bright contrast to the rest of his face. "My name Lucas, Mistah Jacob."

"I haven't seen you at the Waterford's before."

"Just hired for the day, sir."

The blood leaves my face and I feel chilled. Hired servants, music. What else awaits me inside the house? I can only imagine.

I glance back at Spencer. Amelia's at the party though. Inside along with… who else?

Lucas watches me closely. He extends an arm, again indicating the way I should go. Straightening my shoulders, I step inside to a great foyer area. I've never been inside the Waterford home before.

The shine on the wood floors is such I can nearly see my reflection. A great stairway leads to upper levels.

Lucas points me towards a room filled with many voices. The jumbled conversations become louder. I tug on my red coat and stand in the open doorway.

No one notices me. An expanse of tables, draped in white cloth, sit in the center of a long room that seems larger than my family's entire home.

Perfectly spaced chairs are placed on each side. Enough to accommodate the twenty-five or so people that congregate in small groups scattered about what might be a ballroom.

All involved in their light and airy conversations. All oblivious to the intruder, me.

Wedged into one corner, three musicians play a cello and two violins. They sit in a small cluster of chairs, instruments, and music stands. The notes waft over the gathering as though this were a great party filled with lords and barons.

Red uniforms, at least four or five, glitter. Most of them cluster in a single group. Amelia's laugh emanates from within it.

I gaze from one side to the other. Still unable to take the spectacle in, I reverse, staring at musicians, linens, china… and impeccable English nobility in army uniform.

What is expected of me?

Another servant glides by, a tray of stemmed glasses deftly balanced on his hand. He pauses here and there, offering refreshment and carrying away used goblets.

Is there any chance I can manage this without looking like a fool?

There's Amelia's laugh again. My face warms as it seems she is the only girl in that cluster of red coats and gold lace.

It could appear she's flirting with them. I'm outclassed. I should leave, but I'm not going to.

From the corner of my eye someone walks my direction and I know I've been seen.

Mr. and Mrs. Waterford. I smile. Should I give a little bow? Respect for the hosts?

Mrs. Waterford's expression is filled with alarm. Mr. Waterford, not extending a hand, starts a serious explanation.

"William is occupied, as you can see, Jacob. Can he schedule a visit with you some other time?"

What? I try to stammer out some kind of response, staring at Mr. Waterford trying to understand his meaning.

They didn't expect me. They didn't invite me. I have to go.

I glance back at the merriment in the room. I hear Amelia's laughter.

"Um, sorry, I-."

"Jacob!" William's familiar voice calls as he appears through another door. He strides quickly to the awkward meeting.

William throws a reassuring arm around my shoulders. "We're in the same unit," he says directing his gaze to his parents. "I told you that, right? Party wouldn't be complete without the best soldier in the company here."

Mrs. Waterford stares at the floor, then William, then over her shoulder at the party. Her face draws into tense lines and a mouth that flares sharply down at the corners. She's a trapped animal desperately seeking escape.

Mr. Waterford makes a noise in his throat. "Alright, William. I suppose you should introduce Jacob to the other guests."

The older Waterford's, somehow diminished in size, melt away into the social gathering.

William pulling me along, I meet the other guests. So many names. It's impossible to remember them all.

A reverend and his wife from Boston.

The man nods his head as I give a short bow. All this protocol. I have no idea. He seems mollified and his wife makes a small curtsy.

One mayor. Then two. By the time I've met the third mayor I'm almost giddy that they're all out of earshot of each other and don't realize I say the same thing to each of them.

"Where are you from?" Mayor Smythe asks.

"Just two or three farms over, sir."

He's looking over my uniform and losing interest already.

William introduces me to a couple of merchants who have little time for me. They are discussing important matters with each other. Are exports up or down so far this year.

William seems to be saving the officers for last. Amelia however, spots me as I finish acknowledging my introduction to some important man who owns three ships.

"Jacob!" she calls and immediately leaves the cluster of red-coated officers and hurries to me.

She lays a hand on my arm. Her twinkling gaze studies my eyes. Amelia's auburn hair hangs in ringlets just past her shoulders. She wears a pale green dress that flares from the waist, one I've never seen before, decorated with white lace and collar.

A small bell rings and Amelia sings out, "Time for dinner." She keeps my arm. Full of gaiety and excitement she encourages the retinue of officers to follow.

Other guests, goblets in hand and still conversing, make their way to the chairs.

"Sit by me," Amelia suggests.

I hold her chair and chastise myself for not memorizing more stringently the things Mother has tried to teach me about proper etiquette.

Amelia settles into her seat, the red-coated officers collecting directly across from her. She smiles at them. They smile at her.

The table fills as guests find their places. An abundance of shining dishes and utensils glitter across the surface.

I breathe a sigh of relief as William claims the empty chair beside me. It seems I'm anchored on either side by allies.

Keeping my eyes low, I take furtive glances about the table.

Amelia and William sit and chat with ease on either side of me. I watch them.

Dinner was announced before I met any of the British officers. William begins introductions. A Major Harrison sits directly opposite.

What should I do? Stand up? Salute an officer while seated?

No, that doesn't seem right. But neither does forgetting all the formal signals acknowledging ranking superiors just because I'm at the Waterford's house.

Better too formal than not formal enough.

I start to stand. William turns his head quickly to stare at me. He smiles and places a hand on my shoulder. I nod to the major.

Lieutenant Helmsley on the Major's left.

"Yes sir. You are our officer, correct?" Helmsley's the one that rode the spirited gray mare.

"Am I?"

"Jacob is in my unit, sir," William explains.

"The provincial unit. Yes. Well, for now I suppose I have a supervisory role, don't I Major?"

"You do indeed, Silas," Major Harrison affirms.

"Well, then..." Helmsley gives a slight wave of the hand as he glances absently at the end of the table.

Introductions to other officers follow. I struggle to remember the names.

A combination of light from the windows and from candles glints off the gleaming silver butter knives. Guests use them to dip into bowls placed at intervals in front of them. They spread the mixture on slices of warm bread displayed in baskets.

Such a knife lies on the table before me, along with other utensils. I glance up and down the rows, sneaking surreptitious glimpses of the other guests.

I decide to rest my hands in my lap.

Lucas, who had met me at the front of the house fusses over the tables. The servant who had busied himself serving sherry works with him.

Slowly they proceed down the row of guests. The other servant, the one whose name I don't know, carries a large silver tray. Lucas either serves or offers the delectable dishes balanced on it.

It appears they won't reach me for a moment or two. My plate. Two forks. Two spoons.

Sidelong glances to other place settings reveal the same arrangement. Amelia chats gaily on my left. What should I do with the extra eating utensils?

Something touches my shoulder and I jump to find Lucas' elbow has bumped my arm. He stares at me.

"Perhaps you would like to serve the young lady, Mistah Jacob."

I grab the serving utensils and proceed to offer helpings to Amelia. A small snort sounds from across the table. Lucas turns his head that direction.

"I don't believe it was clear who escorted Miss Amelia," he says in that smooth and gracious voice of his. Helmsley just watches.

I curse Lieutenant Helmsley under my breath. At the same time, I'm crushed by the weight of the moment. Jacob Greyson is in a place he has no business being.

Most of the people don't want me here. William and Amelia, though my friends, have not yet realized how helpless I am.

"Lieutenant Waterford." Helmsley sits directly across. "You invited the entire company? Or, is it Colonial custom to invite a representative from each societal class to participate in social gatherings?"

A hot retort forms in my head.

"Jacob— Jacob's been my friend for years." William replies, his expression uncertain as though he too is beginning to navigate unknown waters.

"Mine too," Amelia adds. "Smartest student Mr. Potts ever taught."

She turns and gives me a naive smile.

"Mr. Potts?"

"The school teacher."

"You have a school?" Helmsley asks innocently with raised eyebrows. "How nice."

Major Harrison clears his throat and shoots a glance at Helmsley. "So, Jacob. You serve in the same company as Lieutenant Waterford. How do you like it?"

"I'm learning a lot, sir."

"Good."

All the guests have been served. Now what?

Amelia picks up the fork farthest from her plate. Watching her, I do the same. Lieutenant Helmsley smirks and proceeds to take a bite of his food.

Pangs of jealously threaten to overflow my ability to contain them as Helmsley's attention focuses on Amelia. She's beautiful. Charming. Entertaining. A great conversationalist.

She would make a perfect addition to the London scene, freeing her from this provincial society.

I bristle.

Amelia thanks Helmsley for his compliments. She doesn't think she could ever leave Massachusetts.

Servants clear the used plates and guests break off into their own groups again.

The ballroom fairly glows with gold decorations and crimson, tailor-made uniforms. I tug, smooth, pull, and desperately try to appear as though I belong in the same army.

The light and practiced banter all but excludes me. Amelia's ease with the officers could almost seem like flirting, but she holds me close and never lets go.

Guests begin to drift away and the party to wind down. The British officers are returning to Boston tonight. It will cause them to travel much of the way in the dark. But where would they lodge in Blackham?

Helmsley will stay at the one tavern in the village. I allow a satisfied smile to myself. That will make the arrogant snob angry. He's only a lieutenant. Senior officers still command him. He will lead a group of soldiers transporting something back in the morning.

I say my goodbyes to William and Amelia. With a mischievous twinkle, Amelia bends close to my ear.

"Meet me in Thornby's tomorrow!" She squeezes my hand.

Lieutenant Helmsley brushes by me on the way to the front door of the house. William is with him.

"If you'll look in the regulations, you'll find officers and enlisted men do not attend the same gatherings on equal footing. It's absurd." Helmsley glances at me and continues on his way.

William protests weakly that this was not a military function, but a private celebration.

The voices trail off as the two cross the cavernous foyer and step through the open doorway. The Lieutenant waves William off and bolts from the house leaving my friend standing in the front portico.

# Chapter 14

I stand at the front window of my home, watching. The rest of my family clambers into the farm wagon and lumbers awkwardly down the lane to the Boston Road.

Mother glances back at the last minute and catches me looking through the glass. She's disappointed. Her efforts to change my mind were half-hearted though. She understands.

I could go to church without wearing my uniform. It won't matter. Certainly, word has spread that I am now one of the King's Men. Maybe the whole colony knows.

I'm not really. I'm in a provincial unit, not one of the regulars. My friends and neighbors in Blackham will be unable to distinguish or understand the difference. I wonder how many friends I have left.

I slip my plate into the bucket of water still sitting in the kitchen. I pick up a scrap of bread and nibble on it.

Oh, make yourself useful, I think. I wash and dry the few dishes left from s hurried breakfast and throw the used water out the back door.

The house is so silent. Stepping out to the front room I feel lost and uncomfortable in my own home.

My choices. I hover between regret and irritation.

The villagers won't understand the difference between a provincial soldier and one of the King's men because they don't have to. To them, there is no difference. Regulars or provincials both symbolize the same things. They represent the same power.

I inspect the sitting room, low flames still flickering in the stone fireplace.

Simple wooden furnishings. Table. Chairs. No tablecloth. No glass dishes. No multiple forks, spoons, knives.

No butter dishes.

The stone fireplace is impressive. But my father built that with his own hands. Mother says it took weeks.

It's the British that so distinguish the differences. More scales on the social ladder. Provincials belong on a rung well below anyone from Britain.

And within the ranks of regulars, the Irish rank below the English-born. The officers from families with titles rank above enlisted men from places like London's east end, and on and on.

And I'm voluntarily part of it.

What can be done? I didn't create this world. There seems little choice but to make the best of it.

I shake off the muddle of questions, ambiguities, and contradictions. This afternoon I'm meeting Amelia in Thornby's apple orchard.

#

The trees nestle closely together, the thick trunks attesting they've been here for years. Leafless branches reach for the sky.

Here and there, new grass recognizes the change of season. It pushes through the residue of a too long dormant season, ready for a new start, a new battle with nature. I pause long enough to assure myself the buds on the trees are not swollen. It's a little early for the apples.

Soon though, the orchard will be green with white and pink blossoms that will perfectly complement Amelia's beauty. I look forward to those future visits.

One hand on the top of the stacked rock wall, I easily leap over it.

The branches of the trees, though bare, are thick enough to prevent seeing much more than a few rows. I start to search when Amelia appears.

As she steps into the open, the sun falls on her. Amelia's face, even from several steps away glows with the warmth of it.

The yellow light beams from behind her and flames through her auburn tresses like a halo. The independent strands of hair that refuse to stay with the rest, sparkle radiantly in the light.

Her face had been serious when she first stepped into the open. Now it breaks into a smile more eloquent than any sonnet. It invites, celebrates, loves.

I run to her.

We embrace. Face buried in her soft shining hair; I whisper how glad I am to see her. To see her without the competition of the tailored and suave British officers.

Amelia laughs. She grabs me and forces her mouth to my ear.

"They are no competition for you," she whispers.

I grip her hand and feel the intensity of her fingers meshed with mine.

"Is William in trouble for letting me come to the party?"

Amelia looks at me in surprise. "Should he be?"

I think back to the frosty reception of the older Waterford's.

"Well, I think it was a bit of a surprise to your parents."

Amelia shrugs.

There's a weed that grows a dry boll at the top the color of a persimmon. The dried stalk has lasted all winter. I snap off the attractive little seedpod and twist into Amelia's hair behind her ear. Her hands rest on my sides, under my unbuttoned waistcoat.

"So how is your adventure in the army?"

I pause looking for an answer. I can't lie to her.

"It's— it's slow," I say. "Becoming an officer…" I peek at Amelia's expression. "Well, it won't be overnight."

Amelia frowns. "How long will it be?"

Yes. How long will it be?

I watch my feet. What can I tell her? Six months? A year?

And why will she think my progress is so slow? She still can't grasp the difference between her station in life and mine. Will she think I'm the problem? That I'm not capable of becoming an officer?

"I— I don't know."

Amelia throws her arms around me, burying her face into my chest. "We could still go away. Just the two of us."

I hug her about the shoulders. I kiss the top of her head; all I can reach in this position. My heart thrills at the thought of marrying Amelia now, today even.

I let my mind linger there for a moment. Almost, I can cast aside all worries about tomorrow. But dark clouds shroud such rash action.

Where would we stay? How would we live?

And what would life be like in a year? Five years? Ten years?

"Don't worry. I will work this out. For you, I can accomplish anything."

Amelia looks up at me, a weak smile on her face.

"My parents are trying to find me a husband, Jacob. I don't know how long I can put them off."

There it is. That time has come. I don't have six months. A year.

I search for the right answer but I don't have it. I try to conjure up something to stay what feels like a death sentence long enough for me to find a miracle.

A wagon clatters down the road. The steady beat of a half-dozen marching men accompanies it. I edge closer to the sounds. The red coats of a small army detachment are impossible to miss.

Still gripping Amelia's hand, I bend to peer closer. As I do, I hear someone speak in slurred tones, interrupting.

I spin in the direction of the voice. An officer steps into the open.

He's not wearing his coat, no wonder I hadn't seen him through the thick trees. His hands are occupied fastening his breeches. How embarrassing. The man just relieved himself. Lieutenant Helmsley.

"What would you two be doing out here, wandering about?"

Helmsley stumbles, almost falling. He continues to button his breeches.

"Not wandering, sir. Just a bit of a walk."

"Enjoyed the party, did you?"

"Yes sir."

Helmsley finishes his fastening. Leaning a little to one side he examines us as though he labors to assemble the pieces of a puzzle.

"I see," he says staring at Amelia. "Your mother sees you with someone other than a Blackham farm boy."

Amelia inhales sharply.

"He's not a Blackham farm boy. He's going to be a British officer."

Helmsley chuckles. "Look at him," he says, gesturing with one arm. "He's an enlisted man. No matter."

He turns to me. "You are a colonial, boy. You'll never get far in the regulars. Provincials are not the same as authentic English gentlemen."

I twist in discomfort. Never?

"No offense lad. But, that's the lay of the land, you know." Helmsley tips to one side then regains his balance by reaching out and grabbing the limb of an apple tree.

Amelia becomes flustered. She glances back and forth between me and Helmsley. She seems to want to say something but doesn't speak.

An awkward silence breaks when she announces, "I need to get home."

"Is he going to take you?" Helmsley asks.

"No," Amelia admits, unable to keep the guilt from her voice. Here we are, appearing as two young lovers desperately trying to keep our relationship from being discovered.

I guess that's what we are.

"I can certainly find my way," she instructs the officer.

"I'll take you," the Lieutenant volunteers. He returns his gaze to me. "You had better head off wherever you're going if you want this secret kept."

He smiles slyly. "You skedaddle. I'll get Miss Amelia home and you'll both be undiscovered."

I sort through my options.

I want the secret kept. I certainly can't walk Amelia home myself. As insulting an admission as that is, it's true.

Obnoxious as he may be, Helmsley is an officer. An English gentleman. At least she'll be safe.

Here I am with the beautiful young woman of my dreams. I can't even walk her home. Even for that I have to defer to a real British officer.

I curse my family's social standing. I grit my teeth.

"Give my best to William." I peer into Amelia's eyes. I squeeze her hand, turn, and head cross-country toward home.

Behind me, the officer calls something to a sergeant out on the road.

The anger courses through every vein. I can't even walk Amelia home. Can't look out for her. Can't protect her.

Can't marry her.

What if the Lieutenant is right about being a colonial? What if I can never become a British officer?

There has to be a way. I need to find it. I need to find it now.

# Chapter 15

Destiny sits near the back door as Minister Sones wraps up his sermon with a stern denunciation of sin. The congregation has been warned for another week.

She jumps to her feet and hunches over. Silly as it is, it makes her feel less conspicuous.

She has no dress for Sunday. She has no dress for any occasion. The doeskin trousers and shirt she wears are her only clothes.

Before the meeting comes to a complete end, just before people rise to converse and shake hands, Destiny slips through the narrow doorway. Meeting Mrs. Waterford *inside* the church promises to be an embarrassing scene.

The fact that Destiny has no clothes other than these she now wears will not mollify Mrs. Waterford's shock and disapproval.

Any moment the crowd of villagers will emerge. All will be chatting about whether or not the weather is too dry. Or whose kitchen garden flourished most last year.

Is it just the clothes that evoke such stern disapproval in Mrs. Waterford? Or does she just disapprove of Destiny as a person? Maybe she just can't stand the company of the town's only girl hunter.

Today's sermon continues to flow through her thoughts. Can she hope to be one of the fortunate? The foreordained that will find happiness and joy after mortality? Or is she just fooling herself with wishful thinking?

"Hey Destiny!"

Jackson comes bounding down the front steps of the church.

Just what she needs. A happy diversion.

Managing a small smile, Destiny lets the doubts about eternal things slide from her shoulders. Those are things she can't control. Fears enough exist right here and now.

"I'm worried," Destiny says as she peers solemnly into Jackson's now sobering face. "Mr. Potts is substituting for the magistrate. He says he wants to talk to me tomorrow."

Jackson stares at her, speechless for a moment. Then he begins to reason.

"He'll only want your story. Nothing more."

"Nothing more right now. Won't he believe Jasper and think I should be tried?"

"We," Jackson corrects.

Destiny looks away.

Sweet Jackson. One word. One word to assure Destiny that he will not let her bear this alone. He will share the responsibility.

"We could go to prison, you know. They could put us …. It wouldn't fair to you Jackson. I wouldn't expect—."

"Destiny," Jackson's voice takes on an air of convincing exasperation as he breaks in. "What can Jasper say? He took the money and then was throwing you out anyway?"

"He can leave out the part about throwing us out."

"Good. Then you have a home still. Let him prove who robbed him on the post road." Jackson drops his voice sharply as he realizes his lapse in speaking too openly about criminal things. Both friends peer about them searching for eavesdroppers.

"We can pay the rent now…"

"Then what can Jasper say?" Jackson whispers.

"Jackson. He's Jasper Ellingham representing Lord Ledenberry. That's all he needs." Destiny searches her surroundings again.

Jackson shakes his head. He doesn't think so.

He doesn't think the colony will take a very sympathetic view of Jasper's credentials. Massachusetts has never been as impressed with English nobles as some places and it's even less so now.

Colonists dumped the tea in the harbor after all.

Church meeting over, villagers begin to mount horses and climb into wagons. Time to return home. Gather with the family over a sumptuous Sunday dinner.

"I heard people are sending food to the city since the port closed."

Jackson nods agreement.

"And lobsterbacks are quartering some of the soldiers in people's homes. There's no sympathy for 'em anymore," he assures her.

But it doesn't feel all that reassuring.

"There's still the Royal Judge in Boston. What if Jasper gets me into the city?"

Jackson watches her, expression still doubtful. "Let's see what Potts says. Then we'll know what to do."

Jackson's probably right for the moment. He's sometimes too optimistic about things. She'll have to think about this carefully.

"Hello Destiny." Mrs. Greyson greets her with a great smile and sparkling eyes. She reaches out and touches Destiny on the arm. "Your mother didn't make it?"

"No." Destiny shakes her head. Mother never makes it to meetings, but Mrs. Greyson always asks as though Mother comes every week.

Mother can't take the rejection of people like the Waterford's. She can't be blamed too harshly for that. It's the washing Mother does for those same people that keeps a roof over Destiny's head.

"Come. Have Sunday dinner with us. There's room for you in the wagon."

People don't ask Destiny to Sunday dinner. Mrs. Greyson is being her usual kind self.

Destiny starts a polite refusal without really considering it. But then, Jake's home for two more days. He'll be at home now.

Poor Jake. The colonists who oppose Parliament, patriots they call themselves, feel he's a traitor.

People like the Waterford's, the very people he so longs to emulate, will never be impressed with anything he does. Their idea of greatness is of titles, families with long and storied genealogies, and connections with persons of aristocratic position.

In a moment of bravery, she gazes up into Jake's mother's eyes.

"Thank you, Mrs. Greyson. I'd love to."

# Chapter 16

Destiny sits in the jolting wagon bed, back leaning into one of the sides. Jackson sits across from her as the older Greysons share the seat, Mr. Greyson driving the team.

There's no denying it. Destiny's in trouble. Mr. Potts was deadly serious when he scheduled this 'special interview' with her.

There's only one reason the acting magistrate would want to see her. Jasper has accused her of robbing him on the Boston Post Road. And she did.

Maybe it's already been decided. Maybe she'll show for the meeting, they'll bind her hands and feet and put her in a coach for Boston.

The wagon trundles past the trail to her cabin. She glances. Jackson, sitting on the other side of the wagon box, catches her eye. Without sound but with great exaggerated movements of his mouth, he communicates. "Don't worry."

She smiles at his antics. Jackson won't have power to release her though if she's sent to prison.

Desperately needing a diversion, Destiny looks forward to what awaits her at Jake's house. Will he be glad to see her? Or annoyed?

Even annoyed would be something. He's usually so reserved, as though she wasn't even in his presence. He avoids her.

The wagon turns down the lane to the farm. Within moments Mr. Greyson gives a shout, bringing the horses to a halt.

Jackson leaps from the wagon bed in one athletic swoop. Clambering down herself, Destiny stares at Mrs. Greyson in surprise as she reprimands her son.

"Jackson Greyson! You should assist a lady climbing down from a wagon or carriage, not just leap out by yourself."

A lady? Destiny considers her deer skin clothing. Her face warms at Mrs. Greyson's description of her.

Jackson scuffs the dirt with his toe. "Sorry. I just think of Destiny as a hunting buddy."

The air lightens as Jackson's mother smiles. "She can be a hunting buddy and still be entitled to proper manners."

Jackson is still puzzled. His head tilts to one side, eyebrows arched, mouth drawn together.

"It's not like she's wearing a dress —."

"It's not the dress that deserves the respect. It's the *lady*."

That word again.

She smiles at Destiny, seemingly ending the matter and strolls for the house. "Come in when you're ready."

Across from the Greyson home are rich fields still bearing the stubble of last year's crop. Sure signs of acres of wheat and corn that were harvested, sold, or stored.

Food in abundance.

Mr. Greyson leads the horses towards the barn, a huge structure that holds animal stalls filled with hay and grain meant for their stock. A cow moos. Their own milk cow.

The house is made with wood siding, each plank overlapping the one below it. A painted house. The gleaming white sides set off the green shutters that flank windows. Windows made of real glass.

Following the family, Destiny steps inside to find an interior with multiple rooms, a wood floor, and stairs leading to bedrooms on a second story.

*And Jake thinks he's poor.*

Slowly, as if walking in a dream that could crumble at one missed step, Destiny ventures past the kitchen and dining area, ending up at the foot of the stairs in the sitting room. Jake could be upstairs. His mother has called for him twice.

Jackson bounds up the steps then reappears at the top landing, face quizzical.

"He's not here."

Destiny sets the muscles of her face into tight knots. Knots too rigid to allow expressions that might reveal tightly held emotions.

She just thought —. Where else can he be?

Mrs. Greyson steps into the room just as Jackson descends the stairs.

"I wonder where…" Jake's mother does not set her face into a mask. It's lined with disappointment. Her shoulders slump. She looks at Destiny then Jackson, then Destiny again.

"Well." She brightens instantly into a brilliant and forced smile. "He will miss a great dinner. Destiny, come help me in the kitchen?" She puts an arm around Destiny's shoulders as if they were close relatives.

She even squeezes a little as they pass the doorway to the cooking area.

Mrs. Greyson launches into the several tasks with practiced efficiency. She gives instructions and encouragement.

But Destiny's never made biscuits before. All this niceness, all this inclusion makes her feel uneasy. Thinking back, Destiny can't remember being a guest like this ever.

All her social interactions come at school or church. Some people are nice to her. Others just politely acknowledge her. But no one has ever invited her to dinner.

Tutored by Jackson's mother, the dough feels spongy under her fingers as she presses and rolls it. A periodic glance up assures her she's doing it right. She begins to cut the small circles.

The back door opens and closes. Booted feet make several steps and stop. Mr. Greyson leans into the doorway, watching.

"Well, this is a treat," he says. He just stands there and stares. Mrs. Greyson smiles but says nothing. Destiny returns the look and tries to decipher his meaning.

"Having a girl in the house instead of just two boys," he says. He winks and continues down the hall to the sitting room.

Still staring into a boiling pot, Mrs. Greyson explains. "He loves our boys and really appreciates their help on the farm. But he always wanted another girl after Patty. Just didn't happen." Her complacent expression remains unchanged.

Then, as though startled, she straightens. "Don't tell anybody. He's supposed to be a big, tough man. Being tender about such things will embarrass him." She almost giggles.

Vegetables too. They've been cooked over the fire and Destiny places them in a large wooden bowl as asked. Beef, vegetables and fresh biscuits. Has she ever seen so much food for one meal before?

Dinner is served, grace said. It's hard not to search everyone's faces, to stare at them.

There seems to be some innate need to share the feelings of each one around the table. She has been taken out of the element where she's comfortable.

How to act, what to say become great decisions.

Both older Greyson's include her in conversation. How does she like studying with Mr. Potts?

They don't disapprove.

Jackson speaks highly of her hunting prowess. His parents seem genuinely impressed. Even though she's a girl. They seem sincere.

Still. Her ardent wish had been that Jake would be here. He's not.

She tries to help clean up, but Mrs. Greyson refuses. Let Jackson give her a tour of the farm she insists.

Destiny overhears her remarks to her husband as she goes through the back door.

"That girl can be nothing but a good influence on our boys."

Why does she say that? What does Destiny have to offer? Mrs. Waterford can't see anything about Destiny that's of good report. Somehow, Mrs. Greyson can.

Jackson pulls her excitedly down the lane between fields that clearly held corn and wheat before and clearly will this year as well. He's sure he heard some turkeys only yesterday.

"Jackson," Destiny calls. He stops and faces her. "Have you ever gone hungry?"

He twists his face and tilts his head that way he always does when he's unsure of something.

"I mean like you miss meals for a day or two. Not because of choice or punishment, but because there is no food."

The muscles of his face soften. His head returns to an upright position. His expression sobers.

"No. Never."

"Then Jake hasn't really either."

Jackson shakes his head. "Jake has dreams. He wants to be an important person. A Lord Ledenberry." He laughs.

The laugh carries some derision. Not a lot. But enough.

"I don't think so," Destiny replies. "I think he wants that only because he doesn't understand what it means. To be a Ledenberry I mean."

"What do you think he wants then?"

"Oh, I think he wants what you said. I just don't think he realizes that other people—." She looks at the ground gathering her emotions, carefully keeping them in check. "I don't think he realizes how much other people get hurt."

# Chapter 17

Something's wrong.

In what increasingly seems like a surreal, almost out of body experience, Amelia watches Lieutenant Helmsley approach the road and call instructions to the men under his command.

They are to continue. He will escort Amelia home then rejoin them.

But something's wrong.

It's a feeling. Her vision blurs at the edges, focusing intently on what is before her.

Jacob disappears, blocked by trees and the uneven ground.

Her heart pounds in her chest, warning her. Of what? The threat isn't clear but there's ... something.

Amelia tears her eyes from the spot where Jacob disappeared. It's time to think, to act.

Decision made, Amelia strides deeper into the orchard, a direction that will take her across several fields and home.

No. That's not right. A warning flashes through her mind.

She turns her head, searching her surroundings, looking for direction. The road. The road will be safer. It's open, the other soldiers will still be there if she hurries.

Why does that matter? Somehow it does.

Lifting the hem of her dress, Amelia breaks into a run. She dashes for the open thoroughfare. Helmsley catches her by the wrist.

The officer turned back to her just in time. His men are again beginning their journey to somewhere else.

His grip is strong and she pulls against his grasp.

"Sorry, Miss Waterford," the Lieutenant says. "You caught me by surprise coming up behind as you did. Still, this way is quicker."

He pushes forward, deeper into the orchard, practically dragging Amelia after him.

"You're hurting me," she exclaims. "My mother will like that even less than my walk with a Blackham farm boy."

The pathetic defense brings nothing more than a sneer from her captor.

With a whirl, the man stops and turns Amelia to face him. His face lowers so close to her own she can smell the alcohol on his breath.

His eyes are wild with some inexplicable and dark emotion. They dart as they seem to search her face. His expression twists into a mask of fury and evil. He snarls at her.

"Now give me some of that you were about to give the boy."

Amelia stares at him confused. She would have given Jacob a kiss, but not in front of this man, or anyone else. She's not about to give this man a kiss. She has nothing...

And then the realization. She staggers back, tripping, remaining upright only from the vise-like grip Helmsley still has on her wrist.

Her eyes stare, glued to him, unbelieving.

He wants *her*.

Nothing from her family, nothing else of value.

He wants her.

Panic overflows into a melee of confused emotion and attempted thought. She twists and pulls, trying to run.

He's so strong. Amelia swings with her free hand, like she wields a hammer, crashing down on the arm that holds her.

No effect. Like he didn't even feel it.

He laughs. And in that momentary slip, she hurls her leg in a vicious kick.

She misses her target, but still lands the point of her shoe on the inside of his thigh. He grunts in pain, his grip failing to hold.

Amelia rips her arm from his grasp and darts to find open ground.

Two steps. Then three.

She's anchored from behind. An iron grip ensnares the back of her dress.

She pumps her legs, continuing to run, but going nowhere.

Re-gaining his grip on her arm, Helmsley twists it in a tortuous hold and flings her to the ground.

Amelia's arm where she struck Helmsley throbs. She injured herself more than him. He seems so invincible.

She kicks again and misses.

Throws her aching arm through the air. The bone cracks as she strikes Helmsley's shoulder.

Searing pain blazes through the length of her arm. She screams with the combination of pain and fear. Her arm, now useless, falls limp to the earth.

She opens her mouth to shout for help. Is there no one who can save her?

His hand clamps tightly upon her, covering the bottom half of her face.

In vain Amelia sucks desperately for air, her lungs pleading for oxygen.

Her one arm bound by his grip, her other refuses to obey her commands. She cannot push his hand from her face.

She twists, pulling her body away from him. Her neck arches as she cranes her head away into grotesquely awkward and painful stretches. Anything to get free.

Savagely she jerks. Her head comes free and urgently she gasps for air.

With a desperate surge, she pulls her hips in a twist meant to jam her stomach into the ground.

Helmsley throws his hand violently to the side of her neck. It pins her, shoving the side of her face into the dirt of the orchard floor. Her teeth stab into her lips, her mouth filling with blood.

His free hand tears viciously into her thigh and drives her to her back.

His body straddles her, making it impossible to move, to turn, to struggle.

Amelia clenches muscles in a vain attempt to continue to fight. Her back arches fiercely in an effort to knock him off-balance.

She's losing.

Amelia fights for breath around the grasp of his hand on her neck and throat.

Helmsley's other hand fumbles over her breasts.

Amelia has never been touched intimately before. The shock of the horror— it turns everything to a fog, an impossibility. How can this happen?

Anchoring her beneath him, he continues to grope at her chest. Her dress pulls against the back of her neck as he tries to pull her clothes from her.

With renewed panic, she arches her back once more.

She surges in an effort to push away from him.

His free hand only grabs the neckline of her dress. The material tears into the back of her neck. The sound of ripping cloth freezes her, as Helmsley shreds the front of her clothes.

Amelia swings the useless arm by her side. Like a pendulum, without strength or form, the wrist and flailing hand swing above her.

She clubs the side of the officer's face.

Spasms of debilitating pain sear every part of her.

Her vision flees. Only a flash of white light remains and threatens to leave her senseless and unconscious, unable to resist.

She wills herself to come back and to fight.

But her muffled screams begin to turn to sobs.

Her struggles only seem to bring her further under his control. He grips, covers, holds until she can move no more.

Her body is not her own. She cannot control it, he does. She can no longer tell it what to do, he does.

The horror of the moment consumes her.

The admission that she's powerless overwhelms her.

Sobbing into the grasping hand that holds her mute, she turns her head, memorizing twigs and limbs of the apple tree above her.

# Chapter 18

With two strokes of my hammer, I drive the last nail through the shingle board and into the rafter of the barn roof.

I'm still on leave. Why not help out while everyone else is working?

The uneven roof edge mocks me as I pull back on my knees, examining my work. It's a small flaw, but I should have taken the board down and cut it a hair shorter.

Jackson steps over the peak of the roof, watching his feet. He stops, peering down at me.

"Need me to go down and cut that again for you?"

"I've already nailed it. Bet you can't even see it from the ground."

Jackson's expression turns doubtful, but he remains silent. We slide down to the edge of the roof. I extend my leg into the air searching for the first secure step on the home-made ladder.

My father will see the flaw, of course. But it's worth the chance he'll let it go.

Jackson follows me down and we stare into a sky that's mostly blue, but laced with long strands of thin cottony clouds. We scrutinize our work all the way around the barn.

Jackson's part does look better. We stop and stare at where my last row of shingles laps the edge of the roof.

"I'll fix it," Jackson volunteers. "It can wait a few days."

"He'll see it," I admit referring to my father.

Jackson shrugs. "It won't matter. I'll be here to take care of it."

I stare at my brother. Everyone is being too nice.

"You're not thinking about the roof, you're thinking about Amelia." Jackson's offhand comment startles me, but it's true.

Inside the barn I stretch, enjoying the pleasant feeling of the spring day. Jackson goes out the back to move the horses to another pasture. I turn toward the great double doors opening the barn front to the outside.

Sunlight dims as a gray haze creeps overhead. Startled, I leave the barn, walking toward the house to see dark clouds boiling through the sky, bearing down on the Greyson farm.

The wind picks up and bites into me with a frigid sting. Between the barn and the house, I stop and stare at the onslaught about to bury me.

Approaching on the lane leading from the Boston Road, comes the chestnut mare, with William all black coat and collar and pulled-down hat. No lively canter, no jaunty wave, just a slow approach braving the threatening weather.

Somehow, the icy wind gets inside me. It searches and slices until it finds every opening, sending shivers through my body.

A sense of dread, a feeling unlike anything ever experienced consumes me. Panic expands within, and yet, there's no reason for it.

Wordlessly, William dismounts. He ties his horse to the post, and embraces himself for warmth. I search, waiting to see his face, watching for some explanation.

William turns and I recoil. William's eyes look so vacant, ringed with red.

I take a step backward. I gape at a face that appears gaunt, red, and, somehow at the same time, swollen.

Another step back.

William must be here to see me. But about what?

What could result in the utter devastation written on William's face?

Messages creep into my thinking, warning, pushing me away. They shout to me I don't want to hear what William will say.

But William reaches for me. My face now implores, begs for an answer.

"She's dead!" He cries as tears burst from his eyes.

#

The fire in the kitchen stove crackles. The flames within consume the split wood Jackson brought in.

William sits silent and dejected, his finger drawing unseen pictures into the table-top. I sit across from him without a word to say.

Jackson and Father twist with nervous discomfort in the straight-back chairs surrounding the dining area. My mother doesn't sit.

She fusses around, tucking blankets around the shoulders of both William and me. The downpour began as the two of us stood in front of the house staring at each other, unable to move.

A brooding silence hangs heavy in the room. The "I'm sorry's" having been repeated so many times no one dares say it again.

I stare into a future I've never imagined. Through the corner of my eye I catch my mother's furtive glances, the worry look clearly etched across her face.

Thought, feeling, consciousness even, seem to have fled from me. In my mind Amelia's radiant face contrasts against a backdrop of green apple trees. How…?

William spilled the whole story, including the assault. The exposure of being out all day and much of the night left her with a raging fever. She lasted through that night, but…

The scrape of the chair fractures the silence as I push it against the floor. I rise and step outside.

There's guilt for ignoring my mother's plea to stay, but not so much that I stop.

The rain has ended, an intense yet short spring storm. The sky still looms over my head. Dark and silent.

The twisted cords that tangle into my life tighten, knotting into a jumbled mass. Nothing can be understood for it lies enmeshed with too many incomprehensible ends and loops and twists.

Poor Amelia. At last, the tears stream down my face as I think of her. Not just of missing her. But of the pain she suffered.

Now she's gone and I'll never see her again.

That English officer. The dreams of becoming something akin to that explodes into a fiery death within my heart, burning through my chest.

In my mind's eye I can see him, roaming the streets of Boston. Given every courtesy because he's a gentleman, because of the family into which he was born.

Deserving of nobility, of respect, of deference merely by the chance of birth.

Amelia determines the officer's worth. His victim.

In the scheme of all things, this man, this English officer, this noble gentleman's worth is less than any living thing.

Someday, the world will know that. It has to.

Exercising care not to alert anyone, I enter the house from the rear. I sneak up to my room and back outside to the front of the house again.

As I set the fire, Jackson steps out the front door. Silent.

He stares at me and in that stare, I find a level of support and understanding I've never noticed before.

A minute passes and William follows Jackson from the house. He approaches us and stares for a moment as the red coat begins to disintegrate in the leaping, yellow flames.

My gaze returns to William's and we watch each other for a moment. William reaches out, gives me a small handshake, then turns, mounts, and rides away.

Jackson and I remain, watching the sputtering fire until it dies, unable to find anything more to burn.

# Chapter 19

The stifling confines of the cabin become impossible to endure any longer. As Mother watches her, concerned, Destiny grabs her musket and bolts through the door.

The open air helps her to suppress the bitterness. Still though, dark feelings sweep through her, fighting to take control. She seems utterly incapable of reaching Jake.

Always, Destiny is the different one, the outcast, the one that doesn't fit in anywhere.

The musty yet somehow comforting scent of the forest calms her. She reaches for more positive emotions and pulls them to the surface.

The great trees, fighting for survival over decades, lift their branches and capture the rays from the sun. All is well with them. They survive trauma, disappointment, the overpowering shadow of taller neighbors.

Now they reap the reward of that endurance.

Jake will leave for Boston tomorrow. She hasn't seen him once. Who knows when he will return?

Expectantly Destiny looks down the trail that leads to the post road. Jackson should arrive any moment. She'll focus her mind and heart on the things she knows best. The two hunters will slink through the forest together as though they were part of it.

Something approaches. Destiny tilts her head, listening.

She didn't hear anything. There's just that sense. A sixth sense her mother calls it. From years of practice, she's so in tune with the woods that any change affects her. As though some magical spell were disturbed and communicated with Destiny.

Right again. Jackson comes into view, skirting the last curve in the trail.

Destiny's automatic reaction is to throw a hand in the air to greet her friend, but as she gets halfway there, she stops.

Something's wrong. It's in his step. Jackson doesn't carry his musket.

He's not going to hunt with her. She really needed him today.

Jackson comes near enough that Destiny can better read his face. It's lined with worry. Perhaps even distress. He's not himself.

Leaning her musket against the side of the cabin, she walks towards him, meeting him several steps from her home.

"What's wrong?"

"Something terrible —." Jackson stops. His expression twists, thinking hard, as though he struggles with what to say. "It's Amelia —."

A long pause and solemn gaze. His eyes dull with some great tragedy. His shoulders slump under some heavy burden.

The violence. Then the assault. Then the death.

Destiny steps back, hands flying to her mouth. This is too awful to contemplate. Tears overflow and drip down her cheeks. Poor Amelia!

"Jackson! No!" Another step and her back bumps into a tree she had forgotten was there.

"Are you sure?"

Jackson nods his head. The story came from William, Amelia's brother. There's no doubt it's true.

Amelia.

Amelia had always been kind, very unlike her mother.

She had been so beautiful. Well dressed. Poised. Smiling.

Everything a young woman should be. That was Amelia. How could something so horrible…?

How can she be dead?

Amelia was no older than Destiny.

Jackson kicks at the dirt, still having trouble finding the words he wants.

"The funeral's this afternoon. All my family's going. You should come with us."

No, she shouldn't. She knows it immediately.

She makes excuses to Jackson. He'll never understand the truth. Jackson only sees things at face value. He won't understand the deeper currents of Destiny's emotions.

Now is not the time to appear as though she's trying to take Amelia's place.

And she is. Always has been. But never in an angry or jealous way. Destiny knows about life. Jake doesn't.

He would never have found happiness in the rejection that would have perpetually existed for him in the Waterford family. Never.

Destiny draws herself together and sends Jackson on his way. Don't be late. Take care of Jake.

Turning her back to Jackson's disappearing form, she gazes over her forest again.

Amelia will never get to be one of the tall trees reaching the sun. Hewn down as a sapling. Used by someone who had no idea of her worth.

Used in a dirty, wasteful way. Someone clearing land and viewing all life upon it as things to be used for personal pleasure. Cut it down. Heap it up. Burn it to death. Move on.

Jake will have to wake up now. Now he has seen. This is where aristocratic ideas lead.

Everyone in a class. Either you are in the class to be used. Or you're in the class that uses others.

#

The funeral appears so somber.

From a hillside overlooking the church and the little cemetery nestled behind it, Destiny watches.

She glances down at her clothes. They will be offensive to some. Why add to Mrs. Waterford's discomfort? Despite the miserable person she is, she deserves this brief moment to deal with her grief.

There are others who wouldn't understand. Who will think Destiny has all the same choices they do, and made poor ones.

She twists a little, allowing herself to sit and lean against the towering oak. She draws her knees up to her chest, wraps them with her arms, and rests her chin upon them.

People always judge based on their own experience. They judge others based on what they identify with and easily comprehend. If you are too different from them to be understood, they think evil of you. No one knows this like Destiny.

Almost as though mocking the melancholy scene, the sun burns bright and radiant in an ice-blue sky.

An oak tree even larger than the one standing over Destiny, casts its limbs wide over the entire cemetery. The crowd almost all fits into its embrace.

The whole village appears to be here. The Greyson's stand facing her on the other side of the grave. The casket, a wood box, polished and decorated, sits across two wood stands. The earth piled up on the near side of the grave someone has prepared for Amelia.

Destiny stares at the dirt, envisioning the gaping hole beside it, waiting to swallow up an innocent young woman whose life on earth is now through.

The Waterford's stand on the near side, Destiny sees only their backs.

So somber.

Minister Sones stands at the head of the grave, bible open in his right hand, speaking words Destiny can't hear.

His smooth baritone though carries up her hill. Whatever he's saying, it's meant to comfort. But still, the sounds of occasional sobs roll up towards her.

It's too far to make out expressions. Even so, there's no mistaking Jake's feelings.

His slumped posture. His stare fixed at his feet.

His hands twisting his hat, unconsciously she's sure, as he stands. He needs Destiny, but she can't be there.

And even if she could, Jake doesn't know he needs her. Not yet.

Mrs. Greyson reaches out a hand and lays it on her son's shoulder.

So sad.

And the Waterford's will have nothing to say to him. They'll not help by letting him in. Letting him share with them, share the grieving over someone they all loved.

After all, he's only a Greyson.

# Chapter 20

As Destiny watches, the crowd dissipates. The slow process plays out like actors moving from a stage. The distance makes her feel like an audience.

Mourners, stooped and aged in their posture, pay their respects then amble off to horses or wagons and slowly drift away.

Minister Sones hovers over the heartbroken family. Like a practiced director, he shepherds the weeping mob by the Waterford's, keeping a brisk pace. At last, he ushers the grieving parents to their carriage. William remains.

Amelia's brother and the minister fade into the church, leaving the cemetery empty. The great oak now seems to encompass Amelia's casket, still displayed next to the gaping hole.

The time to go is now. Soon the men will come. They will lower Amelia into the earth and cover her.

That will be too much. Destiny can't bear to watch the dirt being thrown over Amelia. And she wants to say goodbye. To pay respects. To sympathize. To mourn. To …

To say she's sorry.

And what is she sorry for?

Destiny eases from her place under the tree and takes her first tentative steps downhill.

She's what? Sorry about what had happened? Sorry about the violence that crushed and killed someone so like her.

As different as they were, there are more similarities between Destiny and Amelia than there are differences. People will be unable to see it. Some people.

But it's true. Both young women. Both about the same age.

What had Amelia wished for?

Jake for one. That's something she had in common with Destiny.

Surely there's more. Beneath the clothes, the appearance of wealth, the always visible social standing, did not their hearts beat in much the same way? Serve the same function?

Did they not experience the same emotions? Love, joy, sorrow, disappointment.

Had they not both looked at the world around them and wanted something more? Yearned to improve life? Determined somehow that they would help the world be a little better place?

Sure they had.

Destiny reaches out and runs a hand along the smooth top of the casket. She stares at the lid of polished wood.

Amelia's in there. Her ravaged body only inches below Destiny's fingers.

Would Amelia not have wished for a system that would hold Helmsley accountable? That would view him as no more important than Amelia?

Could she possibly have foreseen that this was the natural destination of aristocracy? Of the belief that some were worth more or mattered more than others?

Could her upbringing have prepared her for that?

Surely not.

Destiny's hand remains on the lid, feeling Amelia's presence, feeling the insult to all of them. All women. All colonists.

Helmsley cannot be tried here. If tried at all, it will be in England.

The land of the English officer's birth. His home where lives his family, friends, and those who guard his and all other nobility's claim to preference.

"Destiny?"

She whirls, yanked from her thoughts as though by a team of spooked horses.

William's voice is tentative and soft. But she's intruding. Invading a space she doesn't belong. William will be the guardian against such offenses.

"I'm sorry. I —." Her feet stumble a little as she hurries to leave.

"No, wait."

His face almost implores as she stares at him.

"Did you know Amelia well?" His voice cracks as he speaks. The eyes are rimmed with red, the face ashen, the brow furrowed.

Destiny shakes her head. The silence seems so complete they both shuffle a bit as they stare back at one another.

"Yet, you are here." It's almost a question. Maybe it is. Breaking through the shock of being found by William, Destiny gathers her thoughts into a decent reply.

"She's so much like me."

William's brow wrinkles even deeper as his eyes squint, searching hard for understanding, revealing his surprise.

He won't understand.

"I'm so sorry— what happened I mean."

William nods.

A breeze kicks up and moves the shadows about the grave as the old oak swings in the stirring air. Almost Destiny can see the beginning of new leaves as the aged tree prepares again for another rebirth.

The meeting turns even more awkward. Destiny turns quietly to go.

"Destiny?"

She stops and peers at William.

"How were you and Amelia alike?"

Yes, how were they alike? Amelia had never attended school. It wasn't proper in her social circle.

She had always been friendly at church meetings. Those meetings though, were very brief.

They had few common friends. Except Jake.

"The differences— Well, they just seem on the outside. How we look. Were we very different on the inside?"

William stares. It's his turn to stumble and wonder about what to say. Silence rolls in again, so deep this time that Destiny knows there's nowhere left for the conversation to go. She has surpassed William's understanding.

Her smile is small. Meant to be respectful, yet friendly.

William still watches her. Destiny turns her back to him and makes her way down the road until she finds the cutoff trail to her cabin.

# Chapter 21

Amelia will be avenged. Helmsley will pay. I will see to it.

I've made record time stalking all the way from the farm to Blackham. Now that I approach the town, I see William. So, he came after all.

We met yesterday and he was reluctant. Jackson assured us both Potts was acting as magistrate today. I don't know how Jackson knows that. I pressed the question, but my brother avoided a straight answer.

Whatever. I'm here for justice. Potts will file the proper papers. The murderer, Helmsley, will be brought to justice.

William's face remains unchanged as I approach. Hard. Stony.

No longer is he the heart-broken brother who wept in front of my house only days before. Now there's no emotion. Nothing I can read.

His horse tied under a fledgling oak, William shuffles his feet and glances at the ground. The bright white church building seems to almost jump from its deep green background.

"I still think this would be better handled in Boston."

William means the army; the army should handle the question of Helmsley.

I shake my head. "You don't have to stay, William." I stare back at my friend with unflinching eyes.

This is a fight I will have. Friend or no. Either William can help bring Helmsley to justice or stay out of the way.

William shrugs. "Potts has no authority."

I bristle but clamp my mouth shut.

"Then go."

Spinning on my heel, I stride toward the church door. As I turn, something catches my eye.

Jackson has joined me. In silence we mount the wood steps. I grab the door.

"Is he in school?"

Jackson shakes his head. "No school. He's just dealing with legal things."

"How do you know?" I ask, but not quick enough. Jackson slips through the opening. His elbow hits the door frame. I try to grab it and demand an answer.

Too late. My fingers only graze Jackson's disappearing arm.

William stands at the door. So, he'll attend. I open it wider then follow my childhood friend inside.

Mr. Potts sits at his little table-turned-desk as usual. Destiny sits across from him.

Why is Destiny here? More lessons? It seems I can't see Potts anymore without Destiny being here too.

Mr. Potts rises. He nods. "Good morning boys."

His voice bounces around the empty interior. It echoes off the front wall where a near-opaque window arches from floor to high ceiling. In front of it stands the podium where Minister Sones admonishes his flock each Sabbath.

Potts continues. "The magistrate is out, but I'm looking at a couple of legal matters in his absence." His long face, drooping eyes, and grim mouth create a somber appearance.

"Let me finish with Destiny and Jackson. I'll be right with you Jacob. William."

I stop in the aisle between the pews. Destiny and Jackson? What 'legal matters' do either of them have? Is it one legal matter? Or two?

With slow steps, I move to the front bench, only a few feet away from my teacher. I gaze at Jackson but my brother refuses to look at me. Jackson sits on the other side of the desk just like I do when I have lessons here.

"Jasper Ellingham accuses you of robbing him on the post road," Mr. Potts says.

Whoa! Robbing him? Who's Jasper Ellingham? What has Jackson gotten into?

I lean forward, staring at my brother's profile. At Destiny who also refuses to look my direction. I glance at William, back to Potts, then again at the side of my brother's face.

He can't have robbed anyone. Jackson isn't a thief. He loves adventure and spends a lot of time away from the house looking for it.

But a highwayman? Robbing someone on the Boston Road? Impossible.

Jackson squirms in his chair. "Did Destiny tell you he took their rent money, then told them they had to leave anyway?"

Mr. Potts is nodding. Yes, Destiny told him that.

"I don't know who robbed him, but it shouldn't have been his money anyway. *He* robbed Destiny."

Mr. Potts pulls up his hand and strokes the side of his face, deep in thought. He reaches for and shuffles some of the papers on the table. He finds nothing. Selects none of the writings.

He merely rifles through them and then turns back to Jackson and Destiny.

"So, Mr. Ellingham had money belonging to Mrs. Morris. That's the money that was stolen, or seems to be the money that was stolen." He drops the words slowly, each one well-considered.

Jackson and Destiny nod emphatically.

Potts turns his gaze to Destiny. "Does your mother have money to pay the rent now?"

"Yes. Normally Mr. Ellingham would come for it this week."

More nodding by the substitute magistrate.

"I'll draft a letter to Mr. Ellingham inquiring as to the source of the money that was stolen."

Again, the shuffling of papers as his gaze remains on the table. "I'll ask him if you are still a tenant or if he is issuing an eviction. Once we understand where the stolen money originated, we will have a better understanding of the robbery."

He peers at Destiny. She nods her understanding of her tenuous hold on her home.

Potts leans back in his chair and takes a long look at both Destiny and Jackson.

"I hope my letter will clear up all the loose ends in this affair. Robbery is a serious crime. It carries heavy penalties. If Ellingham has any evidence of who the perpetrators are, it could be a bad business."

His look is stern, worried, and compassionate. He nods again and reaches down to grab his chair. The legs scrape the floor as he turns toward the pew in which William and I sit.

Potts leans forward, elbows on his knees.

"I am so sorry about your sister, William. Is there anything I can do?"

"We know who did it." I blurt.

Potts' eyebrows arch in surprise. His face asks the question.

"Lieutenant Helmsley of the British Army. He's in Boston."

Potts now reverses his expression. "We haven't much authority with the British."

"But. It happened here! Right here in Blackham. Doesn't that mean you have the authority?"

My voice is pleading rather than explaining. I want it too much. Want to bring Helmsley into the village and punish him.

I glance at William who sits beside me, stoic. Why?

There's never been a hanging in Blackham. But this seems like such a sure thing. A gallows will be built. At the appointed time I will make sure I'm right in front, staring into the eyes of a frightened and chastened officer.

In disgrace, Helmsley will be stripped of his red uniform and all the accoutrements that mark him with any distinction. Like a pauper he will stand there. Maybe he'll even cry from being so frightened. Beg for mercy.

And I will be the witness. I'll remind the criminal of Amelia. Of her suffering. Remind Helmsley that he richly deserves everything that's about to happen to him.

I will twist it like a knife, pushing to inflict every morsel of guilt possible upon the man.

"Jacob. Do you remember when we talked about the Intolerable Acts?"

I feel like my heart plummets to the floor.

Mr. Potts sounds so instructive, just like the teacher he is. As though he's delivering a lecture and is absolutely certain of the material he shares.

Destiny looks straight into my eyes. Her expression one of great compassion, of great sorrow as though something awful is about to happen to me.

I'm a caged and tormented animal. Everyone stares at me. They're about to do something terrible to me.

"That's the colonial term. There are four acts of Parliament that fall into the category. One is the right of British officials to be tried in England."

I gaze blankly at Potts, Destiny, William at my side. Then more rapidly I glance at Jackson, back at Potts, at the pile of papers on the desk.

"The Administration of Justice Act, to be more precise. Helmsley will never be tried in the colonies."

Silence looms as though the world has stopped. No one speaks. No one breathes. No one moves.

How can this be? I dismissed the colonial concern over the Intolerable Acts. The tea had been dumped into the harbor by some lawless hotheads. What did everyone think would happen?

This is different though. I didn't dump any tea. Neither did Amelia.

Amelia.

I can't stop it.

The happy face I'd seen in the orchard. Her embrace. Her kiss.

The injustice of her death. That was enough.

But there was more. The dirty part. The crushing violence of Helmsley. How she must have suffered!

Someone speaks. More than one. Destiny maybe. Potts.

I can't really hear.

My footsteps echo as I stride down the aisle. The tears can no longer be contained. They stream down my face as I slam the door open and escape.

# Chapter 22

A sliver of Boston shows through the glass. Jackson and I share the little extra bedroom above my brother-in-law's failed shipping business. The same room where I first tried on the uniform and joined the provincial company in the British army.

I stare through the little pane, past the obstructing building that is our neighbor, and off towards the waterfront.

There are no hard edges. Even the figures on the street blur through the grime smeared across the glass, thickening in the corners.

As though the dirt of the British-held town is finally exposed. Keeping the city from looking clean. Distorting the façade of elegance. The muck revealed underneath.

The fire that burns within me and brings me to Boston not only rages, but flares in violent eruptions.

Where are those who loved Amelia now?

She has died, wounded and used, left in the dirt to suffer alone. Left like a useless toy after Helmsley was through with her.

The Waterford's grieve.

Now though. Now I understand William's reticence.

The Waterford family fortune is inseparable from the British system. They can condemn Helmsley, but not the system that created him.

I descend the stairs and pause at the bottom. Patty's greeting silences a hushed conversation. Jackson and Meacham sit at the small round table.

Everyone turns and looks at me. Patty's expression is enough to send me back upstairs before the emotion overcomes me again.

Jackson pulls out a chair. "Sit down, Jacob. Biscuits and bacon."

Biscuits and bacon. Jackson must be in heaven.

The bread's still hot. The butter and honey Jackson and I brought from the farm sit in front of me.

Patty sets a cup at my place at the table. Where did she manage to get fresh milk?

"I —." Patty clasps her hands together as she stares at me. Standing in the middle of the kitchen, she seems unable to phrase what she wants to say. She tilts her head into an imploring pose.

"Helmsley can't be tried here. Only in England. The Intolerable Acts, you know?"

The chair scrapes a protest as I shift my position. This is a conversation I refuse to have. I'm through hearing about the Intolerable Acts.

"I know." The words come out barely more than a whisper. The tightened muscles in my throat nearly blocking any ability to speak.

The dull knife slices through the soft biscuit, splitting it instantly in half.

Patty stares at me, eyebrows arched. She settles into the last empty chair, leaning forward over the table.

"We'll think of something." I direct the soft words towards my stricken sister. I nod to her then return my gaze to my food.

From the corner of my eye, I see the look that passes between Patty and Jackson.

I can't look at her. What can I say? I haven't formulated a plan yet. I just know I have to act. All I can offer are stuttered excuses.

Perhaps admissions I'm not prepared to utter yet. Maybe Patty was right all along.

#

It's a gray day in the city. People shake rugs out their front door, place signs in front of shops, and conduct business as though it were any other day. The lack of respect for Amelia only increases my anger and need for vengeance. I will not allow her death to be inconsequential, to leave no mark upon the world at all. As though nothing had happened.

Jackson is matching me step for step. I look and, from the side, and I can see the hardness of his features in his profile. His determined strides match mine. Why?

"Why are you doing this?" I ask.

Jackson gazes at me and seems positively stumped by the query.

"Well —." Jackson raises his hands as though embracing a larger question. "He's gotta pay."

"You barely knew Amelia."

"No, but I know you." Jackson averts his gaze for a moment then brings it back to my face. "More than that. The damn lobsterback assaulted *all* of us."

There's fire in Jackson's voice. Profanity. Mother would be furious.

Lobsterback? When did my brother pick up the derisive slang of the rebels? He's a pretend Wampanoag Indian. When did he decide to involve himself in such issues?

My surprise freezes any response before I can form it.

"What's your plan?" Jackson asks.

I gather my thoughts. Jackson's really going to be my ally in this.

"Get him back to Blackham," I reply. "I don't know what else to do."

Letting out a long and labored breath, I stop and lean against a wall next to a shop-front window.

We're on Tremount Street. The window belongs to a gunsmith. In it a neat little stack of gunpowder kegs stands on the floor. A pile of lead bullets sits on a table. An embellished, hand-crafted musket.

Jackson sidles closer, allowing some pedestrians free passage up the side of the cobblestone way.

My mind flashes images of Helmsley dying. The depraved criminal begging forgiveness in his final moments.

Me rejecting his pleas, reminding him of Amelia's suffering. Finally exacting the ultimate punishment.

That point, the moment Helmsley slips away in death, fills with a lack of fulfillment.

Unsatisfied, the pictures fall through my thoughts again. I concentrate on the moment where I tie the suffering of Amelia to the suffering I inflict on the Lieutenant.

Still. It never seems enough.

"Any of those Indians ever teach you how to kill a man?" I ask.

Jackson's eyes grow so large I can see white all around them.

My brother shakes his head slowly. "Do you think we should go that far?"

I consider. We would definitely be caught. Jackson and I would hang. Our mother would be heartbroken.

Jackson though, Jackson looks as though he might try.

"We can't." I straighten from my leaning posture against the store wall.

"Well then, we need to catch him and drag him back to Blackham. Ready?"

We set out again, heading south. In only a few blocks we turn left, then right.

The circuitous route ends in a narrow alley. I slink forward, watching the sliver of light between the buildings that mark Common Street.

Jackson creeps into position beside me. His hand falls on my shoulder as he crouches in the alley. We're wedged between a candle-maker and a closed shipper of New England-made furniture.

Boston Common lies across the way. The voices of sergeants bark orders that echo through the air. I not only hear but understand the commands.

The scarlet formations wheel. They stop in unison at the sound of the shouted orders. All this is gone from me now.

My heart burns with the need to exact punishment on Helmsley. Ultimate punishment.

But seeing the troops… Knowing I can never be part of that again…

I lean forward, turning my head to catch a view of both directions. A smattering of citizens walks the paved street. They enter and exit small establishments that print, sell, advise.

All normal. As if Amelia never existed.

What's wrong with them? Don't they know?

"We need to go farther down the street," Jackson suggests.

The obscurity of kneeling in the shadows is comforting. Being recognized by anyone, especially someone from the provincial unit will crush any hope of surprise.

Measuring and anticipating the movements of the soldiers, I calculate the least conspicuous moment.

A dark horse snorts at us as we slide from the crevice between the buildings. Down the street we venture, still searching.

Ahead a great open doorway, almost like a barn, gapes at us. Inside hammers and saws ring throughout the furniture manufactory. The clattering of boards increases as we pass.

As we pull even, a great crash of dropped lumber hurtles through the air.

Startled, I jump away and into the street.

A gray mare skips sideways as I collide with her. Her rider, a red-coated, gold-embroidered officer, curses at the mishap.

"Watch where you're going, stupid boy!"

Ice clambers over my bones sending frigid spikes into me. I grab my tri-corner hat with my hand, obscuring my face. Eyes glued to my feet; I stammer an apology in a voice far deeper than normal.

A shiny black boot digs its heel into the horse's side.

The alley? Or Helmsley? For a moment I freeze with indecision.

I have no weapon. The result of a physical contest in which I'm bare-handed and the officer has at least his pistol —.

I retreat toward my hiding place.

The ring of the horse's hooves dance over the stones. I raise my head and peer after the rider.

"That must be him." Jackson stares the same direction I do. I only nod.

"You need to get back to Patty's."

Emotions are so raw that at first, I bristle at the command. But then Jackson is here on my errand.

In the seclusion between the two buildings, I examine my brother's expression and find only loyalty. I wonder if I should try and calculate my debts. To Patty. To my parents. To Jackson.

I can't risk Helmsley seeing me. Jackson's right.

The walk back to Patty's stretches long. Jackson, unknown by anyone in Boston other than family, will reconnoiter.

My thoughts tumble with feelings of inadequacy and failure. Will my family understand?

Will it work? Can I really carry out something so bold and daring? Will I freeze at the final moment?

Seeking courage, I force my thoughts back to Amelia.

The soft green dress she wore at the party. Her laugh.

The cobblestone street under my feet fades from my vision. Before me looms the Waterford's home, the ballroom stretching long from the door where I enter. Sophisticated British officers clustering around Amelia.

But she calls to me. She leaves all others and runs to clutch my arm. I can feel her even now.

I pause on the street and realize my arm is extended foolishly in front of me. I'm reaching for her.

But she isn't really there. And never will be.

The fury rises like bile.

# Chapter 23

Hugging the side of Patty's house, I wonder if I can slip through the darkness with the same stealth Jackson and Destiny possess in the woods.

Jackson nods as I look back. The two of us leap into the night.

The misty, damp cobblestone street seems to sleep as it unrolls into the city center. Vacant.

A blanket lies upon the neighborhood, night seeming to silence everything around us. The air, wet and heavy from the sea, nips at my cheeks, nose, and ears. The smell of salt, diluted somehow at night, still creeps around the Boston houses and shops.

The need for silence, to be unseen, seizes all my emotions. Shadows are my friend. Silent footsteps imperative. The mission, well outside the capabilities of two Blackham farm boys.

An intersection looms. A nod from Jackson. I turn left.

Distant yells. A call for someone to come home. Cursing at an errant mule.

The sounds seem far away. Part of the muted emotions of a city under siege. Occupied by the enemy.

Hanover street. A quick crossing back to the shadowy side.

Treamount again.

Common street.

Ahead, light spills out the front windows of The Bronze Bell. According to Jackson, this will be the favored tavern of the officers.

I stop and examine our destination. Music. Light. Men's voices.

But no one on the street. No witnesses.

Several storefronts this side of the tavern, a shadowy doorway hides. Sliding along damp walls, I inch along until I dive into the hideaway. I'm a mere half-block from my enemy's entrenchment. Undetected.

The entryway lies recessed in from the front wall. Breathing comes easier in the secluded alcove. I clutch the brick building, damp and slippery. Down the street, three or so storefronts sleep in the dark.

Beyond them, a narrow alley intervenes. Just past the alley, yellow light flows onto the street from the windows of the tavern. Despite the temperature, the door stands open. Too many bodies for one enclosed space? Fire too large? Or maybe too much alcohol consumed by too few in a short period of time.

Men's voices in conversation, singing, laughter, all escape into the night air. The sounds ring eloquently enough to paint the picture of buoyant, uniform-clad celebrants hefting pewter mugs and sparkling goblets.

I stare at the tavern where two dozen or more ranking army officers make merry, celebrating their charmed lives.

And I'm going to do what? Kidnap one? Murder one of them in revenge?

Shadows alternately block then release the tavern's light. The pool of illumination in the street ripples from bright yellow to a shadowy gray.

Jackson's elbow hits my ribs.

"The plan is to get him back to Blackham, right?"

I nod. "How long is that alley?" I whisper.

Jackson shrugs.

"I thought you checked this out?"

Jackson gives me a hard stare. I take a breath.

A moment's silence and Jackson whispers. "I only found out where the officer's like to go. Hold on."

"Wait!"

But Jackson's gone. He slithers out the alcove and strides down the street as though he belongs there.

Won't someone know he's about to commit a heinous crime? Does he not look suspicious in some way? I stare at the shadowy shop fronts across the street.

All quiet.

With excruciating slowness, I twist my body and search the street behind, the way we came.

Nothing.

A painfully slow return to my original stance. Pressing my face against the wet wall of the building I watch my brother.

Crossing the alley Jackson glances down its length.

He presses on. Past the front of the tavern. He examines the front windows and the open door as he passes.

I hold my breath. Surely someone will call out. They'll stop him and demand to know his business.

Nothing. Only the rollicking shouts and singing of the half-inebriated officers.

My brother disappears from view.

I lean back against the wall behind me. Now what?

Sounds of celebration fill the damp air.

>*...And guardian angels sang this strain:*
>
>*Rule, Britannia! Rule the waves*
>
>*Britons never will be slaves.*

I risk looking around the corner.

Two men desert the party. It's impossible to see their rank from here. They stumble down the street away from me.

As I watch, Jackson materializes from the mouth of the alley. He strides toward our hiding place.

No one shouts. No one turns our direction.

Coming even with the opening, my brother dives into the shadows and leans against a wall.

"Alley's black as pitch," he reports.

I can almost hear his heart hammering from three feet away.

"Helmsley's inside. Pretty drunk."

The enemy is here. In his lair.

And drunk.

"Could you see what he's drinking?"

"Ale." Jackson raises his eyebrows and tilts his head inquisitively.

"If he's drunk and he's been drinking ale, he'll be needing the necessary."

Jackson's face illuminates.

"It's right behind the tavern. The alley will get you there."

Mentally, I measure the distance.

Intermittently, enemy officers leave the tavern. The thought startles me. When had the King's men become enemies?

Exiting the tavern, some turn their backs to me, making their way back towards their quarters. A few turn down the alley leading to the necessary in back.

I stare, carefully studying each face. No Helmsley.

Time creeps. I fidget in the cramped sitting position.

I fight the doubts.

I'm a farm boy from Blackham. It's not what I'm going to be. But, to be completely honest, that's what I am now. And I'm going to apprehend an officer in the King's Army?

From the tavern, a solitary, red-coated figure stumbles from the door. The man turns directly facing us, and negotiates the few steps to the alley, then lurches into it.

I spring from my hiding place. Jackson follows.

A mad race to the corner.

We spin a quick left turn and find ourselves in the muted light of the alleyway.

A glance behind. Nothing.

Hurried steps after Helmsley.

The staggering man, disheveled, but still all red coat and gold lace, can't seem to hear us. He stumbles along his way, occasionally reaching out and using the wall of the building for support.

I pause. I examine the length of the alley back to the lighted windows that flood the street-end of it.

Vacant.

I touch the man's arm. Helmsley spins to face me. He throws out an arm as though to defend himself, catching me with a shove in the chest.

The effort throws the lieutenant off balance. He reaches for the wall to steady himself.

"Remember me?" I ask.

The wildness drains from the eyes as they fill with confusion instead.

"Try to rob an English gentleman and you'll hang for it," he threatens.

My hands tremble as I unwind a length of rope from my waist.

Even my voice quivers. "We're not here to rob you, Lieutenant Helmsley. Do you know who I am?"

The man squints and stares hard into my face.

"What did you say?" he slurs.

"I said, do you recognize me?" Another glance at the length of the alley. I tighten the muscles in my throat, laboring for control.

"It's clear," Jackson confirms. He waits patiently, watching and protecting, allowing me a moment of revenge.

The officer shakes his head, bewildered. "Should I?"

Feelings stretch to a tautness that threatens to snap. Almost I feel like an audience, watching another self accost a British officer and noble, a man of power and consequence, in a dark alley next to a city tavern.

I lean into the man's face, barely noticing the overpowering smell of alcohol. "We met at the Waterford's. Then in the apple orchard near Blackham."

My heart hammers inside my chest.

The brief conversation seems to go too fast for the soldier. Then a flicker of recognition sparks in his eyes.

Confusion as well. He searches for a connection between the apple orchard and being accosted in an alley near his favorite pub in Boston.

Then. Then the expression of wonderment evolves into recognition. Then remembering.

Then fear as pieces begin to fall together.

"Oh, that's right." A quick, nervous laugh.

Slurred words spill, swimming in alcohol-laden breath.

"You were with that lovely Waterford girl. How is she? I got her back to her home alright, I know that much."

"She's dead."

My vision blurs but I can still tell Helmsley's shock is genuine. The officer's mouth operates more quickly than words can escape.

He stutters as he tries to grasp his predicament.

"What! I mean— she was alive and well last I saw her. What happened?"

It's overflow. The fear. The rage.

I drive a fist into the man's gut, needing to release the pent-up stress threatening to overpower me.

"You disgraced her! She lay in the dirt until the night air killed her—." I break off, the tears falling now. Muscles so tensed I feel wooden. Mind exploding with images of clasping the man's throat and squeezing with every ounce of strength I can muster.

Jackson sidles between me and Helmsley. He takes the rope, whirls Helmsley about, and shoves him against the wall. He grabs the soldier's wrists and begins to wind the rope around them.

The Lieutenant's words stumble all over each other now.

Face jammed against the side of the tavern; he tries to proclaim his innocence. He sputters that the little provincial had no cause to do such a stupid thing.

She needn't have felt bad about anything—. That surely there was something else—. He was, after all, a gentleman—.

"Silas? Silas, you down there?" A voice calls from the mouth of the alley.

I whirl and stare back toward the tavern front. I drag my coat sleeves across my eyes to clear my vision.

One shadowy figure stands in the light of the window. It peers down the alley trying to make out what might be there, making noise.

My heart sinks.

"What the bloody hell!" The figure begins to come down the alley waving a pistol in one hand.

We're caught.

The lieutenant bumps into me as he shakes his hands. The rope unravels from his wrists and falls to the ground.

"Arrest these two! They were going to rob me!" He staggers and uses the wall for support.

The intervening officer, Major Harrison I now see, points his pistol and glares at the two of us.

"That so?" He looks quizzically at me, examining me from my feet to my face. "You were at the Waterford party. Where's your uniform?"

"I'll not be part of an army depraved enough to protect this man."

"How's that?" the Major asks.

The burning and swelling can still be felt about my eyes, but I don't hide them.

"Lieutenant Helmsley forced himself on the Waterford's daughter and should go to the magistrate."

The Major's gaze follows mine to the loose rope now lying on the ground. His shoulders sag as though a great weight has been placed upon him. He looks at Helmsley, Silas I suppose, and sighs.

"How much money have you got on you, Silas? I've been buying your drinks for the last hour."

"They didn't know that," Helmsley spits the words out with an angry kick at the loose rope.

"If we'd wanted to rob him, we would of took the money and run." Jackson offers.

The Major peers back at Silas even as his words address me. "I know Silas has conducted himself as a gentleman, but I'm not sure we want wild accusations flying about. Do we Silas?"

Helmsley stares at Major Harrison. Slowly he shakes his head with an air of resignation.

"You boys go on home. We'll all forget this happened." The major takes Helmsley's arm to pull him back up the alley.

"He has to pay," I say through gritted teeth.

Everything's falling apart. I'm being treated like a school boy. Helmsley too as if it had all been some harmless prank.

I grab Helmsley's coat, jerking him back.

The Lieutenant swings wildly, trying to land an angry punch. He misses and stumbles. "I'll see you in prison you stupid boy. Dare to strike your betters—."

The major drives his shoulder between Helmsley and me. I stare down the barrel of the pistol pointed at my face.

"He won't be appearing before any magistrate. The local authorities have no jurisdiction over the King's men. If you insist, which I advise you don't, take the matter up with the army commander."

The Major leads the stumbling Lieutenant up the alley toward the light of the tavern.

"If the army won't prosecute its murderers, maybe we need to punish them ourselves!" I call. The major glances over his shoulder.

"Do that and you'll hang from an army gallows."

I kick at the loose rope that would have led Amelia's killer to justice.

Dismissed. Again. I have no power. No authority.

In this world I'm irrelevant.

I have failed her.

At the very least, Amelia can witness my efforts to avenge her. Still, she hasn't seen anything to make her proud this night.

But this is not the end. It's the beginning.

# Chapter 24

Fuming, I stalk through the streets of Boston. As though I have blinders on, I see nothing but my destination.

What little night was left after the episode with Helmsley I spent pacing the floor and planning my next move. Jackson and I jostle through a smattering of pedestrians, making our way down the city street. I burn with humiliation.

The red-coated, powdered wig, barely-more-than-a-servant man had peered down his long nose at us. Disapproving. Condescending. We'd been refused a meeting with General Gage. He's a very busy man. A quick recounting of what happened to Amelia brought no sympathy whatever.

The orderly had been almost amused at such accusations against one of the King's officers. I clench my fists and rage within myself.

I confronted imperial arrogance last night. Despite tremors and premonitions of disaster, I'd held my ground. I hadn't prevailed, but I held my ground. The experience emboldens me.

A monolithic house turned into a headquarters of some sort, sits across the street from the Common where a number of artillery pieces sit. The giant brass guns glint in the vivid sun. Pale blue limbers, wagons, and other equipment are parked in neat rows near them. Piles of cannonballs. Mountains of gunpowder in wooden kegs.

The white-painted clapboard walls of the house gleam. A sentry, expertly clad with every military accoutrement neatly in place, stands at rigid attention on either side of the door.

Jackson halts at my side. He places his hands on his hips.

"Alright. Crashing Gage's office might not have been the best idea."

The admission dulls the edge of my fury. I turn to my brother.

"Tempting though, wasn't it?"

"It would have gotten their attention."

We stare at each other a moment, each of us seeing the partnership. How much we agree. How united we are at righting a dreadful wrong.

Am I becoming a patriot? No, not yet. This has nothing to do with politics, laws, rights, or any of the philosophic arguments some like to debate.

This is about Amelia.

Taking a deep breath, I straighten my shoulders, and march up the steps. The red-coated guards angle their muskets so the barrels cross in front of the door. I'd expected the challenge.

"Jacob Greyson to see the officer in charge." One of the guards disappears through the door and returns a moment later, sergeant in tow.

"Jacob Greyson?"

"Yes," I answer.

"State your business."

"I want to see the officer in charge. An English lieutenant is guilty of abusing citizens of Blackham."

Abusing. It's an insult to Amelia's memory. But I just need enough to get in the door.

The sergeant raises an eyebrow as though to say, 'and they sent you to see about it?' He stands two steps higher, peering down and studying us.

The sergeant continues his withering gaze for a moment, but neither Jackson nor I budge. He turns and enters the building with a curt command. "Wait here."

Jackson climbs the one step separating us. "I think you're actually going to get in," he says, his voice betraying his surprise.

I steel myself against nervousness and mentally practice my presentation.

The latch clicks and the door swings open to reveal the sergeant extending an arm towards the interior of the house. "You may enter."

Jackson follows and we step into what must have been a sitting room at one time. It's richly furnished, the rug on the hardwood floor extends almost to the walls.

I stand nervously fidgeting and twisting my hat in my hands. Through a closed door, the sergeant disappears into a room. After only a moment, he comes back out, and takes up a position in front of the interior door.

The man stares straight ahead, looking at nothing.

Rubbing his hand on the rich fabric of the furniture, Jackson gazes around the room in awe.

I mentally practice my presentation again. I anticipate the questions that might arise. Carefully, I craft answers for each one.

It seems I'm ready. But everything about the British is so… big. It overwhelms me.

The interior door opens and I jump.

Angrily, I reprimand myself. Pulling every sinew together, I steel myself to be poised, calm, assured.

The sergeant holds the door and a jumble of four officers emerge, still in conversation. The cluster of red and gold drifts to the front door. There's a flurry of hand-shaking and brief salutes. They step outside and the sergeant is motioning me into the room.

Summoning the courage I've been building so diligently, I march to the door. I turn into the entryway and freeze.

Several steps deep into the room sits a massive walnut desk. A matching table sits nearby along one wall. Maps and papers litter the table and much of the desktop.

The clutter leaves only a small working space directly in front of a resplendent major that I recognize from last night. The major smiles.

"Ah, yes. Come in my young friends. All the way from Blackham and I suppose you feel you have much to discuss with me."

Jackson and I step into the room. The door closes behind us.

"Sit. Sit," the Major orders. I drift into one of several chairs that face the officer. The Major, already standing, comes around to the front and, clearing a corner of the desk, eases onto it.

"So. You still are pursuing what you think is your case against Lieutenant Helmsley."

"Yes."

"Well. The Crown decides the guilt or innocence of its own men, not the provincials." He seems to peer right through me. "Jacob, isn't it?"

I nod.

"Jacob, unless you are an eyewitness," I feel my heart sinking toward my feet, "or can provide me with one, there is no case."

The Major stands and paces a few steps before turning and facing me again. His face harder, eyes boring deeper.

"I'll warn you. Lieutenant Helmsley comes from a very fine family in Cornwall. No one wants to be their enemy. You would be wise to drop this ill-advised crusade you have begun."

I open my mouth to speak, but before I can make a sound the Major interjects.

"You can't win."

Jackson bolts from his chair, standing tall and staring at the major. His face shines with anger.

I sputter, unable to proceed, to make my case. I glance at my brother, then back to the major.

I tried to anticipate every question. I fashioned volumes of answers. But I didn't prepare for this, this outright dismissal.

"He killed Amelia!" The words spit from me before I can even measure what I'm saying.

"I don't believe it, nor will anyone else," the major retorts. He makes his way back behind the desk and sits in his chair.

"Now, leave it alone. And, leave Boston."

# Chapter 25

Destiny perches herself on the outcropping of granite that tops the forested hill. She's about a mile from her house. Her favorite place.

She and Jackson often meet here. From where she sits, she can gaze through the tops of the trees that stair-step down the hillside and see all the little homesteads about Blackham.

The wind soughs through the woods. Her woods. Her forest.

She doesn't have title. But no one knows them like Destiny.

She's so free here. No other sounds, no recriminations. No judgments. No classes.

Destiny can just be Destiny.

Along the length of the great, monolithic stone runs a crevice threatening to split the mountain in two. She sits along one edge. The granite here crumbles a little under her hand.

Really, the only bad part about being Destiny is the loneliness. And there is loneliness.

Her musket lies across her lap. She isn't interested in shooting anything for the moment. For now, the peace is what she needs.

"Hey."

Destiny twists her head and finds Jackson mounting the stone refuge behind her.

"You're back."

"Just last night. Thought you might be here."

Jackson settles in next to her.

"What happened?"

Jackson shakes his head. "Nothing really. I think Jacob might have been able to kill Helmsley. He was that close."

Kill. It's difficult to visualize Jake so upset he could do something so— so predatory. So aggressive.

Jake always seems so in control. So planned in everything he does. So opposite of Destiny.

"What did he do?"

"We ended up trying to catch Helmsley and bring him back to Blackham. Just to try and get him arrested here."

"I don't think that would work."

"Me neither. But Jacob has to do something. I've never seen him so ready for a fight before."

Destiny rises and glances once more about the personal panorama of her world.

"Let's head for Moorehouse Creek. Our pantry's bare."

Staying away from the fissure where the granite flakes and crumbles, Destiny works her way off the rock and back into the soft cover of the forest floor. A few twigs snap as she carelessly trudges into the woods.

"So, what's Jake going to do now?"

Jackson shakes his head. "He's got nowhere to go, nothing to do. Dead set on becoming one of the snobs before. Now…" He shrugs.

"He never would have been happy."

"No. But he needs something else to think on."

A hundred yards into the trees and Destiny shakes off her carefree moments. Finding food is serious. Twigs no longer snap under her feet. She's silent. A ghost.

Now there's no conversation. No thoughts even of Jake.

She needs to eat. To provide for her family. Just like all the other predators in the woods.

Eyes were upon her when she entered this world of unseen dwellers. She felt them. They're always here, most people just don't know it.

Now she takes care to slink through the narrowest of openings. She places her feet so she avoids the alarm bells rung by most visitors clumsily trudging through.

The eyes lose sight of her. The ears no longer track her. Soon, something will be astonished at her presence.

Two squirrels scurry acrobatically over the branches of a majestic oak. A quick check. Jackson has seen them as well.

With a language of their own, the two communicate in gestures.

The barrel of her gun rises to meet her eye. She sights down the long iron cylinder.

The gun barks loudly, shattering the silence. Jackson's a second after hers.

Destiny's target falls, limp and instantly dead. Jackson's struggles, caught in a drift of old and decaying leaves, clinging to life. It's sad, but there's really no other way to provide food. None that Destiny has ever found.

The squirrel goes limp. What happened to that spark of life? Where had it gone, that special something that had animated this now lifeless body?

The physical parts are all still there. Even if they were uninjured, those parts themselves are not enough to create a living thing. Moments ago, it dashed through the canopy overhead. It had been alive, a breathing part of the world she knows. Now, it's food for Destiny and her mother.

"Teach me to shoot." Jackson demands. "I want to be able to hit my targets like you do."

"There's three things I have that you don't," Destiny replies.

"What?"

"If I don't hit my target, I starve. And my mother."

She pauses and lets that sink in a moment. Jackson's eyes go deep, almost like they can't see the outside anymore. Just looking in and reflecting on the significance of Destiny's words.

"Two. I do this every day. It's like you doing your chores."

Jackson brightens and his eyes animate again. "I'd trade chores for hunting. Maybe I could convince—."

"Not if your life depended on it."

Destiny thinks back to the rich fields of grain surrounding Jackson's house. The milk cow mooing behind the barn. Hunting could never supply the steady supply of food that those fields of wheat and corn provide.

Jackson shifts impatiently. "You said there were three things."

Destiny lifts her musket and holds it in front of her. She smiles.

"This is a special musket. Yours will never shoot as straight as this one."

Jackson's face turns quizzical as he tilts his head in that unique Jackson way.

Destiny explains the rifled barrel of her gun, the way the long grooves have been cut inside. It came from the Pennsylvania frontier.

Her father made it his prize possession before he sailed off to sea on that last journey. The one from which he never returned.

Jackson watches her. Destiny can tell he's measuring to determine if her father's passing is a safe topic. But it's been years.

"I never want to be a sailor. Spend all your time on the water—." Jackson grimaces.

The shooting lesson seems to be forgotten for a moment. Jackson draws his knife and goes to work on the squirrels. His mind seems to race from rifles to sailing to whatever Destiny can coax out of him.

"What *do* you want to do Jackson?"

"I want a farm in the Mohawk Valley. One—"

"New York? Why do you want to go there?"

"Land is easy to get along the Mohawk. Wouldn't have to rent from the Waterford's."

"I thought there was Indian trouble."

Jackson shrugs. He admires the Indians he occasionally runs with, the Wampanoags, one or two tribes of the Wabanaki Confederacy.

Mohawk Indians are their mortal enemies and will often kill them on sight. It would be a risk to Jackson for sure.

"These squirrels won't last past today. What then?"

Destiny eyes the two carcasses, now skinned and cleaned.

"Hunt again tomorrow. Like always."

# Chapter 26

I fling the sweaty harnesses onto the braces fixed onto the barn wall. The leather stinks and the odor clings to my clothes.

Little flecks of the foamy horse-sweat tremble on my sleeves. A strap of the saturated harness tries to slip off the brace. I jam it in place with a disgusted shove.

Horses in their stalls, I grab the pitchfork stuck in the pile of hay. Eyes squinted so tight I can barely see; I hurl the feed to the animals.

Chaff billows about my head. It fights to pierce the tiny slits between my eyelids. The sweat on my face and the backs of my hands is glue. I'm littered with tiny bits of straw, stem, and dried leaves.

The cow bellows. It's early, but it will be my turn to milk tonight.

Plow horses fed; I crash into a back corner of the barn. Sitting on the ground the weathered wood that makes up two feed bins and several animal stalls all but hide me from the world.

Sunlight floods in from the great open front doors. It strikes me in small geometric shapes, much of it blocked by the bins and stalls. I watch the misshapen rectangles slide up my arm as I raise it.

I lower my face into my knees and weep.

The need to cry angers me. I'm not a small child anymore. But this. How could my life become so… broken?

Amelia is dead. My dream of a military career is dead. My path to a profession that will allow me some sort of place in the world?

Dead.

Everything. Everything I have worked for has blown away in a furious wind. A wind that appeared unbidden and unseen, impossible to foretell.

I can't even return to my useless life here on the farm. My old acquaintances view me with distrust. I joined the enemy, the British Army.

William, once my best friend, lives in Boston, still a lieutenant in the provincial regiment. Or more. Maybe he's been promoted.

The world moves inexorably forward. I sink into oblivion.

Once I worried about being a mediocre nobody. Now I'm an outcast.

Little different than Destiny.

"Jacob?"

I jump to my feet, dragging my sleeves across my eyes. I venture out into the open.

"Just finished feeding the horses," I explain to my anxious mother.

"Jacob what's wrong?" She reaches for me, towards my face. I take a step back.

"Just the hay."

Mother stares at me doubtfully but doesn't press the issue. Her eyes look deeply into mine as though she can communicate in some non-verbal way. Reaching with her eyesight deep into my soul to pry out the truth.

"How would you like to take a ride on Spencer?"

When parents say something like that…

Internally I retreat. Certainly, there's more. Without explaining, Mother is trying to accomplish something. Something she feels is best for me.

Usually, I have a different idea about what's best for me.

With a shrug I offer the first excuse I can think of. "I have to milk in a couple hours."

"I need your help, Jacob. I've got a big basket I need you to take to Destiny and her mother."

"Basket?"

"I've filled it with food. A ham, some other things. Jackson says they're having a very tough time."

"Jackson should take it." Milking the cow doesn't sound so bad right now.

What does Destiny think? All those times I tried to keep my distance from her. Tried to make sure I was too much a gentleman to keep company with someone like her.

Now Destiny is bound to know everything that happened. Most of it anyway. Jackson will have told her.

Now she can gloat over a beaten and humiliated Jacob Greyson.

"Jackson's going to milk for you. I need him for something else." Mother looks at me, face shifting suddenly from that of an instructive parent to one of compassion. "The ride will do you good."

It's true. The ride would do me good.

*So, let me take a ride and you take the basket to Destiny.*

I can't say it out loud of course. At this moment my mother's face is so sympathetic. To respond so callously...

I sigh. Mother touches my forehead, brushing back a lock of hair.

"Be extra careful. Despite the season, Mr. Coombs says he saw a sure case of hydrophobia the other day."

I nod.

"Any animal doesn't look right, stay away."

#

Shadows stretch long across the ground. The pale half-orb of the moon hangs over the treetops seemingly marking the way to Destiny's house.

It's impossible not to think about the upcoming meeting. There are so many things life denies Destiny. Somehow, she's found a place. A place near the bottom rung of society, but a place nonetheless.

It's more than I have.

Spencer leaves the Boston Road and begins to navigate the path to that lonely cabin in the woods. How can I handle the coming exchange without seeing Destiny? Maybe I'll just leave the basket at the door and ride away. They'll find it soon enough, next time they come outside.

But, it's a desperate thought. Out here food will be consumed by raccoons, skunks, or foxes in no time. The story will surely get back. Everyone will know I left the basket outside. It was ravaged before Destiny or her mother found it, not a crumb left for them.

There's no way around it. I'll have to face her.

The white moon, about half of it shining in the night sky, has risen well above the treetops. Coupled with a vast sea of glittering stars, a soft glow lights the path.

It's people. People make the world complicated and competitive. No wonder Jackson and Destiny want nothing more than to wander the woods, away from everyone else.

The path twists to the right. Just past the curve, the cabin sleeps in a little clearing, framed by the forest like it was the subject of a fine painting.

There are no windows, but light glows around the edges of the front door. Smoke clambers out of a stone chimney and climbs into the dark sky.

Last chance. To find an escape I could —.

A snarl of intense ferocity startles me. My eyes dart to a thicket of dense brush.

Spencer jerks his head. He nearly punches me in the face with it.

The horse snorts and backs away. His muscles tense as though ready to bolt.

I search deep into the blackness. Where did the growl come from?

Spencer backs another step then another. His hooves scrape the ground throwing dust into the air.

His ears press forward. Head jerking up and away from danger. A throaty protest sounds an alarm.

I lean to the side searching.

There.

In the dark underlying tangle, smoldering eyes. Two flaming beacons sparking from the undergrowth like alarm fires.

The growl continues. Primal. Deep in the throat.

It's a warning. A threat from something sure it is endangered.

Mad from apparitions that produce a kaleidoscope of threats, enemies and menacing adversaries.

The dog leaps from the darkness.

Gleaming eyes spring toward my face.

A wet, drooling snarl turns blood to ice

I jerk back and away.

Spencer, frantic with fear, jumps to his hind legs.

From somewhere, a musket shot and I fall from Spencer's back.

The ground rises swiftly and as I smash into it the air explodes from my lungs.

I reach up with my hands. I can't breathe. The world dims.

Pain sears the back of my head.

Desperate, I try to focus and find the wild dog. I can't be bitten. I have to fight —.

The world turns black.

# Chapter 27

I'm swimming. Nearing the surface but the deep water clings to me, pulling me back.

Muddled and confused I pull at my thoughts. I twist my shoulders slightly and despite the way all my senses are muted, it feels like being in bed.

Riding Spencer.

The dog attack.

I open my eyes and immediately clamp them shut in pain. Light has become excruciating.

As I listen for clues, the distant crackling becomes a fire.

I try my eyes again. Bare slits allow minimal light.

I remember now. The fall from Spencer. Hitting my head.

So where am I?

Leaping flames fill a great stone fireplace. A blanket covers me, no two. I lie upon a bed against a wall of logs.

In tiny increments, I open my eyes further.

"You're awake." Destiny sits in a chair beside me.

"I think so," I mumble, not entirely sure.

I'm lying in bed in Destiny's cabin. It must be her bed. Or her mom's. Either way it's embarrassing. I pull on the blankets to get up.

Blinding white light floods my vision. With a gasp, I fall back on the pillow. Destiny reaches out a hand and rests it on my shoulder.

It feels... warm where she touches me.

Mother's voice starts from across the room. It draws nearer as she comes into view. She looks tired.

"The doctor says to lie still. You won't be moving much for a couple of days." She smiles weakly and stares at me, eyes nervous and searching.

Destiny's mother stands on the far side of the room.

"When was Doctor Jamison here?"

"We've all lost a night's sleep," Mother forces another smile as she speaks. "It's no more than an hour before sunup."

An hour before sunup? I've been unconscious all night? That's… I don't know. Hours.

"I feel like I'll be fine," I say, still not sounding like it's my voice that speaks.

Mother smiles more warmly.

I've never been inside Destiny's house before. The bed stands a little off the floor, and seems to be attached to the wall.

Another, the same as this one, is attached to another wall, both wedged into an inside corner. On the far side of a packed dirt floor, a rough-hewn counter and shelf mark where the kitchen should be.

I work my eyes. It *is* the kitchen. There are no other rooms. The only door is the entrance. Everything is in this one tiny space.

On the counter sits a wooden bucket, wet with oozing moisture. A hodgepodge of wooden dishes and utensils are stacked neatly against the back of the shelf. Two or three fire-blackened pots and kettles dangle from hooks in the log wall behind it.

This is Destiny's house. Her whole house.

One straight-back chair sits near the fire, the other holds Destiny near my side. The sum total of all their furniture it seems.

I reach up and touch my head gingerly. It's bandaged. My mother speaks again.

"Jacob, you weren't bitten by the dog, were you? We didn't see any bite marks."

"No." The answer spills out slowly as I still reach, remembering. "Someone shot it."

The distant images sharpen in focus. I can see the gleaming eyes, fiery in their madness, peering from the ground, hidden in brush and darkness.

The animal leaped at me, causing Spencer to rear on his hind legs. The musket shot. But the dog had already sprung into the air, hurtling towards my throat.

I inch my view to the side and gaze at Destiny. She still sits in the chair beside my bed. Her blue eyes gaze at me.

"Did you…?"

She nods soberly.

She may have saved my life. The dog was in the air. In my memory it seems as though it was mere inches from me.

Mother touches my forehead. "I'm glad Destiny got the dog before it got you. Your father's sure it had the sickness."

No one would even try a shot like that. Yet, if she hadn't…

Bad news follows. With no bite from the dog, only my head injury is a concern. That's going to keep me in bed, not to be moved, for a couple of days.

Destiny pats my shoulder. Again, that warm feeling of her nurturing concern.

"It'll go by fast." As though she can read my thoughts.

I allow my eyes to close. I'm not going anywhere. Suddenly, I feel tired, sleepy.

Destiny keeps watch beside me. Her arm drapes across my shoulder. The warmth from that touch tingles through me.

A conversation between Destiny's mother and my own seems to fade into a place far distant.

#

I drag myself out of a deep sleep. It's a repeat of my first awakening, my eyes closing immediately upon finding light.

It's much less severe though. I work my eyelids open and orient myself.

Destiny stands with her back to me. I mumble a good morning.

She stirs something in a black iron pot suspended over what's left of the fire. The flames have shrunk since the last time I was awake.

Now, red sizzling coals glare from the stone hearth. Destiny turns and smiles.

"I was just going to wake you for breakfast. The doctor says not to let you sleep more than a few hours."

I consider that, watching Destiny, then pull myself up, leaning on an elbow.

"Where's your mother?"

"Picking up some laundry from the Waterford's. She makes a little money that way."

By the time she finishes her reply, Destiny is across the room and sitting in the straight-back chair.

She seems unembarrassed by the admission. Her mother does other people's laundry. She has to in order to make ends meet.

Had she said her mother went to collect rent on property she owned, Destiny would have said it no differently.

The girl holds a wooden bowl in her hands. It steams with hot oatmeal she's just cooked over the glaring coals.

She looks… content. Grabbing the spoon, she dips several times into the heap of cereal.

"I'm sure I can feed myself," I say, trying to warn her off before she can try to feed me like a child.

"I'm sure you can't."

Her blue eyes are still warm, but filled with mirth. So, Destiny has a sense of humor.

Still, I can't let her feed me.

The spoon heaped with oatmeal though, travels straight for my mouth.

# Chapter 28

It's chilly out. Buried in the shade of the forest, the sun has to work a little harder to warm the air.

A half-dozen steps from the cabin door, Destiny built a small fire ring. Ham steaks sizzle in the cast iron pan. The aroma overpowers every other fragrance. She takes the fork and pushes at the thin slices, trying to keep them from sticking to the pan.

"Ouch!" The popping grease catches her, raising a red welt on her wrist.

The steady rub, rub, rub of the washboard pauses. "Do you want to trade for a while?"

A few steps away, Mother hunches over a wooden tub that sits on the ground leaking water. Her hands, draped in dripping clothing, hover over a washboard. She peers at Destiny with arched eyebrows.

"No."

No. No. No, she doesn't want to trade. Mother usually does the cooking. Destiny's job is to bring in the necessary ingredients. Usually a squirrel, a turkey, or something similar.

Still, she's not trading. Mother is a far better cook; they both know it. But the trade-off would force Destiny into scrubbing the Waterford's underwear.

All the burns from all the popping grease that can be imagined will not allow her to make that trade. How awful.

Destiny jerks her arm back protectively, but keeps her mouth clamped shut. The blistering oil gets her again.

"Move your pan a little farther from the flames. It's too hot."

The black skillet scrapes the rock surface as Destiny pulls it to the edge. From here only one side will be heated. She'll have to turn it, or move the ham slices every minute or so.

She's determined. She will have a nice meal for Jake. Already she tried biscuits, remembering how she helped Mrs. Greyson.

The Morris' though don't have an oven. Nor do they have all the ingredients. It was a complete disaster. The congealed mess lies scattered some distance from the cabin. Some animal will be desperate enough to eat it.

Jake coughs from inside. Destiny glances toward the door then back to her cooking.

She jumps when her mother touches her elbow.

"Go check on him. I'll watch your cooking." Mother sends her such a warm smile; Destiny gives her a quick kiss on the cheek then goes to check her patient.

The blankets lie piled and crumpled at the foot of the bed. On its edge, Jake sits in a slouched posture. He touches the bandage just above his eyebrows.

"Was I bleeding?"

Destiny shakes her head. "Dr. Jamison laughed about the bandage, but your mother insisted."

Jake fumbles with it, looking for a way to unravel the swathes of cloth.

"Wait." Destiny moves her hands but is afraid to touch his head. They waver around Jake's, trying to find a way to stop him.

"If I don't really need it…"

He isn't cut. He has a huge lump but how does a bandage help that?

"Here. Let me help you."

Jake's hands lower.

The tucked in part is in the back. Destiny stands close, almost leaning into him. Or, him into her.

He'd fallen into infant cedars when Spencer bolted from the rabid dog. Even now a sharp coniferous fragrance lingers faintly.

Jake glances at her then stares at the floor. Destiny's fingers tug softly at the fabric, loosening the end of it.

All of a sudden, their nearness makes her nervous. Her hands tremble a bit making them too awkward to remove the wrapping. The job seems so much more difficult and intricate now.

"Thanks— Thanks for taking care of me," Jake mutters in a voice so soft it can't carry to the outside. Thank goodness Mother won't hear it and guess the tenderness of the moment.

"Of course, Jake." Jake's shoulder presses into her side as she bends over his head. Her fingers find the rhythm and, despite her nervousness, the bandage begins to slip easily from him.

Around his head her hands circle, left hand gently pulling the cloth loose and winding it around her right. The silence when neither speaks seems huge. It fills everything.

"I fried some ham. It's a little early, but I thought you could use the nourishment."

"Is that the one I brought yesterday?"

Why did he have to say that?

Destiny had lost herself in her endeavor this morning. Imagining that she could cook a nice meal for him, all on her own.

She nods even though Jake probably can't tell.

"I considered biscuits but -. Well, we don't have an oven."

She almost admits the biscuits didn't turn out, that she threw away the attempt, leaving it for some scavenger in the forest to consume. For some reason it seems important to be more guarded in admitting her failures.

Jake sits silent for a moment then he utters a soft thank you.

The bandage is off. There seems to be no reason to continue standing so near to him. She delays for a moment, but there's nothing for her to do but to step back.

"There you go." She hands him the coil of wound-up cloth. "I better check the food."

Jake lifts his gaze to meet hers, but he only nods.

Outside Mother has already taken the ham from the fire. She's forked it onto a plate and stands fussing with it, accomplishing nothing. She looks up as though startled.

"It's ready."

Her gaze is as soft as Destiny has ever seen it.

# Chapter 29

Destiny's foot sweeps toward the fire, throwing dirt over the dying coals. She blinks back hot and angry tears.

Jake is impossible.

Every glimmering ember now dead, she stops shoveling soil with her foot and slumps against a tree.

Her preparation of the meal didn't turn out that well, but still. The ham was all there was! The biscuits failed to even cook right. But there was the effort.

She tried to make something special for him. Even if she failed in the cooking couldn't he see the effort? He wasn't insulting, but it was a very quiet meal.

The moment seemed so special when she removed his bandage. It seemed to touch him too. His voice was soft. He stuttered twice as though he was nervous. Like he didn't know exactly what to say but tried to keep the moment going.

Did she imagine that because those were her own feelings?

No. It wasn't her imagination or wishful thinking. Jake had been nervous.

*Not* liking someone doesn't make you nervous, *liking* them does.

But then he pulled inward just like a tortoise pulling into his shell. Sometimes… Sometimes he just isn't worth it.

Mother smiled benignly, but her eyes could hardly be still as they flitted about the room. She always knew everything and she knew what misery engulfed her daughter.

Well. That's the end of the food. She'll have to go hunting if there's to be anything for this evening. She grabs her musket from against the cabin wall and steps several paces from her home.

All this advancing and retreating as Jake tries to find just the right distance where he wants to keep her...

She pauses. She has to get her mind right. Has to be thinking about her world, the world that feeds her.

Destiny tilts her head. It's not that she actually hears something. But she kind of does.

Jackson appears, rounding the last curve of the trail. He carries his musket.

Smiling, Jake's brother holds up a hand in greeting as he sees Destiny.

"We're a little low, too. Couldn't bring food, so I brought the means." He holds his musket out in front of him.

Destiny laughs. His eyes shine, full of fun. His mouth turning into a great, happy grin.

"Sure of yourself, huh?"

"Yep. 'Specially now that I know you're only a better shot because of your gun."

"You think."

"No. Not really." It's so good to hear Jackson's laugh. A relief from more complicated emotions.

With Jackson, little is complicated. It's like having a caring older brother, even though he's a year younger than Destiny. With him, she can relax, be herself, and not worry about impossible, non-verbal communication with Jake.

"Let's head west," Destiny says. She throws a quick glance back at the cabin then plunges into the woods.

# Chapter 30

The woolen blanket falls to the foot of the bed as I throw it aside. I've hurt Destiny's feelings. Again.

Sitting on the edge of the bunk, the bed, whatever it is, I stare at the floor and try to make sense of what just happened.

I'm not cold-hearted. So why does everything I do seem to hurt others? Why am I constantly blamed for misdeeds, unknown and unintended?

What about my loyalty to Amelia? It feels like an obligation that should never end.

Destiny sacrificed for me, sure. Saved my life. She's diligently nursing me back to health.

But I left Amelia. Left her in the apple orchard with a murderous wretch who savagely attacked and killed her. I've done nothing to atone for that.

Spring has come. New green leaves everywhere you look. Colorful blooms on some of the earlier fruit trees. The ground moist and softened. The weather warmer, more inviting.

Nothing has changed for Amelia though. She lies in the ground, perpetually asleep.

That's where the story ends. For now.

The fire inside grew too big, or was left burning too long, or… something. The cabin door stands open. Pulling myself to my feet, I lean into the side of it.

I didn't know Jackson was here. He didn't say anything. All I see are their backs as my brother and Destiny slip into the forest as silently as a pair of Wampanoags. The two hunters walk close. They lean their heads together talking and planning.

I keep watching until they disappear. Maybe I should have called out. Maybe offered to join them.

I feel envy. It's time to be honest with myself. I'm lonely.

I've lost everything. Amelia. Military career. Position. Purpose.

I keep staring at the point where the two friends disappeared into the trees.

This isn't helping. I'm drowning. Back inside the cabin I search under the bed, looking for my shoes.

"I'm really feeling much better Mrs. Morris," I say as I search.

She stares at me a moment.

"Your mother wanted you to stay another day."

"I know. But I'm really feeling much better."

Resigned, Mrs. Morris reaches under the other bed, if one can call it that.

"Here are your shoes, Jacob." She moves the chair so that both of them, all the Morris furniture, face the fireplace. Not too close though.

I sit and reach to fasten my shoes in place.

Short flames burst now and again from the bed of glowing coals. I stretch my arms and shoulders after too many hours lying down. Mrs. Morris sits in the other chair.

"We've enjoyed your company," she says awkwardly as though she's trying terribly hard to start a conversation.

I stutter my appreciation for the compliment.

She pulls her long gray hair over her shoulder, letting it cascade down in front of her. She stares into the fire as though looking at something far away.

"You know Jacob, Destiny really likes you." Mrs. Morris smiles as though she's revealing some great secret.

Finished with my shoes, I fidget in my chair and look at the dirt floor. "She's a nice girl."

Mrs. Morris watches me for a minute. She leans closer. "I know about Amelia."

She pauses. "I know *all* about Amelia. All that happened to her."

It's my turn to stare at the flames. They glower at me. Accuse me.

*You left Amelia.*

A musket shot rings out in the distance. Then another.

"Jacob. It's a terrible burden. Don't keep it. Don't hold on to it like I did. My husband, you know."

Her voice quavers a bit. She draws a deep breath and continues. "Destiny has carried the weight of this family ever since because I couldn't. I failed both of them."

She rises from her chair, pulls a blackened pot, then two from the rough log wall.

"I suppose Jackson and Destiny are about back. They'll have something for dinner. Destiny always does." Her voice sings with a false cheeriness.

Collecting my jacket, I walk toward the door and peer back at Mrs. Morris. "Thank you, ma'am."

I don't know what else to say.

# Chapter 31

"Turkeys," Jackson speculates as the two friends set a brisk pace toward the planned hunting ground.

"How did you know?" Destiny asks.

"They wander into Blackham sometimes. I think they're usually back in that stretch between the town and Morehouse Creek."

Jackson reaches out an arm, throws it about Destiny's shoulders and gives a little squeeze. She can almost imagine him calling her Sis.

A woodpecker hammers ferociously. Destiny's shoulders dip. Her breathing slows.

"Still dream of the Mohawk Valley?"

Jackson's eyes acquire a distance, as though he can see all the way to the Hudson River and beyond. Yes, he tells her, he does.

He imagines a place where a plot of fertile ground can be cleared, the fallen trees used to erect a home. The river will glide past, silent yet powerful.

The waterway winds its way through green cultivated fields and little wood houses with smoking chimneys. All the way to the Hudson.

Game in abundance fills the forested slopes nearby. And it would all be his. He would not rent from the Waterford's or anyone else.

Destiny stops and peers at her friend.

"You wouldn't want that if you had to be alone."

Jackson just gazes at her as though he's confused. Or he doesn't know what to say.

"That's where the Scullard family moved."

"Could be." Jackson's voice stretches. Destiny has stumbled onto something.

"Surely you would know. You and Verity were thick as thieves."

Jackson starts walking again and Destiny hurries to catch up.

"Has she written you?"

Silence.

"It's me you're talking to," Destiny reminds him.

He nods. Verity Scullard's older brother George posted a letter on a trip down the Hudson to New York.

All the time they spend together and Jackson still has secrets. Destiny wouldn't have guessed it.

Listening carefully, she can make out the sound of the creek now. The two friends slip farther apart, treading softly.

Destiny searches. She studies the gaps and openings between the trees.

Her ears tune intently to each sound, straining to catch the first hint of her quarry. The scents of the woods are explored and studied for the most insignificant of clues.

There's nothing else. If she doesn't find game, they won't eat tonight. It's not like it would be the first time, but it would be the first time with Jake as a guest. Having to admit that to him will be the most embarrassing moment ever.

This is Destiny's life. Not Jake's. He won't know how to handle it.

That distinctive gobble sound floats to her on a frail, gasping breeze. The hunters are downwind.

Turkeys are difficult. It takes real skill to get close enough for a shot.

After some skilled maneuvering Destiny kneels and leans her shoulder into the rough trunk of a chestnut tree. The hunters are in place.

As she has done so many times, Destiny sights down the barrel of her rifle. She doesn't have to look; Jackson will follow her lead.

The birds seem a bit skittish and keep moving. Destiny takes careful aim and fires.

Her target collapses to the earth. The blasts from both muskets shatter the peace of the wooded glen. The rest of the flock either takes flight, or scatters and runs.

Jackson starts a wild attempt at re-loading then gives up as he watches the escaping turkeys. He grimaces and shrugs his shoulders looking at Destiny.

Oh well. Even one turkey is a large meal. It will be enough for both families.

Her optimism returns. She pushes out the earlier disappointment and clears the doubts.

Jake will be happy too. Excitedly she plans the evening.

She'll use the fire inside the cabin this time instead of trying to keep the cooking a surprise. Let him watch the golden bird, or half of it, roast to perfection over the flames.

Maybe Destiny should give Jackson the credit for the turkey. Might be better. She makes the suggestion to her friend.

At first Jackson resists. He stumbles with excuses before admitting, yet again, "Sorry, Destiny. I'm just not as good a shot as you are".

"Please Jackson. Just say you shot it. I don't think Jake likes me being a hunter."

Jackson's mood turns from apologetic to irritation. He leaps quickly to her defense.

It's alright. This will all work out. The past is just that. Past. Forget about the failed ham dinner, this will be much better.

Destiny flies into her cabin first, Jackson close behind. She grins pointing to the prize Jackson carries, looking in Jake's direction.

The bed is empty. It's made. The blankets folded neatly at the foot.

Mother is in the kitchen corner and as Destiny turns to her, she looks so sorrowful.

"Jacob left. He said he was well enough to walk home."

Jackson curses.

# Chapter 32

The wagon rattles and lurches across the ground in front of my home. I rein in the two plow horses and come to a halt.

Wheat is in the ground, already turning the fields green. Corn will be in within the month.

All that work. Last year I planted, weeded, harvested. Just like thousands of other nameless, faceless people all across Massachusetts. We all perform the same tasks, in the same ways, at the same times.

Next year, we'll all do the same thing. The same tasks, in the same ways, at the same times. And the year after that. And the year after that.

I'm hauling a load of flour from last year's wheat to Boston. Picked it up at the miller's yesterday.

Less than a week ago I left Destiny's cabin. I'm sure she's still mad at me. I know Jackson is.

A horse turns off the main road. It comes trotting down the lane towards me.

William's father.

Mr. Waterford rides a beautiful buckskin gelding. Even from here I can see the glistening of the horse's coat as the muscles underneath ripple with each step.

Waterford sits erect and straight in the shiny brown saddle. A pair of reins loop from his hands to the horse's mouth on both sides of the gelding's head.

I stare. The man appears so proper. Tan breeches ending in glistening black riding boots. A tailored cutaway coat keeps him warm.

His hat. I'm not sure what it's made of. Some type of fur. I've never seen one like it.

Waterford reins in a few steps from me.

"Good morning, Jacob." As always, proper and officious.

"Mornin', sir."

"Is your father at— ah, there he is now. Good morning, John."

"Mr. Waterford."

Waterford doesn't dismount. He peers down at us from atop his tall horse.

He wears shiny leather gloves. His hair, more silver than gray, peeks around the edges of his hat. His face, clean-shaven and thin, always has a serious look to it. Has he ever smiled?

"John, news is that you're gathering donations for those rebels in Boston. I applaud your Christian spirit."

Waterford adjusts his hat and tugs on one of his gloves.

"But law-breakers must be disciplined. They deserve their fate until they can make amends and change their ways, don't you think?"

I twist uneasily wondering where this conversation is headed.

Waterford owns miles and miles of lands. He owns farms managed with caretakers. He owns land he rents, like part of our farm.

He has business interests in Boston I know nothing about.

And yet, his loss is similar to mine. Amelia was his daughter.

I try to imagine myself so woven into the business interests of the Crown, to be so tied to a class of people that the loss of someone like Amelia would not allow me to take revenge. If not revenge, to at least try to forcibly bring the perpetrator to justice.

What would happen to Waterford's empire if he no longer had the right friends?

I examine the kid leather gloves, fine cutaway coat, high-priced buckskin gelding and all the right polished accessories.

It all suddenly seems so much more expensive now. Too expensive.

"My daughter and son-in-law live in Boston, Mr. Waterford. They haven't broken any laws."

"Yes, well." Waterford smiles. "Surely the local donations that will fill this wagon are not for your family." He reaches with the riding crop in his right hand and taps the side of the wagon.

"No. I would assume many others are in the same difficulty."

"Perhaps."

I never noticed the color of Waterford's eyes before. They're gray, the color of steel. They assume the hardness of the metal as well.

Philip Waterford peers around him expansively as though surveying the entire farm. "Half your farm is rented from me. We must work together to be sure we have common goals."

Waterford pauses. His face continues to peer distantly across the fields as though measuring every acre. "For the good of the colony, of course."

The farms examined; Waterford returns his gaze to my father. "Good speaking with you, John. You had a good harvest last year. We like to see that. Good day."

He touches his hat as though finishing an agreeable conversation with an old friend. He turns the gelding and trots towards the Boston Road.

A silence so deep I feel the weight of it, descends upon me. I gaze at my father who watches Waterford ride away.

Father speaks without altering his view from the retreating Waterford.

"We left England after the war to be rid of barons and earls. Now we've got them right here in America."

I look back at Waterford's diminishing form. What should I say?

My pat answer for years has been that barons and earls are needed. Common men lack the ability to govern themselves. It's never been done.

Is Waterford smarter than my father?

In some ways.

Amelia's father continues to diminish in size as his horse trots down the lane.

Waterford can't avenge his daughter's death for fear he will offend someone of greater nobility than himself. Then he will lose business.

My father had only been a sergeant in the French and Indian War, had only served as a common soldier, not an officer.

Yet his men, at their own expense had a medal of gratitude cast for him. They were thankful to Father for risking his own life and saving them. They respected him.

Amelia can see my efforts to avenge her. From wherever she is, she can. I know that.

Can she not see her own father's actions as well?

No one will cast a medal to Philip Waterford thanking him for risking… well, anything. Not his life. Certainly not his worldly goods.

# Chapter 33

Since when are there roadblocks? I sit, stalled, waiting in a line that doesn't move, and watch Lily and Ginger hang their heads, probably wondering when the trip will be over for them as well.

If I can get past the checkpoint, it's only a short distance through the Neck and I'm in Boston. I'm looking at the city from here.

One wagon remains ahead of me. It creaks in protest as the driver clambers around the stacks of goods in the wagon bed.

"Open that crate," a red-coated inspector demands.

The colonial merchant throws his hands up in despair. The barking sergeant offers to confiscate the goods, in which case, they will not need to be inspected.

Slumped in resignation, the man pries at the nailed down lid.

Shovels. The redcoat soldiers, peering over the sides of the wagon made the merchant pry open a crate of shovels.

I glance back at my load of flour sacks, then ahead. The guards fuss over the wagon in front, asking more questions.

A pale and drooping sun is giving up for the day. It hangs, just above the horizon line on my left, waiting to surrender to the darkness of night.

To my right, a salt marsh is punctuated with clumps of reeds and nervous shore birds searching for dinner.

Annoyed at the delay, I turn my attention back to the front wagon. At last, the guards back away to let it pass.

Just as I'm about to flip the reins and get Ginger and Lily moving again, my limbs turn to ice. An arrogant call pierces through a stiffening breeze.

"Make way on the road!"

The chill freezes me all the way to the bone. It's as though the marrow itself has frozen, then begins to leach out into the rest of me.

An officious English Captain on a memorable gray mare approaches.

Silas Helmsley has been promoted.

Enlisted men pull and tug, dragging two small carts around the waiting wagons. The shallow carts lurch forward. They're laden with several game birds and two deer with impressive antlers. Helmsley's been hunting.

The captain looks up and catches my stare. Immediate recognition.

He pulls even to the wagon as his entourage of servants pull at the carts.

"Told you to pull aside there, boy."

Helmsley's riding crop flicks towards my shoulder. I'm so astonished I grab the short whip. My palm stings as I grip it.

Helmsley thinks he can drive me like cattle or sheep? Angrily, I jerk the leather strap as though to pull it from him.

Helmsley stares at me in surprise. He works the crop to pull it loose. I release it.

"You better learn your place boy." The man pushes the words through the narrow slit of his mouth.

His eyes burn with… something. He's been drinking.

"Time you colonials learned your place. You think I hurt that ridiculous wench of a girl? And you there, hidden in that little grove of trees. How many times had you ravished her?"

The world floods red.

I spring from the wagon seat like a great African lion capturing its prey. In mid-air, I grab the captain about the neck and shoulders. Both of us as one struggling mass, tumble off the horse.

The ground hits hard and the flighty gray mare bolts.

I struggle with tears. Tears of rage. They flood my eyes, impair my vision.

I pull back scrambling to my feet. The captain gets to his as well.

Without a moment's hesitation, I let loose.

All the blinding red emotion within me focuses. Every injustice. Every recrimination I have flogged myself with over leaving Amelia in the orchard…

My livid right fist smashes into Helmsley's jaw.

The English officer grunts in pain. The top half of his body twists from the blow. His feet tangle in the turn and he falls to his knees, his back to me.

Again, I draw back my fist. I'm ready to strike again. My vision still hazy, but clear enough to find a target. I wait for the hunched-over captain to turn and face me.

Instead, Helmsley leaps to the cart loaded with dead game. He spins back and throws his arm in front of him.

Even in the low light, I spot the swelling where I struck him. He bends at the waist, as though unable to stand straight.

His extended arm points a pistol at my middle. I take a step back trying to consider my next move. He's going to shoot me?

Almost Helmsley breaks into a triumphant smile, but only half of his mouth reacts. His eyes blaze.

As though the rest of the world has stopped, the silence is complete. Deliberately, his right thumb reaches and pulls back the hammer. The click of the action is near deafening.

"Captain Helmsley!"

The shout flies from the Boston side of the roadblock. It lands with such volume and such command that even I pull my eyes from the pistol barrel.

It's the familiar major. He rides towards us. The superior officer reins in his mount only a few steps away.

"Captain Helmsley, I believe you were to conduct the change of the guard?"

Still holding the pistol at me, Helmsley spits out a reply. "My guide got lost on the way back."

The major shifts on his horse and sighs. "Yes. And, now I am conducting the change."

He searches the onlookers gathered about, then focuses on Helmsley and me.

"Captain, I think it would be best if you retired to your quarters. Greyson, you need to return to Blackham."

In fury the captain sputters. "I'll not be treated—."

"Silas, you've placed me in a position between you and General Gage. Would you like to explain the background of this— of this feud to his Excellency?"

Abruptly, Helmsley drops his arm and slings the pistol back into the cart. Only inches from the man pulling the two-wheeled wagon, he glowers into the soldier's face.

"Well don't just stand there! Recover my horse!"

The man drops the cart handle. He sprints in the general direction the gray mare escaped. Captain Helmsley stalks off towards Boston.

Shifting his gaze from the retreating British officer, the major turns to me.

"And you are to leave Boston immediately."

"But—. I have a wagonload of flour. I've been driving all day. My sister—."

"I know your sister Jacob." The major leans forward. He slumps like someone who has assumed a great weight. His voice carries an air of resignation.

"Unload your goods. Leave before first light."

I open my mouth to protest.

"First light!"

## Chapter 34

For what must be the hundredth time, I glance over my shoulder.

No one. I'm alone on the post road back to Blackham. There's been no sign of pursuit, though I've watched for hours.

I delivered the flour in Boston. Spent a short night at Patty's and left before first light like the major said.

In an admission I'll never reveal to another, my insides chill with fear. It never occurred to me that Helmsley would try to kill me.

I'm pleased how I defended Amelia. Leaped off the wagon and bruised the face of the cowardly Helmsley. At the same time, an image so stark, so real, it seems to be in front of me even now, I see the gaping hole in the barrel of the pistol.

It stares right at me. One twitch of the captain's finger and the gun would explode, sending a lead bullet tearing right through me.

I'd be dead.

I've entered a new world where contests like this result in someone getting killed. So, now I know the stakes. This will end only when Helmsley is dead.

The thought makes me shudder.

Lily, the right half of the team, is lagging. I flip the rein in my right hand to prod her along, convincing her to pick up the pace.

Above a spring storm threatens. Clouds overhead congregate, thicken, and darken. The angry sky blocks the sun so thoroughly not a shadow can be found anywhere.

The road curves, and there it is. Thornby's apple orchard.

Lonely, chilled, windswept. Nothing but solitude and gray sky greets me there.

The wagon creaks to a halt as I rein in the horses.

Happy pictures of Amelia dance in my mind. My eyes sting at the memories.

Jumping to the ground, I take the lead and maneuver the wagon to the edge of the road. No one will come by. But, just in case.

I cross over the loose rock wall.

It was here. Right here is where I left the road only a couple of weeks ago. It seems so much longer.

There, several paces ahead. That's where Amelia stepped from behind an apple tree. She swept into the sunlight of a warm pleasant day.

Despite the calendar, it's not spring now. There's no sun to shine upon that beautiful face, a face I can almost see.

Still leafless, the apple trees are almost dead in appearance. No leaves. No fruit. No life. Just like her grave.

I draw a ragged breath and wipe my sleeve across my eyes.

I watch the ground, unable to look upon the place she last found me. So radiant. So beautiful.

Haltingly, I walk until I stand in the place where she stood.

She will never stand here again.

I meander through the trees, remembering our walks. I measure the distance from the road. It's clearly visible through the skeletons of trees that once secluded two young people in love.

I find the spot to my best recollection. The place where we stood when she kissed me. Where she said she would leave with me even if her family withheld their permission.

I fall to my knees. My feelings and emotions tell me to give in. To break out in sobs that will rack me body and soul.

But I don't. I dab at the tears that fill my eyes, grit my teeth, and cling to that portion of me that will not completely release my grief.

Something else happened here.

I stand and glance to the side, in a direction I remember. The cold wind sweeps through the dead-looking trees. I see with my mind, not my eyes.

I see the sophisticated and haughty officer of noble birth. This is the place Amelia and I found the English Lieutenant.

An emotional fist plunges into my mid-section and I double over, hands on my knees. The images now course through my memory as though thrown at me.

I left her. Left her in Helmsley's care and my insides erupt in fury.

The man should be dead. Instead, it's Amelia that's gone.

I should never have left her.

My face turns upward, I stare into a dark and brooding sky. I make a vow.

I will never fear Helmsley again. Let him come with his pistol, with his saber, with his size and military training. I will meet him.

Surely Amelia witnessed from somewhere my fight with Helmsley. I've not yet avenged her death, but neither have I forgotten. She knows that. She has to.

#

The lead unties easily as I return to the road and the wagon. I give the reins a small shake and the horses readily move forward. They sense the nearness of home.

With relief, I turn into our drive all jangling trace chains, rattling wagon, and clomping, big-footed plow horses.

As I near the house, Jackson throws open the barn doors. He fastens them so the wind won't blow them shut.

My brother circles around the corner where I park.

"How was Boston?" Jackson begins to unfasten the harness that connects the horses to the wagon.

"I hardly saw it."

"Figured."

I climb out of the seat and begin to help with the harness.

"Went in after dark. Came out before light." I consider for a moment. The story of my fight with Helmsley can wait. I'm emotionally drained for one day.

The horses, still covered with straps and leather bands, are loose from the wagon. Jackson and I lead them, still locked together as a team, into the barn where it will be warmer.

"There's a bit of a surprise for you in the house," Jackson says.

"What?"

My brother finishes leading the horses into the barn and begins to unharness them.

"Destiny's here."

# Chapter 35

Jackson's deft hands remove the straps and buckles that bind the team together. I step back and release the harness.

"What's going on?"

"Destiny and her mother are here for dinner. Don't be rude to them."

*Don't start Jackson.*

Why is Destiny here?

At the sound of the harness falling to the floor, I turn back to help Jackson finish.

My brother swats the horses on the rump, moving them to the back of the barn. We throw the leather contraption onto the hangers in the barn wall together. Jackson raises his hands shooing the horses into the big stall. Several pitchforks of hay complete the chore.

We close the big double doors and latch them shut. The wind bites into me as I glance at my brother.

"Just be nice to them, okay?" Jackson orders.

"I'll do my best," I say, but I think my brother missed the sarcasm I intended.

A raindrop falls on my shoulder. I peer at the now black sky. Cold air pushes me. My ears begin to sting.

"You coming?" Jackson has his hand on the side door.

It seems strange asking Jackson about such matters. But inside I have nothing but questions.

"Is— is she mad at me?"

Jackson shakes his head. "She should be. She's stuck on you."

My brother releases his hold on the door. He leans closer to me.

"If you knew her, you would see she's a better person than any rich Boston aristocrat. You are blind, brother."

I feel a flare of irritation. As though Jackson would know what's best for me. I start to speak, but not quickly enough.

"She's better'n either one of us." Jackson throws open the door and goes inside.

I enter the kitchen-side of the house as though scouting hostile territory, trying to find out if it's safe before going too far. There's a small alcove just inside the back door.

No Destiny.

I stare deeper into the house.

No one I can see.

Stepping lightly, I reach the opening to the kitchen and jump when Mother speaks to me. "She's in your room, so don't go in there."

"Who?"

Mother smiles and it appears as though she winks at me.

"Her mother is in by the fireplace. How was Boston?"

"Fine, I—." But she's gone. Whisking into the pantry for something. In her right hand she grasps a large wooden spoon, her left stretches under it to catch anything that drips.

A small clatter. Then mother comes hurrying back.

"Why is Destiny in my room?"

"She should be down in a minute. They've been here all day. We've had a marvelous time."

This is going to end in some embarrassing way.

Father's voice carries over the crackling sound of a large fire. I venture into the sitting room. Destiny's mother and my father sit and keep up some kind of small talk.

No Destiny.

Mrs. Morris greets me. "Hello Jacob. How was Boston?"

Father looks amiably in my direction, waiting for an answer.

"It was fine." But that satisfies neither of them.

I spill a short, rehearsed version of my trip. A version without meeting Helmsley.

The great field-stone fireplace covers one entire wall. It barely contains the raging flames within its gaping mouth. I step back from the heat.

"Here she is," Mother calls. I turn to look up the staircase.

It's Destiny, but it's not.

Gone are the doeskin hunting shirt and trousers.

A striking blue dress with small white flowers imprinted on it fits her perfectly. The collar ruffles around Destiny's neck. The soft blue material fits trim to her waist then cascades artfully to her feet.

Her blond hair, always tied behind her, falls softly about her shoulders. It has a luster I have not seen before.

The smooth skin over her face bears just a hint of pink on her cheeks.

The warm blue eyes look the same. They contrast completely with the gray and dreary way the day has ended.

I'm gaping. I know it. I struggle to catch my breath. She hardly looks like Destiny at all. But she is.

She smiles. She stops three stairs up. Now she stands there. Upon her lips a smile as radiant as I have ever seen.

She returns my stare. Her eyes lock onto mine. They ask questions I'm not prepared to answer.

She descends the last few steps.

"Hi Jake. You like it?" She twirls in a circle sending the hem of the dress skirting across the floor.

I'm on a stage. Everyone around will hear my answer.

The fire still rages as I glance back at it. The back door, still in the same place. The front windows.

I try not to stare, but Destiny is actually... she's beautiful.

A croak comes from my throat as I try to answer in a muted voice. I give up trying to keep my words from other ears.

"I— It looks nice."

Over my shoulder I catch my mother's disapproving expression.

"You look real nice," I elaborate.

"You certainly do," Mother gushes. She goes to Destiny and grabs her arm.

It's dinner at the Waterford's. I'm as uncomfortable as I was that night, though now I sit at my own table. Without the support of Amelia and William, I feel alone, an outcast.

Destiny makes conversation, unflustered and calm. I stammer and stutter each time I'm asked a question. When I'm not asked, I say nothing.

I do, though, cast furtive glances Destiny's direction. It's impossible not to.

Dishes are gathered and carried to the kitchen. All three women seem to work away merrily. Their voices carry through the entire house.

I stare into the fire, now diminishing to a more comfortable level, bewildered still. Sparks fly up the chimney as Jackson places another log on the blaze.

"It's starting to rain," he says as he straightens.

Through the front windows I watch a few large splatters appear on the glass. Within seconds the heavens open. A downpour pounds on the roof and windows.

Mrs. Morris looks dismayed. Only now it occurs to me I don't know how they got here. How will they get home?

"You'll stay here, of course." Mother responds to something from Mrs. Morris I didn't hear. "You and Destiny can stay in Jacob's room."

The house occupants wander to their different sleeping spaces. Good nights are said.

At last. I feel the pressure lighten. I long to hide in the room of my brother. Mother calls before I can escape.

Alone, the two of us sit near what's left of the fire. It's dark except for tiny, short-lived flames that burst occasionally from the pile of shimmering coals. An orange glow paints the room. Shadows are long and dark.

"What did you think of Destiny?"

I find the edge of my shirt and twist it in my fingers. "You really changed the way she looks."

"She's been here all day. We made that dress for her from an old one of mine. I had always thought I would, one day, be altering it for another daughter. Not that I'm disappointed with my two sons."

Mother smiles and reaches out a reassuring hand to me. Her eyes search my face. She seems to hope for some kind of response from me.

I grope for something to say. "It's nice she can look more normal."

"Jacob Greyson. Looking normal is not a great attribute to be proud of. There's nothing wrong with it, but it accomplishes little. That child is the bravest person I know. I have nothing but respect for her. I wish she were my daughter."

I stare at Mother's expression. I can read the truth of the words she speaks.

She has a wistful look about her. The fire sparkles in tears that form in Mother's eyes. She continues softly, yet with conviction.

"Destiny is the leader of her family. The child and yet the leader. She adapts. She doesn't hunt and shoot because she hates being a girl."

She almost harrumphs at the thought and flicks her hand across her cheek.

"She does it so she and her mother don't starve. She looks at life and does what needs to be done. Regardless of what people like Mrs. Waterford might say."

# Chapter 36

A red fox trots diagonally across the plowed earth, the brush-choked ravine at the end of our fields its' destination.

The animal glances my way. It's thin. Its fur matted and rough.

It carries no food in its mouth. Seemingly little to show for what must have been hours of hunting.

Hungry and unsatisfied, it continues to the protection of the creek bed.

I pull my coat a little tighter. The sun, barely peeking over the horizon is white and impotent. Winter has lost its battle. There's no snow, no frost.

The warmer days are welcome, but the cold nights and early mornings demand warm clothes and fires.

Jackson shouts at the horses. Reins slap. The wagon rolls forward, creaking under the weight of a full load. Sacks of flour I picked up at the mill yesterday.

By the time we turn onto the Boston Post Road, I already feel the change. Like an iron stove just heating up, the sun struggles to add warmth to the spring day.

Lily and her 'teammate' Ginger pull the heavy wagon up the grade. The road levels and reaches the gentle bend that skirts Thornby's apple orchard.

I stare off, wanting to forget. Knowing I never can.

As we pull abreast of the first of the apple trees, Jackson abruptly stops the wagon.

"She's not coming back Jacob. Just because you lost Amelia, doesn't mean you can treat Destiny like dirt."

Brittle emotions splinter. Just like with Helmsley, I lose focus and the red floods my vision.

I spring across the seat, driving a shoulder into my brother.

Over the side both of us tumble from the wagon. The ground smacks me hard. I push into the wet earth, struggling to my feet.

I knocked Helmsley down. Maybe broke his jaw. With Jackson, I can end this fight before it really begins.

I hurl my weight into a vicious shove meant to free myself from Jackson's grip. One step and I will finish this fight with one punch.

I stumble into a stance, but Jackson grabs my arms and twists. With his weight added to my own, I'm sent tumbling across the ground, out of control. My shoulder drives into the dirt. Needles shoot up my neck.

Back on my feet, I pull both hands in front of me for another shove. Jackson is so much stronger than I remember. He simply holds on.

Again, I'm rolled, my brother toppling me into the wet spring grass. I beat my fists into his ribs. The blows are harmless.

Tumbling to one side, I get my feet underneath me. I start to gain my balance.

Jackson tumbles the other way. Like a rag doll, he pulls me with him. The ground beats at me as much as my brother.

In a move that flashes too quickly to see, Jackson pushes at me and springs to his feet.

He's so quick.

Instead of putting up his fists, he crouches, open handed. I hurl a punch aimed straight at his jaw.

Jackson spins and grabs my arm. Over his shoulder I sail limply through the air. The ground slams into my back again.

The fall drives the air from my lungs. Jackson places a knee squarely on my chest, pinning me to the ground.

"What say we call this a draw?" Jackson asks.

The falls, the tumbles, the complete loss of control drains the adrenaline from me. My brother is being generous. The kinds of moves Jackson used. I've never seen them before.

I'm outmatched.

The Wampanoags. Where else would Jackson learn to fight like this?

My brother stands. Both of us take a deep breath. I pull myself to my feet.

I see the road and recognize immediately where I am.

This is the spot. Less than a month ago, Amelia was here.

Smiling. Offering to give up her family to be with me.

This time I can't hold it. The tears win the battle and drip from my eyes. I turn my back on my brother and pull my sleeve across my face.

"I left her. I left her with Helmsley and he killed her." I lift my eyes toward the sky. "But, I'm the one who left her."

Placing my hands on my hips, my breath comes in ragged bursts and I labor for control.

"Jacob. It's not your fault. Anyone would have done the same. It's Helmsley's fault."

Still brimming with emotion, I swing around and face my brother.

"And he will pay. I will not rest until her death, her— her attack is avenged. Not before then."

Jackson peers back at me. His eyes have lost their ferocity.

"Okay brother. But– you don't have to marry Destiny. Just be nice to her. She deserves that much."

I peer into Jackson's eyes for a long moment. I nod.

I take a step forward and hold out a hand. We shake.

Emotionally drained for the moment, I walk back to the wagon.

After climbing into the seat, Jackson whistles and orders the horses to move again.

I won't admit it. But I'll never best Jackson in a physical contest again.

The alliance seems to have returned though. At least for the moment.

We're headed for Boston. Jackson is with me.

Helmsley is in Boston.

# Chapter 37

I chafe at the slowness of the big freight wagon. As we near Boston, I let my mind race ahead, wondering if Helmsley will be there. Will I see him? Am I prepared to defend myself?

Jackson has his musket. He always has his musket. I, though, am unarmed. I wonder if I can save enough to buy a pistol.

Ahead, a road angles in from the south. It crosses the one we travel. Past the intersection, it proceeds north. Several miles away, it will intersect the main turnpike from Boston to Concord.

A farmer's woodlot spreads over a plot of ground near the intersection. The trees grow close together, like a thicket. Trees that are cut sometimes sprout multiple shoots from the stump. These grow thick, looking more like bushes than trees.

The branches sway a little. Some small movement seems out of place.

In a flash Jackson throws the reins at me. He ducks under the seat, grabbing his musket and aims toward the woodlot.

I pull the team to a stop, alternating glances between Jackson and the trees ahead.

"You really think there's something dangerous there?" I ask.

"If not, why is someone hiding?"

"Could be anything. Deer, raccoon… anything."

"It's a man."

"How do you know?"

There's little explanation for that. Jackson places great store in the woodsman sense he tries to develop.

"Don't shoot!" A man's voice calls from the woodlot.

Rustling. The sound of someone crawling through low trees and brush. A hand extends from the edge of the clump of trees and waves.

A man emerges holding a musket in his other hand. He extends it over his head where it's harmless.

He's a scarecrow. The arms he extends are thin. They appear as though they belong to a boy. The man though is near six feet tall.

He comes closer and I see his face is gaunt and grizzled. He moves with an animated air, full of short, quick movements and a ready grin.

Jackson lowers his gun.

I squirm. This is embarrassing. Threatening a man who appears every bit the Massachusetts farmer, innocently going about his daily routine. He may be the owner of the woodlot.

"Sorry," Jackson says, returning his musket to its place under the seat.

"No harm." The man strides over to us and holds out a hand. "Pretty good eyes there, son. I'm the one s'posed to be watchin'."

He peers about as though looking for anyone who might overhear.

"You boys seen the redcoats?"

I look at Jackson who's staring right back at me. We both shake our heads. No, we haven't seen any redcoats.

"Good. That's what I was a'watchin' for. Rest o' my boys'll be up any minute. If we'd a' seen 'em 'round here, we'd a' knowed they was sendin' reinforcements."

Again, the man twists his head, searching the fields and roads.

Redcoats? So what? Before I can ask a question, the man begins to speak again.

"You know the war's started, right?"

"War?" Jackson and I exclaim in unison.

"Yessir," the man continues. "We just got word a bit ago. Their on the march to Concord lookin' to steal all our muskets and supplies. Word's a goin' out to all the militias. You boys with an outfit?"

I grip the side of the wagon seat.

War? Redcoats? An outfit?

I haven't even thought about militia. They aren't real soldiers. They never even have something to fight unless a poor stray Indian steals a farmer's horse or something.

Still. I'm not with an 'outfit'. We both shake our head no.

"Well. You're gonna miss the fight I suppose. We're a goin' up to Concord an' send them lobsterbacks right back across the ocean."

The man, Alvin he says, grins. His face shines under the black and gray stubble, alive with excitement.

"Here comes the rest o' my group." Alvin waves his arm.

He motions several similar appearing, musket-bearing men, forward and across the road.

"You boys have a safe trip and be a' listenin' for news. You'll hear it for sure." He's off.

Across the road he dashes. Catching the group of men, they all hustle up the route to the Concord turnpike.

Watching them go, butterflies swarm inside me.

Rebellion. War. What if Massachusetts raises a real army?

Jackson pulls his musket from under the seat. He jumps to the ground and turns to face me.

"This is a one-man job, brother. I'm going with them."

"What?"

"I'm going with them. You deliver the flour. You don't need me. I'll see you at home in a day or two."

Jackson skips a couple of steps towards the far edge of the road, anxious to get going.

"You can't do that— you're going to walk all the way home? Spend the night out— ?"

What's he thinking? What am I supposed to tell our father?

"What if you get shot? What do I tell—?" I continue to sputter. "Father will be furious."

Jackson grins. "I'll be fine. Tell them I promise not to get shot and I'll be home straightaway."

He touches his hat as though saluting, turns and runs off to catch the others.

I call his name one more time. No response. Just a fleeing Jackson, musket in hand, heading off to war. Without me.

I sit in the wagon, reins draped across my lap. Lily and Ginger stand in the road, tails swishing flies. As though nothing has changed.

What's Jackson done?

# Chapter 38

"There's war!" I burst through the door of Patty's house without knocking. I almost stumble in my rush over the threshold.

The room's empty. Where are they?

Footsteps thunder down the stairs.

"Jacob!" Patty holds a hand to her chest as if she just survived a terrible fright. Meacham follows her.

"Sorry," I gasp. "I should have knocked."

"No. That's alright." Patty hugs me. Meacham offers a hand in greeting. "You just surprised me. You were so excited… well, I was afraid maybe you brought terrible news from home."

I shake my head. "There's war with England."

I expect— I don't know, shock, disbelief. Instead, Patty watches me for a moment, her face cautious and impossible to read. Quietly she gestures to the table for me to sit.

"I know about the skirmish." Patty isn't secretive exactly, but she speaks in low tones. "It's not outright war yet. But it could be."

I stare at her, speechless. She's calm. As though this is routine, or… or like she knows all about it. Before I can form a question, she continues.

"Word's all over about Lexington. We haven't heard anything from Concord yet."

I just stare blankly for a minute. "How do you know…?"

"Everyone knows about Lexington. The word's all over. All the militias are being called up."

True. When I unloaded at the warehouse the talk was of Lexington and nothing else. I had trouble getting a receipt.

"But what about Concord. What's going on there?" I ask, since it seems my sister has all the latest news.

Patty appraises me for a moment. She rises and moves to the counter across the room. "Meacham, could you get me the crock of butter from the pantry?"

It's only steps away. Meacham retrieves the dish. Patty brings bread to the table with a knife and cutting board. She begins to slice the loaf.

"Maybe nothing. But, the size of the British force that left Boston seems too large to just arrest two men."

I sit, mouth open, trying to figure out what she's talking about.

"Mr. Hancock and Mr. Adams are staying in Lexington- were staying in Lexington."

"How do you know where John Hancock and John Adams happen to be?"

"Not John Adams. Samuel."

She slices more bread. She holds it out asking if I would like some. I shake my head no. How can one eat at a time like this? She seems to be almost teasing me with bits of information.

"Patty —."

"Lower voice, Jake." Patty gives me a serious look. "I doubt we're being spied upon but let's not take chances."

She hands the slice of bread to Meacham, letting him fix it however he wishes. Turning to look behind her, she starts to rise. Meacham presses her shoulder down then grabs a pitcher and three mugs from the counter.

"I've been a little involved in the patriot cause in Boston." She pauses. "Let's just say that for now."

I stare at my sister incredulously. A part of the 'patriot' cause? She's a rebel?

"You know my feelings." Patty looks pointedly at me.

She extends her hands across the table and gestures for mine. She clasps it.

"I would think you might have grown sympathetic to this cause as well."

The sudden shift in topic startles me. From explosive news of war, or maybe war, back to… Well, back to my political leanings. Again. I breathe deep allowing some of the excitement to drain away.

She's right. About my feelings that is.

There's no defense for what Jackson would call Lobsterbacks anymore. I mean—, the way Amelia was treated. The way Jackson and I were treated as we tried to find justice for her.

Still. Armed rebellion? Against the Mother Country?

"We are just as important as anyone else, Jacob." Patty's gaze hasn't left mine.

Of course. I nod my agreement, but still assemble a mental puzzle.

"Even if the law as it is written, the law mind you, had been applied in Amelia's case, that officer would only have been sent to his home."

And even that didn't happen. The monster is still here, in Boston.

All my efforts. If I'd been able to get the law applied to Helmsley the way it should have been, he would have been sent home. Amelia will sleep forever under the oak by the side of Blackham's church, and Helmsley would have gone home.

"It's all the Amelia's we fight for," my sister asserts. "We will have a nation of laws, not titles."

# Chapter 39

The tension in my home is too much for me right now. I've escaped to the woodlot.

Only hours ago, I returned from Boston. Explaining why Jackson wasn't with me was no easy task.

Mother's hands flew to her mouth. Father sighed and shook his head.

It's unlikely Jackson will come walking down the drive at this very moment. Still, there's the anticipation.

What will my brother say? What's happened? What has he seen?

I can't help it. It's in my blood. I picture ranks of men. Formations. Weapons.

If war has started, Massachusetts will have to raise an army. What color will the uniforms be? Certainly not red. Maybe white like the French.

No —. No one will want to look like the French. They've always been our enemy.

Maybe blue. Or green.

Scrambling to my feet I search the shadows blanketing the farm. The dirt lane makes a fine parade ground. I march several steps down it.

I consider how I might look in a dark blue uniform, like the Prussians. I still remember the drills from my short stint in the provincial company.

My musket feels natural in my hands. I bring it up in front of me. Just like in the drill exercises.

I thumb the hammer as though readying it to fire without really pulling it back.

My mind gives the order. Present!

I step back about six inches with my right foot. I bring the musket into my shoulder ready to fire.

Fire!

It's a dream I've been mourning.

Left face. Right face. Column. Line. Port Arms.

Without all the British arrogance surely, I can be an officer. Massachusetts will have a place for me. They'll need me, young men who know how to command army units.

"Hey."

I whirl around, startled. Like a ghost Jackson materializes from nowhere.

"Jackson! Where did you come from?"

"I came up behind you. You do too much thinking. You don't know what's going on around you."

"I know what's —."

The fight's not worth it. I'm more interested in what Jackson has seen.

"What's waiting for me inside?" my brother asks.

"Not good."

I'm not waiting. I insist Jackson tell me what happened.

The nearer the men came to Concord, the more they met up with other militia units. By the time they neared Lexington, there were hundreds of militia. Maybe thousands.

Word came down the road that the English column was approaching. It was on its way back to Boston.

Militia scattered everywhere. They searched for cover away from the road. As the English column passed, they fired at the opposing army.

It wasn't all that easy. They had to flee parties of redcoat troops that stormed into the thickets, buildings, and fence rows along the way.

"Not in formation?" I ask. "They searched wooded areas… Did they wear cocked hats?"

Jackson shakes his head.

"No, they wore those leather cap-things," he says as he runs his hand up over his forehead indicating the vertical front of the headgear he tries to describe.

"Light troops."

British light infantry, men who operate independently, out of formation. They could scour the colonists out of their most secure hiding places.

"And the bearskins formed the columns on the road."

"Grenadiers," I muse.

Grenadier companies. Big men. Strong men. Heavily armed. No one can stand against them when they charge.

I gaze back at Jackson. "You guys were up against the best they have."

"Yeah, well. We must've outnumbered 'em ten to one." He smiles with a nonchalance that seems almost genuine.

I have to admit it. I'm jealous.

Jackson has participated in a real battle. He was a militia man without uniform or proper military training, but a battle, nonetheless.

"Did— did you shoot anyone?"

Jackson nods. "I did."

He pauses for a moment as though remembering.

"Not up close. But, a couple of times I saw redcoats fall when I fired into the column."

I stare into Jackson's eyes trying to measure his reaction.

"It's not a great feeling," he finally says.

It's the most somber statement I can recall ever hearing from him.

"We're really at war, aren't we?"

Yes, Jackson agrees. Massachusetts Bay Colony is at war.

"Well. I'm sure they're still up." Jackson jerks his head toward the house. "I better go face what's coming to me."

"I'll be in after a while."

Jackson smiles. "Smart."

My brother seems different. Aged. He trudges off toward the house.

He's changed I think again. Will that happen to me?

Perhaps it doesn't matter. I think maybe everything has changed.

# Chapter 40

I hesitate again as I stand in the door. Part of me is so impatient to go I can hardly keep still, the other part of me…

Mother's tears have started and stopped several times already. They seem to create permanent tracks down her cheeks.

Jackson and I stand, muskets in hand, haversacks over our shoulders.

"Let me walk with you a ways." Father's hand is on Jackson's shoulder. His comment seems to offer a way to bring the emotional farewell to a conclusion.

Mother grabs each of us in fervent hugs. We start down the drive. Mother waves eagerly, smiling through a fresh batch of tears.

"So, you're sure about the Blackham militia?" Father asks.

Jackson nods. He doesn't want to join the local group. He has friends. He's fought with a unit of militia already.

We all walk in silence a few moments.

"Boys," Father finally says. "It's serious business. I've been there. I know you feel like you need to go but listen to the others. Don't go looking to fight a war by yourself."

I shove my hand into my pocket. The medallion is there. The one praising my father for saving his men.

We all stop as the Boston Road meets our little lane. Father holds out a hand to each of us.

"You're men. You don't have to prove that to anyone. You are." He turns quickly and heads back toward the house.

Light barely peeks over the eastern horizon. But it's enough to see that lone solitary figure walk down the long lane to our home. He walks slow. As though he were carrying a burden.

I watch his back. How's he going to plant the fields by himself?

A low mournful cry from the milk cow rolls across the landscape. I won't be milking anymore.

My father disappears around a corner, heading for the back door I suppose.

While relieved of the odious task of milking, I won't have fresh milk either.

The house sleeps silently. It huddles, nestled in the arms of three old trees. An oak, a maple, and a chestnut. I study the image as though I were leaving an old friend.

"Harder than you thought, isn't it?" Jackson says.

I shrug, turn my face, and begin the trek to Boston. We labor our way up the road in silence. My marching feet find the familiar bend in the road.

Thornby's apple orchard.

Emotionally, I just can't do it again. Can't go back there. I've flogged myself enough.

Still, it's almost as if Amelia were a beautiful, benevolent ghost. A spirit inhabiting the special place.

I can almost see her here, unfettered by the disadvantages of mortality. Smiling, looking after me as she would have done in life.

I push my gaze to the road and press on. A couple of hours pass and Jackson points.

"Let's stop up here," he says.

A little brook tumbles in a shallow ravine. A bridge carries the road over it.

There's a musical quality to the tumbling water. I toss my knapsack into the grass. We pull a scant meal of bread and ham from our haversacks. A mockingbird sings from a nearby tree limb.

"I have a little surprise." Jackson says as he takes a bite of the ham. His eyes seem to measure me and I can tell immediately, this is no small thing.

He looks away. Raising his voice, he calls.

"Destiny!"

# Chapter 41

Destiny? I spin in my sitting position, turning to face the direction Jackson stares.

Destiny. She comes walking out from a thicket of Witch Hazel.

I don't know what to say. I'm glad to see her. Enough so that it surprises me. I've missed her company, rare as that has been.

But —. What's happening? Surely these two can't think Destiny's going to join the army.

I get to my feet, still puzzled.

"Hi Jake," she says. Her uncertainty makes her voice quaver.

"Destiny." Like a fool I stop there, breaking off my words as I struggle with what to say next. I look at Jackson. The silence forces me into saying something.

"Are -. Um, you've come to see us off?" It's lame but it's all I can think of.

"She's coming too," Jackson says, a defensive tone already in his voice.

"What?" I turn back to Destiny in confusion. "Why would you even want to do this?"

She stares at me as though I've just said something really stupid. Like, how could I even ask that question.

"*You're* going," she starts. Probably realizing that makes her sound like her only motive is to follow me, she changes direction. "Why are you going, Jake?"

Now I stare at Destiny like *she's* said something stupid. "Well. After all that happened," I say, holding my hands up in what must look like a helpless gesture.

"You mean Helmsley? The English officer that attacked Amelia?"

"Killed Amelia," I say.

"Killed Amelia. You're going only to fight him? Is he meeting you?"

The last part is insulting. I start to get angry and fix a hard stare at her. Destiny seems to realize she pushed too hard and looks at the ground.

So, I stand speechless. Water from the brook tumbles and cascades over the rocks. It's unique music seems to challenge me to find the right words.

"No," I admit without defensiveness. "No, I guess I'm hoping to see him. I guess I think he's a symptom, a symptom of a corrupt system."

She stares at me, silent. She knows I'm smart enough to figure out she would want to change that system as well.

In my exchange with Destiny, I forgot about my brother. Jackson reinserts himself into the conversation.

"I imagine Destiny feels the same way."

I ponder that. Taking a step to the side, I idly kick at the haversack I dropped into the grass when Jackson and I stopped to eat.

What they're saying— it's not quite enough for me. I have a clear purpose. Helmsley killed Amelia. I'm here to make sure he pays. He and others like him. Destiny's had no such experience.

I'm trying to find the words. Destiny watches me. Reading my mental stumbling, she tries another explanation.

"Jake. Remember all the things we read in Mr. Potts' classes? How our parents and grandparents thought for decades they were British citizens. They just happened to live in America."

Her eyes have taken on a lustrous blue tint, her expression one of deep conviction.

"Now we know that's not the case," she continues. "We are colonists, provincials. In the eyes of Parliament, we no longer have the same rights as British citizens. We're a lesser class."

I sigh and glance behind me. The conversation is taking a turn I haven't prepared for. These philosophical discussions have their place I guess, but -.

"It's worth risking your life for that?" I ask.

"Just like it is for you," she says. "At the very least we'll have the same rights as an Englishman in Britain. Or, we'll have a new country. One where aristocracy doesn't exist. You, Jacob Greyson will be a gentleman because of actions, not birth."

I smile at the thought.

"Then I guess you're a lady."

"Yes, I am."

# Chapter 42

The first view of Boston is always the best. The city surrounded by sea and harbor. Ships on the water. Canvas spread before the wind carrying goods across the mighty Atlantic. The sharp whiff of strong ocean air.

I can't get a real grip on what I feel. Resignation, I guess for giving in to the arguments of Jackson and Destiny. Indecision at how this will affect my future.

I mean, we may all camp about Boston like pretend soldiers, the leaders will straighten things out, we'll all go home. Maybe I will be forever remembered as the guy who over-reacted and jumped into an unnecessary fight.

Unsettled maybe. We're going to join the militia unit Jackson fought with at Lexington and Concord. Militia often has the reputation of being unreliable and undisciplined.

So, I'll either join them and be unreliable and undisciplined with them, or I'll be the arrogant one that tries to change things.

Destiny walks beside me as we crest the last little rise to catch our first view of the great city.

Tent villages lie mired along the inside perimeter of the harbor. Yards of canvas drape over tree limbs or fence poles. They lean awkwardly in jumbled masses.

Chickens run loose through the grounds. A dog lopes through the grass, enormous pink tongue dangling to one side. It chases a protesting rooster that runs, flapping its awkward wings, and squawking loud enough to be heard across the bay.

Even worse than I feared.

"Jacob." A note of exasperation fills Jackson's voice. "Stop judging by how straight the tents are. All that matters is if they'll fight. They will."

I nod. Jackson means well, but that's far too simplistic. One volley by the professional British army ...

As we approach the encampments, I can't help but wonder. Are there no officers? No sentries? The men I can see seem to have no duties except to fritter away their time. I'm no prude, but where's the military discipline?

It takes a little searching, but we find the unit Jackson fought with at Concord.

"This is Caleb. Some of the men are off to find tent poles." Jackson introduces us.

Caleb stands about my height. He's thick through the torso. A jutting chin gives him a look of belligerence.

His face is round, what some would call a baby-face. It's grizzled though. In the dark eyes, I sense that nobody actually calls him baby-face.

Short black hair tops his head.

"Imagine Alvin'll take all the new recruits he can." Caleb measures us closely, peering up and down with his eyes.

"Brought yur own girl, huh?"

The remark is so absurd I just gape at Caleb trying to find a reply.

"Destiny's one of us. Just like me and Jake," Jackson states defensively.

"She ain't like you and Jake," Caleb replies with a chuckle. "'sides. Militia don't take no girls. Lessen they're washin' 'r something."

"Yeah. Like you're in charge," Jackson retorts. "We'll let Alvin decide."

"Everyone gets a vote." A new man with a narrow face and bloodless thin lips walks up behind Caleb. "Look. No offense or anything, but the army's no place for a girl."

A few hours ago, I was the one telling Destiny she shouldn't come. Her rejection though makes me angry.

"Isn't there an officer around?" I ask.

"Told ya. Alvin's off findin' tent poles," Caleb replies.

"You call your officer Alvin?"

"Well, that's 'is name."

I wave a hand in disgust and pull Destiny into a retreat up a small embankment. Jackson follows.

"No company supplies 'r shelter till this thing's decided," Caleb calls out.

I glance back but make no reply.

"I knew this was a mistake," I mutter to my companions.

"Let's wait for Alvin. We can count on him," Jackson says.

"Militia votes for their officers. They're little more than politicians," I reply. I'm losing faith in the whole idea. I should have waited until the colony organized a real army.

# Chapter 43

A twig snaps under my foot. The sharp crack earns me a sour look from Jackson. Destiny, mercifully, makes no visible reaction.

The woods are moist and silent this morning. Maples, chestnuts, birch, as well as clusters of pine stretch a canopy overhead. The sharp fragrance of the pines seems to mingle with the damp odor of the moss clumps growing in shadowy wet pockets.

The unfriendly reception at Jackson's militia unit yesterday resulted in a long night of discussions. There are other militias. They're all over, around the inside edge of the harbor.

Nope. Jackson wants this one. Jackson and I argued. Destiny tried to make peace and finally came up with this idea. We'll make a very early morning hunting trip and return to the camp with fresh meat.

I bristle at the idea of working this hard to get into the militia. I mean, normally they take just about anyone. It makes me feel… I don't know. Debased in some way, I guess.

Jackson and Destiny begin shifting right. From several yards behind, I match their direction.

I'm relegated to this position, according to Jackson, because my observation skills are inadequate. My approach awkward and noisy.

I almost slugged him. Destiny only giggled.

We creep through the forest in the gray light of pre-dawn, about a mile from the militia camp. The misty morning air is so moist I can feel it on my skin.

Both Jackson and Destiny freeze.

I ease to a kneeling position, hugging a tree, straining to see what the others have found.

Like hunting dogs on a scent, those two. Jackson shakes his head no and points to Destiny. She pulls her musket into her shoulder, sinks to one knee.

Motionless, she watches… something.

A small cloud puffs near the hammer of her musket. Then, instantly, the gun fires sending smoke belching out of the barrel.

Jackson jumps to his feet. Animated, he congratulates Destiny. It should be safe now, so I catch up to my companions.

"Did you see that shot?" Jackson asks, unable to contain his excitement.

"Yes," I lie.

Impatient, my brother runs up the hill. Destiny and I follow more slowly. She keeps glancing without really turning to look at me.

"I wish I had your skill in the forest," I say.

Her glance at me lingers this time.

Finally, she quietly says, "Kind of improper for a girl, don't you think?"

"No. No, I don't."

I know how she feels. She's always wanted something more between us. It just feels natural. Kind of a right time, right place you know? I casually put an arm about her shoulders. She looks like she might cry.

A deer lies crumpled against the trunk of a great oak. It'll feed the entire unit. The head bears a set of massive antlers.

Jackson's already cutting a small tree with his tomahawk. He fastens the deer to the sapling. We sling the carcass between the two of us, the pole sagging with the weight.

#

"I'd a' never thought you'd find such a creature in them woods. Not after half the colony done hunted 'em out." Alvin peers admiringly at the deer.

A fire pit surrounded by stones already sits in the middle of the tents. Even a homemade spit for cooking.

"We been a'talkin'," Alvin continues. "No hard feelings. Some o' the boys not sure about a girl fightin' like a man. They been brought up to always protect their womenfolk. But— well, we're gonna make an exception."

I watch Caleb to measure his reaction. He catches my stare.

"I don't believe the girl shot it," he grumbles, indicating the deer.

"You don't think she's a good enough shot?" I already like where this is going. Someone needs to stuff that big mouth with a great helping of humble pie.

Caleb just shakes his head.

"Maybe you ought to have a contest."

I suddenly have everyone's attention. There's a definite stir of excitement.

A shooting contest. It wouldn't matter who the contestants were, there would be interest. But Destiny against Caleb?

Caleb looks trapped. He's not afraid. But I can see the wheels turning in his thinking. Are we bluffing, or will he really lose a marksmanship contest to a girl? Would that be possible?

His eyes simmer.

"A shootin' contest in front of everyone. No skulkin' off in the woods alone," he says.

"I advise against it." Jackson suspends his work skinning the deer. He stabs his knife into the dirt and stands.

"She's a good shot."

Caleb's apprehension shows. The challenge was accepted too easily. Jackson and I are too sure of Destiny. And the girl isn't saying a word.

He's trapped though. At this point, in front of everyone, what can he do?

"A straight-up contest. Same place. Same time. No luck involved," Caleb says.

Jackson shrugs.

"I insist." Caleb stares alternately at Jackson, then at me.

# Chapter 44

Digging into her haversack, Destiny finds the folded bundle. The sounds of camp seem to fade as she concentrates. She unfolds the fabric, sorting through various strips of soft tanned skins and woolen cloth.

A pan of water simmers on the fire for coffee. Steam lifts aimlessly from its surface. Reaching, Destiny dips a cupful out of the pan.

The tree branch that forms the crosspiece of the spit over the fire has a broken end. Destiny pries and twists a piece loose. She plugs the hole at the hammer end of her gun and pours the water into the muzzle.

Caleb keeps glancing at her, as though she can't tell. Surely, he knows what she's doing.

Now's the time to gain every advantage. Destiny depends on the tight barrel and cut grooves inside to spin her bullet accurately.

Two more rinses and she removes the splinter stopper. With oily rags and the gun's ramrod she coats the inside of the barrel.

A shooting contest.

Just the thing to excite the passions of a bunch of men with little to do. They grin. They search for targets. They wager.

Alvin fumbles with a foot-long strip of torn red cloth. He ties it to a piece of wood. He shows it to Destiny and Caleb. Yes, she nods. It will make a fine target.

The jumble of militiamen tread across the field as Alvin leads the procession away from the tents. Still talking. Still joking. Still wagering.

What odds are being given now?

Destiny gazes across the ground. She'll be shooting inland.

Zach strikes an axe at a couple of small hobblebushes that obstruct the view.

Stepping in a stilted way, Alvin counts his strides and tries to measure the distance. He stops and turns then hammers the stake into the ground.

The red marker flutters in the air currents. It plays with the marksmen, looking as if it could dance away from a speeding bullet before it can be struck.

"I figger' this to be about seventy-five yards," Alvin calls and begins the trek back to the firing line.

Destiny shifts a little and grips the muzzle end of her gun as the butt rests at her feet.

Caleb smirks and gives an impatient shrug, telling her to shoot.

Destiny considers her opponent then peers downfield. It's not impossible to lose. But she is a good shot. The psychological contest seems even more fun than the physical one.

"You first," she calmly says.

"Girls go first."

"It's too close. I'm not wasting the bullet."

Caleb stares at her in disbelief. His eyes dart from Destiny to the target and back again.

If he hits the marker and Destiny misses it farther out, Caleb wins. But, she's tired of being cautious. Pandering to the ridiculous prejudices of others. Competing against herself to the point of anxious exhaustion, just to be accepted.

She'll win with a memorable flourish. Or she'll lose.

In a flash, as though having made a difficult decision, Caleb throws his musket into his shoulder. His head turns as he takes one more glance at Destiny.

His cheek lays into the butt of his gun; he sights down the barrel.

As though peering over the edge of a cliff at some unfortunate climber, the audience stands frozen and breathless.

The target, limp in a moment of stillness, springs to life as a small gust of air hits it. Zach stayed downrange, but well to the side. He quips.

"Don't shoot me Caleb."

Nervous laughter.

Caleb shifts, freezes in place, and pulls the trigger.

His musket jumps and a cloud of smoke explodes from its muzzle. Zach runs to the target. He pulls the stake from the ground.

Even at this distance, Destiny can see him wiggle his finger for emphasis as he pushes it through the small hole in the cloth.

Caleb grins. He looks like a condemned man given a reprieve.

Alvin calls to Zach. "Another twenty-five yards!"

"Make it fifty."

Caleb whirls about and stares at Destiny. He starts to speak then closes his mouth as though he really wasn't sure what to say.

"You sure, Missy?" Alvin speaks to her like her long-lost father. "A target that size… Over a hun'erd yards…" his voice trails off.

Destiny only nods so he puts his hand aside his mouth and calls the instruction to Zach. Zach bends as though he can't have heard correctly. Alvin repeats the order.

Assured he heard right, Zach marches on and hammers the target home.

"You go first," Destiny says to Caleb.

"Nuh-uh. I done shot once. Your turn."

"When I shoot, I'm gonna cut the target right off the wood stake. You shoot first."

Caleb's friends guffaw. It is an audacious claim. A smoothbore musket would have little chance of hitting the target. Of course, Destiny's not shooting a smoothbore musket. Caleb is.

Caleb tries but can't seem to get out an authentic laugh. He starts to aim then glances at Destiny. He starts again. Then he stops and stares at the target a full hundred and twenty-five yards away.

Finally, in a show of bravado, he steps up to the line. He jerks his musket into position and fires, barely taking aim.

"You cain't hit that and unless you do, I win."

Zach runs to the target. He yells something to Alvin. The exact words are lost but there's no mistaking the message. No second hole exists in the cloth marker.

Destiny steps to the line and kneels in front of it. It's as though the entire colony has gone silent.

She leans on her knee. The long barrel seems to stretch out into the fields before her.

Uphill she reminds herself. It's always tougher to hit a target uphill.

The weight of the gun rests comfortably. She has time. There's a mark at the end she always uses for difficult shots.

A hundred and twenty-five yards.

In places, taller grasses sway in the breeze trying to confuse her. They bend over her view of the red cloth then straighten.

The target appears a mere scrap at this distance.

Another wave of air pushes at the meadow grass. She measures its effect in her mind.

A lull in the breeze and the grasses straighten.

Destiny releases the air in her lungs in a long, slow sigh. She pulls the trigger.

The powder flashes in the pan.

The load in the barrel ignites and her rifled musket leaps in her hands.

Smoke and flame burst from the muzzle.

Unmoving, Destiny holds her position and watches.

In an explosion of splinters the top of the stake shatters.

The red cloth, caught in the returning breeze, flutters to the ground.

Zach runs, grabs the cloth, and sprints back towards a stunned and silent group of militia.

She did it. It actually worked.

It's hard to keep the smile from her lips and Destiny stops trying.

Triumph. For the present problem anyway.

What will Jake think of a girl who makes such a spectacle of hunting and shooting? Of besting self-made, domineering leaders like Caleb.

"Missy," Alvin says. "You got a place in this here outfit if I haf'ta go all the way to General Stark. We could shore use a marksman like you."

Jake has watched from the edge of the crowd. Destiny catches his eye.

He stands there, hair tousled on his head. No hat. Looking like… what? Like he can't decide how he feels?

The old longing wells up inside her. The longing to be accepted. To be loved.

To not be rejected because she doesn't conform to someone else's vision of what she should be.

She stares at Jake, the man she has so long dreamed would love her that way.

"What about you Jake?" she asks. "Can you use a girl marksman?"

Jake had shifted his gaze to Alvin. Now he locks onto hers. "More than anyone."

# Chapter 45

I watch Destiny's face as we sit by the fire. I can tell she feels like I do. We're here to *do* something.

It's only been a couple of days, but if all we're going to do is sit around and stare at British soldiers over the water in Boston, I may as well be at home. I could help my father with planting.

"Mistah Jake."

That voice is so familiar. I can't place it. I turn to see a large yet mellow-faced African man approaching.

"Lucas?"

"Thas right. You rememba'."

Lucas. The hired servant at the Waterford's party.

"We in the same outfit. Got back this mornin'. Jus found out."

"You're here in the militia?"

Lucas reaches a paw-like hand and smiles that deep genuine smile I remember.

"I was only at Waterford's for a day." He leans in as though telling a secret. "Needed the money." His dark face splits into a large white grin then sobers.

"I hear about Miss Amelia. I'm so sorry. You two was deservin' of each other."

Amelia. William and I as friends.

The Waterford party. William telling his parents the party wasn't complete without me.

Lucas telling Helmsley it wasn't clear who had escorted Miss Amelia when, in fact, it was clear to everyone.

Amelia, the center of attention from a half-dozen glittering officers in red uniforms. And yet, clutching my arm as though she would never let go.

The pale green dress. Her light scent of what... roses? Lavender? Am I forgetting already?

I'm speechless for a moment. Destiny uses the pause to introduce herself to Lucas.

"I'm so glad you're here," Lucas says, pulling me back into the conversation. "We need you Mistah Jake. I rememba' you in that fancy uniform. A fine redcoat officer you was."

There's a startling statement. One I wasn't expecting.

I shake my head. "I was no officer."

"But you know about soldiering. I ain't never been in no army. Alvin, he was as a young man. Long time ago."

I nod. "Well, we should all be drilling."

Lucas laughs. "May take time ta' get people ta' listen to that."

Yeah, don't I know it.

"Jake." Destiny points.

Jackson hurtles down the lane heading straight for us. Breathless, he pulls to a halt.

"The British attacked."

Attacked? I jump to my feet.

Distantly, I hear the kettle that had perched on a rock near the fire go crashing to the ground, I guess as Lucas flies to his feet as well. Dimly, I can feel the camp area fill with other soldiers as we all clamor for information.

"Last night," Jackson gasps.

When? Where? I look back at my musket as though we might need to start shooting any minute.

The British attacked out of Boston. It seems they were after hay for their animals.

A sortie, I think. A raid. A distinction that will be lost on the others and probably not important.

"We knew feed was short in the city," I interject.

Jackson nods. Out near Noddles Island. A few militia men had been nearby at the time. A battle—.

*Skirmish. Not a battle.*

A battle broke out and men were wounded, several killed.

Lobsterbacks or New Englanders?

"Both," Jackson replies.

*Both.*

The conflict's not dying, it's escalating. More of the King's men killed. More of the colonists. No one will back down now.

Jackson's breathing slackens, but still, he talks in bursts of air between pauses for deep breaths.

"Alvin. Captain Rawlins wants to see you."

With a curt nod, Alvin takes quick strides, re-tracing Jackson's steps towards Rawlin's headquarters.

My head spins. Armed conflict. I know Lexington and Concord were real battles. Many were wounded. Many were killed.

But I wasn't there. This time… it feels different. I'm in the militia.

"We'll probably start training," I say absently. I really only meant to include Destiny. Maybe Lucas. But Caleb must have heard. He lets out a derisive retort loud enough for all to hear.

"Ain't that just dandy. We'll be a army with straight rows. Girls 'n darky slaves fer soldiers."

A departing Alvin whips around in nothing more than a blur. He stomps back into the group.

Using both hands, Alvin shoves Caleb sending him staggering backwards. He points a finger into Caleb's chest.

"Ain't nothin' wrong with bein' a girl. And we ain't got no slaves. Lucas' is my partner. Either remember that or the only thing I want to see out 'o you is your backside leaving camp."

Alvin stands glaring, daring Caleb to challenge him. Caleb's round face droops. His mouth hangs open, eyes round and wide.

Alvin spins on his heel and leaves.

Slack-jawed militiamen look at Caleb, the ground, Destiny, Lucas. Face reddening, Caleb blusters a few syllables but can't seem to string together an intelligent sentence.

He whips around and shoulders his way through the small crowd. The other men glance at one another and, as though escaping a quiet danger, begin to wander from the fire ring in the camp center.

"I guess it's okay for me to be a girl," Destiny says with a wry smile.

# Chapter 46

Only moments after Alvin disappears, I face what's left of the fire, still standing. Lucas sits on a small wooden barrel tipped sideways. Patiently, he begins to rub a thin oil to the stock of his gun.

"Lucas?" Destiny asks. He lifts his big brown eyes and peers at her.

"What did Alvin mean you were partners?"

The big man smiles and returns to oiling the wooden stock of his musket.

"We got a little farm south 'o here. Ain't much, but we do okay."

Men continue to wander away to their own amusements. Jackson, Destiny, Lucas, and I are all that remain. Lucas searches and seems to notice it too.

"Used to be a slave. Ain't no more." He shakes his head slowly at the declaration.

The others are sitting. I lower myself to the ground, still watching the big African man.

"How did you meet Alvin?"

"Used to be my mastah."

Lucas grins at the astonished looks from us, his audience. "We live in Virginia then."

"Really?" Destiny asks. "I've never seen a slave— I mean an ex-slave before."

"Alvin. He own a small plantation. 'Bout six of us slaves." Lucas looks around at his audience and chuckles at our rapt attention.

"One day, a man in very fine clothes come around. You could tell. He was somethin' important. Ordered Alvin ta lock us all up. Everything gonna be sold in the mornin'"

Lucas leans his gun against a log meant to be a seat beside the fire ring. From the ground, he picks up a piece of slender branch. He pokes at some of the embers. A few flames flare into life.

"After dark, Alvin unlock everyone. Tell 'em they can stay or flee. Ask me to come with him." He looks up from the fire, face serious. "I gots papers. But they ain't real. Alvin sign 'em but he di'n really own us no more. I spec' ya'all can keep that under your hats."

We all murmur our assent. Lucas appears pleased.

"We buy a little farm…," he peers into the sky a moment. "'Bout… Mmm, five years ago. Been workin' it ever since."

"What happens if anyone finds out? About the papers I mean," I ask.

Lucas pulls his stick from the ashes and points it at me. "Nuthin' good."

He tosses the piece of wood into the fire ring and picks up his musket. "But that ain't gonna happen." He pauses for a breath. "Miss Destiny. You gotta teach me how to shoot."

"I'll try. I only learned because if I didn't, I starved."

I peer off into the field that served Destiny so well in the contest with Caleb and see Alvin walking down the road toward us. Two men accompany him.

One is a tall, narrow-faced man with a blue hat. A bonnet I think it's called.

"Ruskin MacGregor." Lucas nods the direction of the two men.

Jackson agrees. Someone he met on the road to Concord. "He's something with the company."

It's all Jackson knows. No rank. No position. Just Ruskin McGregor.

The other man is short, dark-haired, and thin. His expression, his walk, his gaze, all have a rather severe nature about them.

Braswell. A lieutenant Jackson thinks. Lucas nods agreement. Both respond to his coming with a measure of distaste.

Ruskin McGregor wears the bonnet of a Scottish Highlander. His sandy hair peeks from underneath it. His narrow face is hard, but wrinkles when he smiles. His eyes are an intense icy blue.

Alvin waves a hand. "Call ever-one together."

It doesn't happen quickly. With some searching and calling, everyone in Alvin's unit congregates at the edge of the camp. Caleb slinks in last.

Alvin glances at him, but otherwise ignores the earlier altercation.

McGregor is popular. The men like him. There are enthusiastic greetings and promises to shove the British into the sea.

"Aye," Ruskin agrees. "If we could'a only kept 'em out of Scotland."

Murmurs of assent.

Braswell watches, intense and silent. He looks kind of like a loaded gun ready to fire.

"Let's get on with it, Sergeant." Braswell moves only his lips. No hand gestures. No shifting.

"You must be Jacob Greyson." Sergeant McGregor peers at me.

"I am."

"Jacob Greyson is now Corporal Greyson. He'll be teachin' ya' to be soldiers," McGregor announces to the group.

I stare first at Ruskin in surprise, then Braswell, then Alvin.

I've been chafing for all of us to get to work. To train ourselves into a unit that can stand with the British. That can maybe find Helmsley's company on a battlefield.

But am I the one to do it? I'm the young kid that thinks he knows everything. The one who's never been in battle, while the rest of them have actually fired on the British and been fired upon.

Still. Imagine the possibilities. Helmsley's an officer in the British army. I'm being given permission, no orders, to prepare a bunch of Massachusetts farmers to meet him. Maybe be better than their professional British counterparts. We could kill Helmsley and it would be legal, celebrated even.

I feel Destiny lean into my side.

"By orders o' Captain Rawlins." A few heads nod. McGregor looks directly at me.

"Trainin' starts this afternoon."

"What's the girl doing here," Lieutenant Braswell asks.

"Part o' our group," Alvin answers matter-of-factly. "A better shot you—."

"She has to go."

"I don't think you understand—."

"*You* don't understand. I issued an order. I expect it to be carried out." Braswell turns to McGregor.

"We're finished here Sergeant."

If someone had not been watching Ruskin's face, they would have missed it. Ever so slightly, his eyebrows rise in an expression of derision.

Off they go on what surely will be a silent walk back to the regiment's headquarters.

"Now don't you worry Missy." Alvin bends a little and speaks low, keeping the words from the ears of the brash lieutenant. "I'll talk ta Rawlins."

# Chapter 47

"This is what you've always wanted." Destiny encourages me as we select a location where marching, turning, forming will be easier. It's the field where she embarrassed Caleb with her shooting.

I have doubts. The other men don't really think they need training. They've all been in a battle, I haven't. A couple of them have even shot enemy soldiers, I've never even seen a red coat in a setting where we were enemies.

But—.

I have, haven't I? Helmsley wears a red coat.

I fought him with fists. Impotently. He pulled a gun and I was outmatched.

I can train a unit of militia. Train them to be as good as British soldiers. Good enough to defeat, maybe even kill the likes of Helmsley.

They may be reluctant, but I'm going to train those that will help me exact revenge for Amelia. Even if they don't know that's what they're doing.

"We need to form a line." Less the browbeating and the yelling, I try to emulate the sergeant of the provincial unit when I first arrived at that dreadful Boston warehouse. With a little stumbling, I manage to place everyone. I explain a few basic marching moves.

"How does this make us shoot better?" An impatient Zach asks.

Yes. Exactly how does this make the men fight better?

To my left I spot a dry stick entangled in the meadow grass. Stretching, I grab it and pull it loose.

"This is a line of British soldiers," I say, placing the stick on the ground where all can see it. "They're shoulder to shoulder, muskets extended."

Grabbing another twig, I break it into small pieces and scatter them in front of the long stick.

"Here's all of you, acting independently, scattered about the field." It takes little description to explain the bayonet I trained with in the provincial unit. They've all seen them.

"The enemy line advances. Their front a solid line of steel bayonets."

I'm not getting the reaction I want. I describe how the glistening steel makes the redcoat muskets a foot longer than the gun carried by Zach.

I extend my hands then stop and snap a branch from the hobblebush beside me and break it at the appropriate length.

Warming to the subject, I become more animated. Zach stumbles as I pull him from the line and order him to hold out his gun. I help position it as though Zach were staving off the thrusts of the enemy.

I poke the stick from the hobblebush into the muzzle of Destiny's musket. I hold it in the position soldiers would use when charging an enemy. I'm facing Zach and look straight at him.

"Imagine you are Zach," I say to my audience. "You're scattered across a field firing accurately."

I look at Destiny's musket in my hands, the stick protruding another foot from the end. "This line of infantry charges with bayonets, making the reach of their muskets this long." I pull Destiny's gun a little higher for emphasis.

"What happens?"

I'm silent. Waiting for an answer.

The implication surely is lost on no one. But they're not admitting to it yet.

"What happens?" I repeat.

"The redcoats win. We retreat," Zach replies.

"Or die with a steel blade in your gut." I want them to get the picture.

And so, we march. Then we march some more.

Right face. Left face. To the rear march.

Maybe it's a bit much.

The afternoon is warm. Once I find my stride, though, I'm relentless.

Finally, even I can see my tiny column and line formations beginning to fall apart and regress.

I dismiss the men. They disperse and in groups of two, or singly, straggle back to camp.

I'm on a mission though. This colony, Massachusetts, will have an army. One to match the British.

# Chapter 48

Pacing parallel to the unit of militia, I survey the soldiers, my soldiers. I'm certain they all think they're standing at attention, so I resist a reprimand. I've driven them hard and can sense I've reached that edge where they could refuse to listen to me anymore.

They're veterans. I'm the kid who thinks he knows military stuff from books and a few days training in the British Army. Best to back off some of the smaller shortcomings, I think.

Sergeant McGregor, with his familiar blue bonnet, shifts his feet as he stands with Captain Rawlins at the roadside. He's brought the captain for a demonstration of our progress.

We have no uniforms. We dress in civilian clothes, some with a rather ragged appearance. Caleb unshaven and unkempt. No one with matching accoutrements.

What a ragtag bunch to call an army.

Drawing a deep breath, I hurl the commands at my soldiers.

Cock your muskets!

Present! Fire!

Handle your cartridge!

Prime!

The line of militia fires three rounds in such unison it sounds like three great explosions. It's a pretty good effort. I'm proud. Just days ago, this would have been impossible.

Shedding his coat, Captain Rawlins paces down the line. The men act like soldiers. No silly grins. No impertinent greetings. They all stand straight and stare forward.

Rawlins stops in front of Destiny. He glances at me then returns his gaze to the one person that has supported me more than all others.

"You're the girl? The one that hunts?" he asks.

Destiny nods.

The captain turns to me. "And you have her here in line?"

"She's been a real help, Sir. And, you've heard about her marksmanship."

"I have." The captain eyes the line of militia in front of him again.

"Sergeant Greyson."

"Serg— Sir?"

"That's right. It's now Sergeant Greyson."

Sergeant. Not an officer, but a promotion, nonetheless.

"Tonight, we are anticipating more enemy raids along the coast. See that farm down there?" Rawlins points toward a weather-beaten building and adjoining fences a good half-mile away.

"The barn is full of hay and a half-dozen milk cows. I want your unit to see that none of it falls into enemy hands."

Under siege in Boston, the enemy army is desperate for fresh food for their soldiers and fodder for their horses. The sorties have come more often as they search desperately for supplies, especially feed for their animals.

"Yes sir." Somehow, I recite the expected response. My mind though is reeling.

"And sergeant?"

"Yes sir."

"The girl's greatest asset is her marksmanship. I don't think she'll help you in a physical contest. Post her accordingly."

"Yes sir."

The captain backs away a few steps. Staring at my little ragtag unit he gives a curt nod of approval then he and Sergeant McGregor turn back the way they came.

Dazed, I manage to dismiss the militia and catch snippets of excited conversation as they meander back to camp. They think they're going into battle tonight and whip the damn lobsterbacks like they did on the road to Concord.

I turn away from them, still sorting my thoughts and feelings.

Real fighting. Or, the possibility of it anyway.

I thought of my first foray into danger as being a small part of a much larger action, just following the orders given me from above. But —.

We'll be all alone out there.

Destiny touches my arm. An eager Jackson clamors to inspect the site of what he's sure will be the coming battle.

In a fog, I walk, Destiny at my side, Jackson pestering me as though he were a child. He can't run out of things to say. He rushes forward, stopping every few minutes to allow Destiny and me to catch up.

He asks me countless questions.

How much ammunition will we get? Is it just the ten of us, or will more join the guard duty?

What time should everyone report? Will they report in camp and then all walk to the farm at once? Or, should everyone just show up at the barn at sundown?

I barely hear him. My mind races through a list of things I haven't thought through yet.

"Jake? What's wrong?" Destiny asks.

"Destiny, I've never been in a battle." I hold my hands in front of me in a gesture of helplessness.

"Isn't that what the drills are for?"

I almost snort in scorn but realize how much I will sound like those that deride my penchant for repeated drills. Yes, I tell her, the drills allow the unit to fire in unison. But when? From what position?

"Where?" I ask rhetorically. "Where will the British come from?"

She hadn't been thinking of things from my perspective. Her face turns serious.

"They'll come from the shore right?" she asks, still deep in thought.

We reach the farm. Destiny and I stand at the front of it, gazing towards the water.

In my mind I envision a dozen British soldiers charging in from the shoreline, my little ragtag group of farmers and storekeepers gaping at the sight.

We're no match for that.

"What if someone gets killed?"

I drift into the barn, still desperately looking for solutions to a problem I've never faced. A problem that will kill the people I know best if I don't find the right answers.

If the British come…

They'll be real soldiers. Professionals. Men who drill every day, commanded by officers with experience. Trained by the best army in the world.

I'm…. I've read books.

There's a loft above. Rawlins was right, the place is stuffed with hay, the cows have only a small space at the back and a fenced in area behind that.

Professional soldiers will mow down my pretend militia section. I can see Destiny kneeling helpless, out of powder, cowering before a British infantryman.

To the enemy's musket will be attached a gleaming, razor-sharp bayonet. The enemy soldier thrusts his weapon at her. She's just another casualty of war.

I've spent hours of daydreaming, winning imaginary battles, defeating the enemy.

But no one died in those battles. No bullets were fired at people who would bleed when struck. No one was ever in real danger.

Destiny is asking what's the matter. She peers at me with those ocean-blue eyes.

My vision of Destiny, dead or wounded, sears my thoughts.

No longer is she the outcast from Blackham. The strange girl that hunts, that wears the clothes of a man. Now she's... What?

My friend?

That's insulting. Alvin is my friend. Lucas is my friend.

Destiny? Destiny is so much more.

Still staring into the blue sea of her eyes, I bend and kiss her.

Her body relaxes and melts into my arms. She clutches me about my shoulders and kisses me back.

I lift my head and stare at her.

"What have I done?" I ask.

"Jake. I'm here. I'm part of it. I'm safest with you." Her arms slide more snugly about my neck. Her embrace tightens.

But the vision of the bayonet plunging into Destiny's body, spilling her blood; the premonition won't leave me.

# Chapter 49

No one's watching. I sneak past the tents to the far side of a tangled thicket. I've been here twice this afternoon already. I bend over and retch.

There's nothing to come up. I haven't eaten all day.

Straightening, I gaze off to the west.

An ominous sun slips low into the sky and touches the far horizon. A white-hot orb, it seems suddenly menacing.

Standing tall, as though that could hide my nervousness, I form our little company into a double column, five soldiers in each row. We turn and I lead them down the long, low hill to the farm we are to defend tonight.

The shadows of my marching soldiers elongate into ridiculous caricatures in front of me. I watch the long arms swing, the long legs march towards… what?

The unknown? Bloodshed? Death?

Reaching the farm, I think through my earlier plans. Head twisting, I review the scenes I've considered dozens of times and make assignments.

There's little cover. The barn and a hodgepodge of plank fencing that won't stop a musket ball. The other buildings were demolished for firewood weeks ago.

I turn to my brother.

Jackson cannot be contained. He shifts from foot to foot with a nervous energy.

I try to turn every weakness to an advantage if I can. Destiny told me that. Something about surviving without a father in the house.

If I try strict orders with Jackson, he won't heed them anyway. Still, I really need him.

"We can't be surprised." I stare into Jackson's face. I push in close forcing my gaze into Jackson's eyes.

My brother nods.

"I mean it Jackson. Surprise will kill us." I grab his sleeve.

"I won't let you be surprised," Jackson insists. "I'll find 'em and tell you before they get here."

He means it. As undisciplined as Jackson can be, he understands his mission.

I release him and my brother turns, disappearing into the gathering gloom.

The barn, cavernous inside, has a huge loft. High up on the front side, great doors swing to the sides revealing a gaping opening. Destiny follows my suggestion without pause and scampers up the ladder.

It will be the last position overrun by a charging enemy. If it comes to that. At the same time, it's a perfect vantage point for a marksman like Destiny.

What else?

I pace the front of the barn.

Destiny calls from the loft. I turn to see her leaning out the doorway that faces the water.

Is it enough? Can I really protect her any better than I did Amelia? What else can I do?

I fasten the ground floor doors to latches that hold them open. Even the smallest movement causes the hinges to creak out warning messages that can be heard far down the beach.

At home Father would oil the iron until the doors move in silence. I need to get a message to my family. They haven't heard from me since I arrived here.

I put my hand in my pocket and feel my father's medallion.

The men.

There's nothing for them to do out here.

I turn in a circle peering at the darkening surroundings. I have it all memorized already.

I could post guards.

But then, Jackson is searching our front. Destiny has a lookout overhead.

If the enemy shows, I'll have to set a firing line quick.

No. No guards. Keep the men together.

"What do you think Jacob?" Alvin appears at my side. "Think these boys might as well hunker down inside?"

I nod. "I think so."

I pull the medal from my pocket and absently rub it with my fingers.

Alvin stares.

"Can I…?" He holds his hand out, staring at the metal disk.

"Where did you get this?" Alvin demands. "Greyson," he says. "John Greyson?"

"That's my father."

Alvin stares at me in disbelief. "I shoulda knowed. All these years."

He stares off.

"Your father was a hero, son. Saved our lives."

"You served with him?"

Alvin nods. "I'll tell you about it sometime," he promises, holding the medal out for me to take. He points to it. "Don't lose that."

I think back to the man who walked my brother and me down the lane to see us off. He told us we were men. Told us not to try and prove it.

Alvin calls John Greyson a hero. Not because he won a battle. He didn't.

Alvin gives me one last piece of advice before retreating inside the barn.

"You're ready for this son. Put your men first, you'll do fine."

'Your men'. Alvin couldn't have said anything more ominous.

I turn back, staring into the night. A white moon, almost three quarters full, casts pale light across the landscape. It's behind me.

A firing line deployed in front of the barn will be in shadow. Anyone coming from the water will be in full view.

Like a ghost, Jackson materializes. He jogs from the beach towards me.

"Nothing," he reports. "See the moon?"

I nod. "It's in our favor."

"It's completely quiet out there. Maybe Destiny should come—."

"Not a chance."

My brother doesn't argue. He turns and trots back into darkness.

The land slopes down from here. I can look across it and view the sea, black as the night. I breathe deeply. I pace down to a corner of the barn. Nothing but empty countryside.

The other corner.

Nothing.

I search in all directions making sure I'm alone. It's silly. Searching as though an enemy has sneaked in behind me and is now stalking about the building.

Inside several men sleep. As I pace in and out the doorway, Alvin looks up and asks if I want company.

No. Nothing's happening. I drift back outside.

I find a small pebble and toss it toward the loft doors.

"See anything?" I ask in a loud whisper.

The loft opening is nothing but a black hole. Destiny's arm protrudes past the barn wall and points. I pivot to look toward the sea.

Jackson sprints up the beach towards me.

"Redcoats!"

# Chapter 50

Stepping back on my heels, my ears fill with the sound of my heart hammering in my chest like some giant machine. I can barely hear.

Redcoats. British soldiers.

They're coming. They're really going to attack us.

I've prayed all day, all day that nothing would happen. They'll kill me. They'll kill my friends. They'll kill Destiny.

Reaching behind me I find the barn wall. It steadies me.

"Jacob?"

"How many?"

"I can't tell. There's two boats, not packed. Maybe twenty?"

Over my shoulder the barn doors stand open, the inside invisible in the dark.

Twenty.

We're outnumbered two to one. Can a militia unit stand against British regulars? Can they stand against such odds?

Jackson stares at me expectantly, his eyes wide with excitement. He never listens to me, never wants to hear what I have to say. About anything.

Now. Now, all of a sudden, he stands there as though he can do nothing unless I decide it.

Turning my body and taking an aimless step, I put a hand to my forehead.

I could order a retreat. The British only want what's in the barn. They don't care about me and the men. They just want to feed their horses.

Is stopping that worth the lives of eleven New Englanders?

"Jacob?"

"Let me think."

"We need to defend this place."

I bring my gaze back to Jackson.

"How far are they?"

Jackson shrugs. "Just a few minutes away."

My voice won't stay steady. It catches repeatedly. I whisper my instructions anyway.

We need to know when the British will close on us. Can Jackson do that without getting too close and getting shot?

"Yes." My brother nods for emphasis.

A signal from me and he evaporates into the dark as though diving into some giant inkwell.

I smooth my shirt-front, take three slow, deep breaths and enter the barn.

Everyone's asleep. I place a hand on Alvin's shoulder, waking him instantly.

"Time?" Alvin asks.

"They're coming."

Alvin nods his head. "You go on back out to the front, I'll rouse ever-one."

Retreating outside I lean forward, staring towards the water.

Nothing.

From nearby an owl calls. Night insects chirp as though all is peaceful.

A general bumping and stumbling against the ground-level doors accompanies the eight men spilling out to its front.

Destiny.

Skipping a couple of steps farther out where I can view the loft, I throw a hand in the air and wave.

From the large indigo square, Destiny's arm reaches out and returns the gesture.

With loud whispers and repeated glances toward the looming danger, I order the men into line. They stand straight, muskets in front of them.

Where's Jackson?

The men fidget with their guns. I command myself to be calm. To present an air of confidence.

I work my mind, talking to myself. I'm the commander. Confident. Brave. Refusing to retreat.

Victorious.

The last part is a prayer.

Someone raises their musket. I conjure up my most commanding whisper and order them to ground it.

The line will only fire or move upon orders. I walk down the front of the tiny formation and issue the order again. Only respond to orders. The unit will fight as a team.

Like an apparition from the water, Jackson materializes before me.

The British are coming.

A small column, with several skirmishers thrown as a screen in front. Even now they approach us.

I look up and see Destiny wave.

Jackson darts to a small rise in the ground. It lies on my left, a position I picked earlier.

My brother drops to his belly and peers over the top of the mound of dirt.

Cloud fragments begin to play with the moon's light. I glance at it, half-hidden, its white light now muted.

I whirl as I hear the sharp report of a musket.

Jackson. The blast from the muzzle flashes fiery light across the ground in front of him. My brother ducks below the crest of the little mound. Furiously he works another load into his gun.

Flashes detonate through the curtain of ink in front of me. The corresponding musket blasts cut through the cold silence.

Only three or four at best.

The skirmishers. I curse myself for not knowing instinctively they would be the first to fire.

Destiny's rifle barks above my head.

No answer from the darkness.

I strain. I can't see anything. Both Jackson and Destiny have better vantage points and are finding targets. The men of the unit shift restlessly behind me.

Jackson pulls the ramrod from his gun. He pushes himself over the top of his dirt wall. A burst of fire flashes from the muzzle again.

The scream of a wounded soldier wails from a hundred yards out.

I stare, doubled over at the waist as though that will make me see farther. I glance back at my fidgeting formation. They rivet their eyes to me as I extend a hand to calm them. A gesture meant to convince them I know what I'm doing. I don't.

*In control, Jacob. You're in control. The men are waiting for you.*

Destiny's rifle barks again. Another man cries in pain.

A loud oath from a surprised voice carries across the field. Then two flashes through the black, the reports of two muskets with them.

Only two.

Jackson springs from his position and runs towards the barn.

I extend a hand behind me and back several steps closer to the men.

Do we need to change position?

"We've pushed back their skirmishers. The column is heading for us at a trot."

I exhale loudly.

Jackson speeds back to protect our left.

I turn my head towards Destiny's hideout.

"Officers!"

She waves.

Fight or die. Those are the only options left now.

I push the men against the barn so tight, their backs touch the wall.

The adrenaline is so powerful I can't steady my voice. I order again and again. Only act as ordered. No independent fire. Only act as ordered.

I catch a glimpse of Zach's face.

Absolute terror.

I slap him on the shoulder.

I can hear them.

Feet hit the ground at a rapid pace and in unison.

I can hear the cartridge pouches and equipment slapping against the sides of the soldiers.

Slings on muskets rattle at the metal fasteners.

Bayonets. Will they have bayonets fixed?

My mind flashes back to the demonstration I gave the first day of drills. The fifteen-inch stick protruding from Destiny's gun. The hopelessness of parrying that pointed steel with a shorter hunting musket.

I stand at the end of my line and raise my hand into the air.

Destiny's rifle barks.

Jackson fires another shot.

They appear. I can see them now.

They come running, as though they expect to clear a few stray militia hiding in the darkness.

"Present!"

"Fire!"

The volley from my men belches out in one great explosion.

There's a sickening *thwack* sound as musket balls find targets.

Several enemy soldiers collapse. Others trip over the ones who fall.

Fire bursts from Destiny's rifle again, Jackson's as well.

The British don't stop. They keep coming.

There's no time. The column will be upon us.

We need another volley.

I yell the commands as I stare with horror at the coming onslaught.

"Handle your cartridge!"

The British column looms closer and my heart is in my throat.

"Return the rammers!"

A mass of gleaming bayonets shimmer in the moonlight. My heart sinks.

We need one more accurate volley. Just one more.

"Shoulder!"

An officer running to the side of the enemy column catches my eye.

Destiny's rifle barks. The man jerks and falls to the ground.

"Fire!"

The night turns all blinding light and ear-splitting explosion. Sulfurous smoke billows about the front of our position.

I fumble for my own musket leaning against the barn. Frantically, my hands search for it.

In the melee descending on me I have nothing. No sword. No gun. Nothing to parry the thrusts of the bayonets.

I can't see.

I can't hear.

I turn to see if some enemy soldier is falling on me.

My line is faltering. Several men retreat into the barn.

Musket fire off to my left.

Then another shot from above me. Destiny.

*Destiny.*

Blind, nostrils filled with the acrid smoke, I push toward the barn door. Retreating bodies stumble about me. I force my way though.

Breaking into the building, I race to the foot of the ladder and spring up the steps two at a time.

Destiny stands at the top.

She smiles. I recoil in confusion.

"They're running, Jake. You did it!"

I scramble to the opening from which Destiny poured such a devastating fire. I can see over the billowing smoke.

Red-coated soldiers run, picking up or dragging their dead and wounded as they leave.

Someone fires another shot and I yell the order to cease fire.

It's a dream.

In a misty haze I start back to descend the ladder.

I fight for control.

Destiny throws her arms about my neck and kisses me.

# Chapter 51

I can hear them even from here.

The men of the militia unit snore as they lie about on stacks of hay in the barn. The racket echoes off the weather-beaten siding and reaches my ears twenty paces away. A small lantern inside throws muted light through the still open front doors. I warned them about fire, but it's there anyway.

I glance back just in time to see Destiny stand in the doorway and stretch. She walks towards me with a faint smile on her lips.

"Can't sleep either?" she asks.

I shake my head. "Jackson's off trying to find where the English boats landed."

The smile evaporates.

"He thinks they might be coming back?" Destiny gazes east where a pink glimmer announces the morning of a new day.

"He needs something to do." I smile. He must get tired sometime, right? For now, he's as unsettled as a caged fox.

"Guess we're all a little nervous. How do you feel?"

I survey the field and sigh. "I'm glad they took their wounded."

I didn't say dead. They took their *dead* and wounded. I peer off as though answers were in some distant yet discernable corner of the universe.

"Is anyone on guard duty?" Destiny asks.

"Not with Jackson out there already. Alvin's off that way." I point the opposite direction. "It's getting light anyway. They won't be back."

She doesn't notice me watching. Destiny searches the ground as she drifts into the area where the enemy was last night. She doesn't seem to find anything at first then her gaze rivets on a dark stain upon the ground.

The glance over her shoulder cinches it. She's judging the distance to the barn loft. Good chance it's one of hers.

"You okay?" I ask.

"It's a lot different than hunting. Last night there wasn't time to think. Now…"

She slides her arms around my middle as though looking for support. I hold her. The warm infusion fights off my guilt as well.

Her head slips right underneath my chin. She jumps when I greet Alvin.

"Don't mind me," the older man raises a hand. He searches my eyes and seems to judge it safe to join us. Destiny reaches out and touches his arm as he comes close.

Alvin throws a quick look over his shoulder, assuring himself that we're alone I think.

"You kids okay?" he asks.

We both assure him that we're fine. Our answers are somber, but it's true. We'll be fine.

The pink in the eastern sky enlarges and begins to turn orange. A rattling wagon sounds some distance inland.

"S'pect they comin' to milk those cows. Good thing we saved 'em."

Men stagger from the barn. Stories are exchanged.

Victory makes the men agreeable. The plan of battle seems to meet with their approval now that the fight is over.

As Alvin, Destiny, and I make our way back to the barn, I notice a mounted Lieutenant Brasswell accompanying the wagon laden with clanging, empty milk cans.

I try to give my smartest salute. "Lieutenant Braswell."

"You held the barn I see. Any damage? Casualties?"

"No property damage, sir. No casualties." Even I can hear the pride in my voice.

Braswell nods.

"Your unit is relieved for the time being. Report back to your camp."

"Yes sir."

"The girl's still here Lee." Braswell directs his gaze to Alvin. "I gave an order."

"I'm not so sure Rawlins—"

"You damnable and insolent farmers! This is supposed to be an army, not a social club. I gave an order."

His horse jumps backwards at Braswell's outburst. Alvin argues in Destiny's defense, but the lieutenant is unmoved.

He spins his horse in a circle and rides away.

# Chapter 52

Destiny takes my arm. "Does it help with Amelia?"

I pause for a moment; the question so startles me. It's been so quiet here near the place we first hunted trying to win over the militia. Far from the violence of last night. Far from Brasswell's outburst.

Alvin is off to see Rawlins, the other men catching up on sleep at camp.

Before I can piece together her meaning, Destiny explains. "Winning against the British. Does it help your memory of her?"

"Some."

"It's not like getting Helmsley though, is it?"

I shake my head. I admit it. I had hoped becoming the consummate enemy of British so-called justice would suffice, but —

It's not even close. The two issues, Amelia's death and British tyranny have become separate in my mind.

Tyranny. I'm starting to sound like a rebel.

I'm not letting go of justice for Amelia though.

Destiny points out a chickadee, balanced precariously on a thin twig and watching us. A squirrel stands erect on a chestnut tree, busy with something clasped in its forelegs.

I identify the call of quail nearby, but I can tell from her reaction that Destiny heard them already.

From our right, the quail flush. The birds streak through the trees in front of us, their beating wings sounding like the roll of drums.

Destiny stares, intent. She scrutinizes the place the quail left. I begin to question her when, from the trees that had obscured them, two men step into the open.

The two are backwoodsmen certainly. Their appearance seems foreign for Massachusetts. Clothes of animal skins.

But so are Destiny's and Jackson's.

These are more worn though. They carry dark stains from sweat and blood.

Each carries a musket in the crook of their arm. Grizzled and dirty, they meander toward us calling a friendly hello as they come.

"What outfit are you with?" I ask.

I don't know why, but the back of my neck prickles with fear.

I can't see anything that should make me worry. But something, something I can't identify yet, just doesn't seem right.

"Maryland." The one man speaks around a wad of something in his cheek.

A hat, the brim pressed down on all sides and torn in places, sits pushed back on his head. He smiles widely, revealing uneven, dirty teeth.

He's clean-shaven. His brown hair sticks like straw out from the bottom of his hat.

The other man stares at us with intense, dark eyes. Black hair, his beard, full and thick, bursts from his face. He doesn't wear a hat and unlike the speaker, he doesn't smile.

Maryland.

Militia from Maryland has joined the New England war? Since when?

"We're from Massachusetts." Destiny's fingers sink into my arm.

So. She feels it too.

"Oh, we know," the speaker replies. "You're the marksman, ain'tcha?" The man's eyes study Destiny as though she were some ancient relic just found.

Destiny nods.

"Well, we're supposed to come git ya."

The man turns his head and spits some disgusting brown liquid from his mouth. He looks square at me.

"You're supposed to go see the captain over yonder." He jerks his head in a direction that would send me some distance from where our section is camped.

Well, maybe. Maybe something about Destiny and her place in the militia. At the very least, the idea offers escape.

"I guess we better get going." I grip Destiny's arm even tighter.

"Oh, no," The man replies. He holds his palm out as though to stop us.

"*You're* to report to the captain, *we're* to escort the sharpshooter back to your unit." The man shifts his weight, peers closely at me, and smiles that dirty, stained smile.

I pull myself a little taller.

"My business with Captain Rawlins concerns her place in my unit. She's coming with me."

"Enemy scouts about. We're s'posed to escort the lady." The man continues to chew on his tobacco.

"I'm not going without Destiny."

"Destiny. That's your name?" The man peers at her with exaggerated sweetness. "I like that."

He turns to his companion. "Her name's Destiny." The man with the black beard nods.

As he peers at me, the smile vanishes from the speaker's face. His countenance burns with intensity. "Now you follow orders."

"I outrank you soldier. You don't give me orders." Even the most backward militia unit knows that. This guy is about to abandon the claim of being militia altogether. I knew it.

What seems to be an inevitable battle between us is lost already though. Two men with muskets. Even without muskets, the hunting knives hanging from their belts will make quick work of dispatching me.

I can't leave Destiny. I glance at her and see Amelia.

Just as she appeared between the rows of apple trees, sun upon her face. In my mind, as if able to communicate from another world, Amelia pleads with me. *Don't go.*

I won't. I won't leave Amelia in Thornby's apple orchard to be brutalized and murdered by a British officer.

At least these two have the appearance of what they actually are. Not disguised as was Helmsley, who only pretended to be honorable. These men are him, stripped of the glittering army uniform.

"Okay," I say and remove my arm from Destiny's grasp.

It hurts to do that.

From the corner of my eye, I can see it. Her distress. The fear that I'll leave her as I did Amelia. I squeeze her hand as I let go.

The musket still rests in the crook of the man's arm.

I spring from my position and grab the gun with both hands. I push desperately.

My feet dig into the earth, finding traction. From my toes in the ground to my fingertips clasping the musket, I launch myself in one great explosion.

The force of the shove drives the speaker into his partner with the black hair. Neither has time to react.

The second man loses his balance and falls. The first one clutches the musket tightly. I can't wrench it loose. My opponent keeps himself on his feet by his iron grip on the gun.

Destiny jumps. She's nothing but a blur in the corner of my eye.

Blackbeard's musket waves through the air. He's on his back, but trying to position his weapon to shoot.

I twist the gun in my opponent's hands. The man twists back and pushes. He gains better footing and sends me reeling backwards.

Destiny shouts.

A musket fires.

I fall backwards. I pull my opponent with me, still trying to free the gun. I twist to keep from falling underneath the man.

The butt of the musket hits ground first, jarring the weapon from both of us.

The gun bounces into the air from the impact.

A glimpse of Destiny running. But running towards me.

The straw hair man lands on the ground with a grunt. I hit a split second behind, the impact driving the air from my lungs.

A fist aimed for my opponent's nose misses, but still drives into his face.

Images flash inside my head. It's Helmsley. No, it's the woodsman.

Destiny's yelling something.

I push myself to my knees and turn, desperate to find the musket. Destiny has it.

It fires. For a moment I'm blind and deaf. My nostrils fill with acrid smoke.

I search and find my opponent and see the flash of the glimmering knife.

Both arms in the air, arching myself back to miss the blade.

My left arm too slow. Searing pain.

Then the butt of the musket crashing into the man's face.

He yells, rolling to his side.

I grab the musket from Destiny.

More confusion. It's Helmsley on the ground. I pound the musket into the man's head.

He wanted to hurt Destiny. He killed Amelia.

All that is evil in the world—.

Again, I swing the musket, then again.

Destiny's yelling. Her arms reach around my shoulders.

No, it's the woodsman.

He lies still. Unmoving. Head surrounded with blood-drenched leaves and dirt.

Blood pours from my left forearm.

The man with black hair lies dead, a musket ball in his chest.

Destiny stands before me, unhurt.

I stare at her, breathing deeply, blood dripping from my fingers.

She springs into action. She rips my shirt, wrapping the wound as tight as I can bear.

It's throbbing now. A searing pain convulsing through me with each heartbeat.

Destiny ties off the bandage. She rips more of my shirt and makes a sling.

Dimly, I can hear her commands to not move my arm.

Destiny's arm encircles my waist. She grabs a quick kiss from me and I realize her face is warm and wet.

She's crying. Destiny pulls me into a desperate race towards camp.

# Chapter 53

He's so much heavier than she expected.

Destiny circles Jake's waist with her left hand. She clings to his good arm and keeps it about her neck.

The weakness of his effort is frightening.

He tries not to lean on her at first, but before they've gone even a short distance, he can scarcely stay on his feet.

Another slope in the undulating forest. Destiny has passed over this uneven ground many times. The ups and downs are easy to navigate. Shallow really.

But Jake stumbles as they start up the incline. Destiny grabs tighter. Jake's weight careens into her. She trips, but keeps her balance.

"Up the hill, Jake."

He mumbles something unintelligible in response.

His arm bleeds too much. She can't get a good look at it. In order to examine it she'd need to stop and lean him against a tree. She may never get him started again.

"Come on, Jake. Almost to the top." Her voice has a catch in it.

Destiny attacks the upper half of the grade at an angle. Jake's weight presses even harder on her.

It gives her a vantage point. She glances at the way they've come.

Her gasp is audible. Just instinct.

It's too much. She can see the red trail. Destiny has tracked wounded animals before. Has found them dead.

This trail wouldn't require tracking. It's a painted marker pointing the way.

He's losing too much blood.

Finally, they stagger over the crest of the rise. As the trees fade back, a small, moist meadow is left in the clearing.

"Downhill now Jake."

A cottontail rabbit fidgets on the shady side of the field. Destiny notices because they rarely venture out into the open during daylight.

There's a tree stump. It's disintegrating near the ground, easy to trip over. Destiny maneuvers Jake away from the obstruction and angles down towards the meadow's edge.

A shadow streaks across the ground behind the cottontail. A chicken hawk dives at lightning speed, dropping from the sky. Its talons stretch out and stab into the unwary rabbit. The hawk climbs steeply into the air. Its prey struggles, the hind legs kicking frantically.

It's no match for its airborne captor.

If Jackson were only here.

Jake collapses.

She can't hold him. He just drops. They both go down together.

He hits the ground, jarring his wound. He screams. The fall must have been agonizing.

Her tears have flowed on and off ever since she'd seen his wound. They start fresh now.

Jake needs her. He needs her to be strong. He needs someone able to carry him to where he can get the help he needs.

Instead, he's stuck with Destiny.

She tugs and pulls at him. They're near the edge of the meadow. A Red Maple with a stout trunk grows only feet away.

She can't leave Jake laying in the dirt as though he were already dead. She'll leave him sitting, expecting her return, waiting patiently to be rescued.

"Come on Jake! Push!"

She doesn't really expect a response, but he bends his leg, digs a foot into the ground, and shoves himself up against the tree.

Leaving makes her voice so unreliable. Destiny tries to explain.

"I can't carry you. Jake. Jake, I'm coming back. With Jackson, and Alvin, and— and Lucas."

He mumbles at her.

"'kay. Get Jackson."

His head lolls off to the side. Help is her only choice. Destiny sprints off, around the edge of the meadow.

It's really not that far. But minutes have become so precious.

The ground slopes up at the far side of the meadow. Destiny races up the incline and over the high ground. She can smell the sea.

To her right. The remaining trees zip by as she escapes the woods and breaks into the open.

She passes the elm grove. Around the little hillcrest and she's at the road. Across it.

She can make out her friends lying about the tents, recovering from being up all night.

"Jackson!"

Her call grabs the attention of several men. Lucas. Alvin.

She races across the last of the open ground, reaching the first tent.

Jackson comes dashing from behind a canvas lean-to.

"Jake!" She gasps to gain enough air to say more. "Jake's hurt."

She describes the wound in as few words possible. Surely the tears on her cheeks describe the urgency. Winded, she draws great rasping breaths.

"Where is he?" Jackson asks her.

"I'll show you," Destiny gasps.

Back across the road, past the elms, through the first outposts of the forests, and into the meadow.

Jake's on the ground. Not sitting against the tree. Lying, collapsed beside it.

Despite the fire in her lungs, Destiny reaches him first.

She can't speak. Her breathing wracks her body.

She kneels and touches Jake's cheek with a trembling hand. She pats it looking for a response.

Jake's head tilts.

"You're back," he slurs.

"Yes!" The reply comes out in one great burst.

Jackson's tomahawk rings through the air as it works on a couple of saplings in the edge of the meadow. Alvin and Lucas' hands fly as they repeatedly throw coils of rope around the felled limbs forming a litter.

Destiny cradles Jake's upper arm, keeping it from sliding. The men lift and set him on the makeshift stretcher.

And the race is on again. Lucas and Jackson carry Jake. They run, their gait awkward as they work to keep the jolting to a minimum.

Destiny runs beside, watching Jake's face. She tries to talk to him, keep him alert.

No response. Should they stop?

No. Time is the greatest enemy now.

She pleads. Jake.

She talks to him. Remember the battle at the barn?

Jake. Wake up.

His eyelids crack.

"I'm okay," he murmurs.

But he isn't okay. She knows it.

If he has to lose an arm he'll be devastated, but he'll be alive.

The alternative is too grim to contemplate.

## Chapter 54

Destiny races ahead of the litter bearers.

The little farmhouse comes into view, the station where the surgeon sees patients, everything from broken bones to axe cuts to dysentery.

Outside the house, sheets of canvas hang over poles creating a cavernous tent. Open at the ends, the protected space is filled with sick and wounded lying underneath.

A man hovers over the patients, moving from one to another. His brown breeches and near-white stockings are quality. He's well-to-do. Probably educated.

A few more steps.

The man's solid brown hair is tied into a queue at the back. He's young.

"Please! Sir!"

He turns and looks at her.

"My— my friend."

Destiny points behind her. Alvin, Lucas, and Jackson all race awkwardly toward the large open tent. The litter with a broken Jake rocks clumsily between them.

The surgeon immediately drops a sheaf of papers and hurries out, he glances back at Destiny as he talks.

What happened? Where's the injury? Any other injuries?

He arrives at Jake's side and those carrying the litter slow to a walk.

The surgeon keeps them moving, directing where they can place Jake on a table for his examination.

"He appears to have lost much blood," the doctor comments in a sober voice.

He cuts the bandages from Jake's arm, speaking to him as he does, trying to rouse his attention.

"Can you hear me young man? Know where you are?"

"What's his name?" he asks Destiny.

"Jacob."

"Jacob? Jacob, do you know where you are?"

The physician extends his arm giving a 'come here' motion. Two men and a woman working in the hospital hurry towards him.

The doctor lays the blood-soaked bandages aside. He glances at Destiny. "Not familiar with a tourniquet, are you?"

Tourniquet. It doesn't sound familiar. She shakes her head.

The physician flashes a quick smile. "No matter. Difficult things to work with."

He turns his head to the woman he called over. "I see no reason for an amputation yet. We'll watch the wound for infection." The woman nods.

"We obviously need to stitch it." She bustles off. The two men jostle their way around the table to opposite sides of Jake. Alvin and Lucas give way, fading into the background.

"Jacob? Did you hear me? We must stitch your arm."

The surgeon lowers his head, trying to get a response.

"Mm-hmm," Jake replies, barely audible.

"I can offer you some spirits for the pain. Haven't much time though. We must be quick."

Jake shakes his head.

"No? Are you sure?"

Destiny searches Jake's face. "Your mother?"

Jake nods. His eyes close.

The muscles of his face set into hard lines. He's preparing for the pain.

She looks up at the surgeon and shakes her head. The coming agony will be intense, it's hard to see him refuse anything that might help.

But he's honoring his parents. His mother especially. There's no strong drink in the Greyson household. Jake's father barely drinks wine.

The surgeon's hands flash about busily. The curved needle with the wicked looking point. The thread strung through it and draping behind.

As if from a signal, the two male helpers grab Jake's legs. Jackson steps near to Destiny's side and holds Jake's good arm. He catches her eye.

Destiny moves to Jake's head. She places her hands on either side of his face.

She strokes the hair back from his forehead. Her fingers caress him.

The surgeon grasps his arm with one hand and draws the needle near the wound.

Jake tenses, his muscles all going rigid at once.

Jackson presses a piece of wood between Jake's teeth.

The point of the needle touches the quivering flesh.

The surgeon pushes through the skin. Jake lets out a muffled cry, eloquent with searing pain and a desperate need for relief.

Destiny hovers over his face, her tears bathing his forehead.

# Chapter 55

"Here. This will be more comfortable." The woman who assisted the physician smiles at Destiny. She places a small chair near Jake.

Destiny sits and runs her fingers through Jake's hair. He's unconscious.

Looking up she sees the surgeon watching her as he wipes his hands on a rag. The woman picks up after the operation. She wipes blood that spilled from Jake's arm. Places the needle and leftover thread in a small wooden box.

"I don't think he's in danger of his life," the surgeon says. "I do think it's unlikely he'll keep the arm. A day or two and we'll know."

Poor Jake. He'll lose his arm. And he did it to save her.

Destiny's fingers twist some of the locks near his forehead as she watches for signs of waking.

Along the two rows in the makeshift tent, assistants bend over men who lie upon the straw-covered ground. They check and re-bandage wounds. Inquire as to how the sick and injured feel. Help them drink concoctions aimed to heal them.

Two hours pass. It seems Jake should have stirred some by now. But he still breathes. His heart still beats.

"Hey Missy." Alvin steps into the tent and puts a hand on Destiny's shoulder. He places an old flintlock pistol beside Jake.

"It's a officer's sidearm," he says. "I think the boy's earned it."

"Thank you, Alvin. I imagine he'll love it." It may be hard to understand, but Jake will definitely be pleased.

"I cain't stay Missy. You watch after 'im. I'll be back in the mornin'."

A reluctant Alvin leaves. As he does, he passes a returning Jackson. The two wave briefly at each other as Jackson strides with purpose into the tent.

"Found it," he says. "How's he doing?"

"Fine." It's Jake. Destiny jumps to her feet and stares into his face.

"You're awake!"

He cracks his eyelids. The corner of his mouth curls up in the smallest of smiles.

"I think so."

Destiny's hand lies on his chest. She can't hug him, but she wants to.

"Look what Alvin brought you."

Destiny shows him the pistol. It's old, much of the finish worn off the wood. The stock bears nicks and cuts from long and hard use.

Jake takes it with his good hand.

The importance of this symbol is lost on Destiny. The pistol won't be nearly as accurate as her rifle.

Jake turns it over as he examines it. It seems to have meaning for him. Some kind of status thing. Officers carry pistols, not muskets.

Jake's not really an officer, but in his dreams…

Destiny pats his shoulder as he admires the weapon. If Jake ends up with only one arm, the pistol will be easier to use.

Jackson's haversack hits the table with a light thud as he removes it from his shoulder. Reaching inside, Jakes brother pulls a gob of tangled plant stems.

The leaves shine a bright, glossy green. Small yellow flowers hide within the heap Jackson places on Jake's chest.

He glances furtively down the length of the tent.

"Unbandage his arm." Jackson puts some of the plant into his mouth.

"How's that supposed to help me if you're eating it?" Jake murmurs.

He barely beat Destiny to the question. She stares at Jackson.

"Not eating. You have to chew it slightly, just to break it down a little. Then put it on the wound. It'll work." Jackson nods his head with assurance and enthusiasm.

"I don't want your spit on my arm," Jake protests.

"You have to—."

"Let Destiny do it."

Destiny laughs as she pulls the bandage from Jake's arm.

Jake watches her as she chews a few stems. Jackson rifles through the cuttings. He breaks off the yellow flowers and throws them aside.

"Just a little," Jackson instructs. "Just to break 'em up. The juice in the stems. That's what works."

Destiny pulls the gooey glob from her mouth as Jake still watches.

His arm lies beside him so red and angry. Blood still oozes from the stitched-up slice.

She places the green mass on the cut then repeats with another batch. Once the wound is covered end to end, she wraps the bandage back into place.

"That, brother, will save your arm." Jackson tilts his head the way he does when he has a question. There's no question in his voice, however. He's sure.

#

Surely no one could sleep in that chair. With a start though, Destiny opens her eyes at the sharp call of a nearby rooster.

Even the gray light of dawn has passed. Long, sharp, well-defined shadows stretch across the grounds. The sun is up and bright.

She raises her head from her arms which rest on the edge of the Jake's bed.

Well, his breathing seems normal. His chest rises and falls. A gentle hand on his heart. It beats strong and sure.

Where did Jackson end up? She must have fallen asleep before he left.

Needing the stretch anyway, Destiny explores a short distance down the road.

Small ribbons of smoke spiral into the sky. Around a clump of birch trees and there's Jake's brother, leaning over a small fire.

Jackson straightens with a tin dish in his hand. He holds it with the flap of his haversack.

"He awake yet?"

Destiny shakes her head.

"Anyone in the tent?"

"No."

The pan holds three eggs just cooked over the fire.

"Let's get these into him before anyone finds out."

Jake stirs groggily as Destiny touches his face. A moment later, he peers at her, eyes clear and alert.

"Here." Jackson hands Destiny the pan of eggs. "He'll want *you* to feed him."

Destiny cuts small spoonfuls of the firm, fried eggs. She puts a bite into Jake's mouth.

"I remember doing this once before."

Jake shakes his head. "That was mush."

"It was oatmeal!"

Jake grins.

Another bite. Then another.

"Uh-oh. Look who's coming," Jackson says.

Lieutenant Braswell.

The pompous officer marches up the road with great purpose. Two militia men follow. This can only mean trouble.

"I've heard about the incident," Braswell says as he stops just inside the tent.

"You are permitted to stay in hospital until released." Braswell is gazing at Jake.

Jackson mutters under his breath. "Nice of you."

Braswell glances at him but doesn't seem to make out the words. He shifts his gaze to Destiny.

"You have been ordered out twice. Yet you are still here."

He throws out a hand indicating the men he brought with him.

"These two soldiers will escort you, *immediately,* two miles out of camp. Don't come back."

Jake lies behind her. She's in front as though protecting him. The two guards grab her arms, one on either side.

The sound confuses her at first. She knows what makes the loud snap as soon as she hears it. But it doesn't seem possible.

Jake limps around the foot of the table that's been his bed since yesterday. His left arm dangles by his side, trailing the bandage Destiny had already begun to remove.

His good arm extends rigidly. The pistol points at Braswell's nose. Jake closes the distance until the barrel of the gun almost touches Braswell between the eyes.

"If anyone is still touching her in three seconds—. Pray now."

No one waits for a command. The two guards release Destiny and jump back as though scalded by the breath from Jake's lips.

Braswell retreats a step, face reddening in rage.

"You will be *shot* for this! I—."

"Everyone take a step back and breathe."

Captain Rawlins. He steps into the tent like an actor walking onto a stage. "Alvin Lee warned me this might happen."

Braswell salutes smartly. Rawlins flashes a quick reply.

"You got here faster than I anticipated," Rawlins says to the lieutenant.

Jake still holds the pistol.

"Son, put the gun down," Rawlins orders.

Jake lowers his arm. Destiny clutches him, trying to push him back to the table.

"Sergeant Greyson, you cannot point guns at your superiors. You are confined to assigned quarters for the rest of the week."

The captain turns to his subordinate officer.

"Lieutenant Braswell. I told you to let me handle this situation."

"She has no place in a military encampment. She—."

"Lieutenant. You are dismissed."

Braswell just stares at Rawlins, speechless.

Rawlins raises his eyebrows peering at the junior officer.

"Dismissed."

# Chapter 56

I can't explain the feeling. Tingling maybe. That might be it.

Destiny wraps my arm and secures it by tying it to my torso. The surgeon instructed her to be sure and keep it immobile.

It's been over a week. I think the required time period has expired, but…

I smell her. Her head bowed, concentrating on her work. Her closeness bringing us into contact as she fumbles with the bandages.

"I'm not sure we need to do this anymore," I admit, thinking I really don't want the morning ritual to end.

She looks up at me and, in her gaze, I see her disappointment as well. We watch each other a moment then Destiny breaks the stare.

"I think you're all set." She gives my shoulder a soft pat.

"Thank you, Destiny."

Prepared for another day, I return to the meadow. Captain Rawlins is thrilled with the defense of the barn. No casualties on our part. Twenty of the King's men run off by ten militia. All soldiers from his command. He's been bragging to every officer that will listen.

He also has me training the rest of the company in the same drills. He sits on his horse, this time with a small audience. Another opportunity to brag.

I raise my hand into the air. A line of sixty-five soldiers stand at attention waiting for me. On my command, every other man steps forward. They bring their muskets into their shoulders and 'fire'.

It's not a deafening roar this time. The hollow clicks of hammers falling echo across the field, but there are no explosions. Gunpowder is a precious commodity and in short supply.

I order the second line to quick march forward through the files left open. The first line, now behind their companions, pretends to reload their guns.

I call out the orders and the front rank raises their weapons and fires. Again, thirty some hollow metal clicks as hammers fall.

The rear rank then advances, as the one that has just 'fired' pretends to reload.

The company is firing and advancing by files.

I wheel the formation to face Rawlins. All the men salute.

We practiced exactly this. It comes off a smart, military-looking maneuver.

"Nice work!" Rawlins crows. He touches his hat as though in a salute.

Taking that as permission to dismiss, I release the men.

I look for Destiny anticipating a leisurely morning walk along the bay. A cluster of horsemen approach Rawlins along the road. The bright red coat in the center of the group can't be missed. I'm intrigued. Has someone captured an English officer?

"I came under a flag of truce!" An outraged voice complains to Rawlins. A familiar voice. William's voice.

Running to the collection of shifting horses and complaining voices, I can't help but wonder. Could William be leaving the provincial unit? Coming back to the patriot side?

"Untie him Lieutenant," an exasperated Rawlins orders Braswell who seems to have taken charge of the party escorting William.

I'm speechless. With short deliberate movements, Braswell fumbles at the rope that secures the British officer's wrists.

William notices me. So does Rawlins.

"Do you know Lieutenant Waterford?"

"Yes sir. Very well."

In my mind unfold colorful scenes of playing army as a boy. William and I marching through the fields about my home, searching for Jackson.

Jackson, always the enemy, always the French.

How the world has changed.

I proudly wore that red coat from my father's service in the French and Indian War. William and I, as schoolboys, always fought the French. There was no other enemy.

Now we stare at each other across an imaginary abyss. William wears the red coat of the British still. I, while not the French, have become the new enemy.

"Sergeant Greyson?"

"Yes sir."

"You have permission to meet with Lieutenant Waterford. He should be the guest of General Ward if he stays after nightfall."

"Yes sir."

Moments pass in silence as the others fade away.

"Is this awkward?" William asks.

"Not with you, William." I extend a hand. I'm lying. It is awkward.

We are, though, on my ground. William ventured through the lines to see me.

The two of us stumble into conversation, reviewing our lives since parting. The provincial unit William and I shared for a time still trains. William is impressed with their fighting ability.

I shift the topic. There are things I have to know, things I still can't fully understand.

After Amelia —. Didn't that change the world for him as it did for me?

"Helmsley's gone. Assigned to another regiment. I don't even see him."

"And nothing's going to happen to him." My words are bitter. I fear I may have overstepped, but I don't care. I *am* bitter.

"Careful Jacob. Amelia was my sister and I loved her as much as you. I don't like it. But I'm not going to rebel against my sovereign because one man escapes justice."

"Are you still outranked by a British Ensign?" I shouldn't ask, but still feeling the insult, I do.

"Does your militia still *elect* its officers?"

William's gaze meets mine and we stare at each other a moment. A stalemate. We each drew blood.

William seems to search his feelings. His countenance softens. His voice still fills with frustration though.

"Out of all the people in Blackham, I think I'm the only one that remains loyal." He shrugs his shoulders and holds out his hands, a gesture that communicates a complete lack of understanding.

"You're the one to feel the weight of British injustice the least," I answer. "I'm not an officer, but I may become one. They won't care about my family's name, or how much money we have. It'll be about merit."

"And winning an election," William mutters.

The repeated insult angers me and I open my mouth to protest. Before I can utter a word though, William adds, "It's alright. I can see the system has been more unfair to you than to me."

I stand down and swallow my retort. We walk down the road in silence.

"I could argue about the chaos and anarchy likely to follow the overthrow of the king, but I know you'd have answers." William places a hand on my shoulder. "I won't go there."

We stop and face each other. William's comment seems to draw a truce between us.

"Have you seen my sister?" I ask.

William nods. "That's the real reason I'm here. She needs your help."

I think back at how much Patty knew about Lexington and Concord. Even before anyone else. She was at risk even then. My expression must reveal my alarm.

"She's alright," William adds hastily. "She just needs your help."

Almost every patriot family, rebel family in William's view, has left Boston. Patty hasn't because Meacham is ill. She needs help moving and asked if I could come into the city.

New Englanders are allowed to pass freely in and out of Boston. I, however, am the enemy. Militia. This requires special permission.

"Can I bring Jackson?"

"Sure."

# Chapter 57

The borrowed horse heaves with a deep cough. It pauses; concentrating on its infirmity then pushes itself into a listless shuffle.

Jackson's mount appears little better. The horses, loaned from undersupplied militia officers, transport us past Roxbury, toward the Boston Neck.

William is carried by the chestnut he's owned for years. Well-kept, spirited, and beautiful.

The swells of the gray Atlantic mirror the sun in sharp bright flashes when the angle is just right. The islands scattered about the outer edges of the harbor are placid.

The masts of British warships rise like a forest.

Comparisons flow naturally through my thoughts as we venture deeper into the enemy's lair. My company marches in straight lines. They obey the commands that make them halt or turn. I fill with pride when they all lift their muskets and fire in unison.

The men I serve with though, are amateurs, novices. In real life they're farmers and merchants. The tools of their trade are plows and dry goods.

The soldiers I pass now wear red coats. In real life they are… soldiers.

They have no other life. This is it. They are professionals.

My eye is drawn to the enemy works near the road's edges.

Huge cannons nestle into safely entrenched positions. They wait to send twenty-four-pound iron balls exploding through ranks of colonists. The mouths gape at me, threatening.

Gun crews hover about the weapons. They watch over piles of cannonballs and wagonloads of gunpowder and other supplies.

Infantry sits behind earthen embankments. Hundreds of muskets stand in pyramids, waiting to be used.

As we enter the city and near the Common, teams of four and even six horses draw heavy wagons filled with military supplies.

Red uniforms, in constant movement, appear everywhere. They march from the wharves along the water's edge, to join other units. The sections grow ever larger in their marching and maneuvering. Entire regiments of professional infantry form in and around the city center.

In silence, we traverse the city streets until we arrive at Patty's home. It sits by the road, worn and tired. The glass of the front windows even dirtier than when I last visited. A windrow of debris clings to the door's threshold.

William and I stare at each other, words on the tips of our tongues. There's so much to say, but no way to say it.

I watch my friend, regal in his uniform, ride away.

Well. Time to concentrate on why Jackson and I are here. A wagon blocks part of the street in front of Patty's house. My brother ties the horses and we make our way to the side entrance. A quick knock and I push the door open.

The familiar kitchen welcomes me, but it's empty. The table still lingers near the wall, its surface bare.

The walls stare back at me, empty of the pans that used to hang on them.

The small cabinet still stands on the far side of the room. Cleared out, one of the swinging front doors hanging open.

"There are a few things left, but most of it is ready to move." As Patty descends the stairs, she catches me by surprise. She reads me so perfectly.

She smiles and hugs both Jackson and me.

"How's Meacham?"

Patty glances upstairs. "Holding his own. He's had a fever for three days; the doctor says he's seen worse." She makes an attempt at a tired smile.

#

I wake, feeling tugging on my shoulder as Jackson pulls me from sleep.

My brother brings the team from the nearby stable. Together, we lug three wooden trunks out the door and strain to lift them into the wagon.

Patty leaves the largest of her furnishings. She's coming back she insists. I hope so.

Jackson throws a rope over and ties the load along one side of the wagon. I drop a few blankets in the open space. Meacham will endure a long jolting ride to Blackham.

Clattering up the street comes a spirited gray mare and half a dozen trotting British soldiers.

"Arrest him!" Captain Helmsley points at me. The redcoat privates under his command run to obey his command.

"For what?" I sputter. "I'm here by permission. Lieutenant Waterford will confirm it."

"Waterford." Helmsley spits the name with distaste. "A provincial."

Surely the captain's bluffing. I break the fiery stare and turn back to the wagon.

"Seize him!" Helmsley screams.

Two British soldiers grab my arms. Swinging to one side, I yank myself loose from one of them. Swiveling the opposite direction, I jerk my other arm free.

The glinting point of a bayonet hovers inches from my face. At the other end of the long knife-like weapon, I stare into the eyes of a third soldier. One who appears unafraid to use force to subdue me.

It takes a moment frozen in time, but I regain some composure as the bayonet retreats to a safer distance from my nose.

"What can you arrest me for?" I ask.

"Desertion. You are assigned to that miserable colonial regiment. Deserters get the firing squad. You'll be dead by this afternoon."

# Chapter 58

A blur of British redcoats surrounds me. I stumble from the pushing and shoving as they force me in the direction of Helmsley.

"Me brother was killed on the road from Lexington ya bloody rebel." A scarecrow thin face spits the words at me. The butt of his musket drives into my midsection before I can clench muscles in anticipation. The blow drops me to the pavement.

A kick to the ribs. Hands with vise-like grips clutch onto me and drag me limply from the ground.

This can't be happening. I look from angry face to angry face.

Patty's voice cries out. I can't make out her words. Jackson's voice. Something else.

I try to look back to find the messages of my family.

What must be the butt of another musket crashes into my back. Fiery fingers of pain shoot through my back, hips, legs.

My sight dims. My head spins.

Saliva flies from my mouth as someone lands a debilitating blow near my right temple.

"Eyes front!" A voice screams in my ear.

I seem to trip on unseen obstacles. The world goes nearly silent. With a mighty effort I raise my head.

Helmsley rides in front. The soldiers march in two lines, one on either side of me. A turn to look in another direction brings another blow.

I stumble again. A blow to the back with the butt of a musket.

"Keep movin'!"

My breath comes heavy and uneven. Each gasp brings searing jabs like needles.

I must keep up. My eyes examine the street immediately before my feet. Straining to see, I glance right and left without moving my head.

Is there a place to run? A side street to break into?

Helmsley blocks the front. Three soldiers on either side just wait for the opportunity to beat on me. Maybe they'd shoot me.

I lift my head higher, trying to see where we're going. Another turn and I'm sure.

The provincials. The warehouse-turned-barracks that houses the unit that once claimed me.

So. No appearance before the Provost Marshal's office. Helmsley means for this to be his decision only. His judgment. His punishment.

The captain means to kill me.

How can I fight back against that? I can barely stay on my feet. I'm outnumbered by what seems like a hundred to one. I have no friends here.

As we approach, New Englanders in red uniforms stop whatever they're doing. They stare. They gape. They're accusing.

The deserter, me, is drug home for a just reward.

"Tie him to the post!" Helmsley bellows.

On the water side of the street, a timber stands along the dock. Worn and chipped, it's well-used, familiar with the horrors of army justice.

I try to appear stoic, but I can't contain the cry that escapes me when they yank my arms behind and around the post.

The still-healing wound in my arm sears with a sharp and cutting flame. Pain bolts up into my shoulder.

The voice behind me laughs.

"Somthin' about that arm pains ye?" The grip loosens, allowing my arm to fall forward several inches, then the restraints are wrenched back as I gasp.

A chain clatters noisily as it's strung through an iron ring. A lock clicks firmly into position.

The voice laughs again. The soldier walks toward the regimental barracks. He spits into the side of my head as he passes.

Dimly, I inspect my audience across the street, lounging against the weather-beaten siding of the old warehouse. Behind me, where they can't see, I pull at the restraints, but all I can do is wiggle my fingers.

Helmsley will win again. He can kill me as easily as he killed Amelia.

The bands clamp my wrists so tight there's no movement. Nothing. Discipline. I've got to think.

What are the possibilities? However remote, there must be something. I determine to start a mental list for evaluation but can't come up with a single prospect.

Horse hooves on cobblestone signal someone coming around the corner. Maybe my executioner.

It's William.

My friend careens through the intersection. The familiar chestnut skids to a halt in front of me as William leaps from her back.

"Unchain him!" William commands in a voice filled with authority. He's clearly learned the art.

The six soldiers who drug me here jump up. They face the men of my old regiment.

"Don't nobody try," one threatens. The man turns to William. "We ain't under your command."

My friend sputters trying to form a threatening reply. He's powerless though, and he knows it. So, do I.

Guiltily William glances at me. He watches the soldiers as though he were my guard. They watch him just as closely.

"Don't worry, Jacob. We'll get this sorted out."

I nod but manage little more than that. William fumes. He maintains a vigilant watch, never straying more than a few paces from where I stand fastened to the post. Finally, Helmsley appears, rounding the corner, entering the row of warehouses.

My friend storms towards him.

"You have no right! Release him," William orders pointing back to me.

"May I remind you Lieutenant Waterford, you are one, a lieutenant, and two, a provincial." Helmsley smiles grimly as he dismounts.

William waves a paper under Helmsley's nose.

"This promises Jacob Greyson safe passage in and out of Boston. Colonel Graham's signature is on it."

"Must not have known he was a deserter." Helmsley sniffs.

"They know you're a murderer. They're just too gutless to do anything about it." William's voice rises in pitch and intensity. I've never seen him so livid. His hand flies to his waist and yanks a pistol from the crimson sash of his uniform.

He throws his arm out straight, pointing the weapon into Helmsley's face. The captain steps back.

"You murdered my sister. Now you plan to murder my friend."

The pistol trembles. The barrel stares into Helmsley's eyes.

William pulls the hammer back. It clicks solidly into place with a firm metallic ring.

"William. Put down the pistol." A familiar voice negotiates the corner. Major Harrison. Calm, unflustered. I wonder if he would have felt relieved of a burden had he been too late, and William managed to end Helmsley's career right here. For good.

William lowers his arm and watches the major approach. "Jackson must have found you." The words come in a great exhale.

Helmsley reaches angrily for William's arm.

"Silas, think," the Major says. He stretches an expectant hand toward William.

My friend hands the paper he'd waved in Helmsley's face only a moment before. The captain drops his arm and peers toward the heavens in exasperation.

"Seems to be in order," Major Harrison continues. He turns his face to the guards. "Release him."

The lock clicks open, the chain drops, and my arms are free.

Pulling the injured limb into a more normal position brings another spasm through my shoulder.

"He's a *deserter*!" Helmsley cries in frustration.

"Then he's a deserter with a pass," replies the major. "Silas, we've talked about this before. I report to His Excellency on these matters. I don't want to try and explain this to him. Agreed?"

Helmsley stands, fuming as though he might explode.

"One stupid, provincial girl—."

In a blur that catches me completely off guard, William throws his fist into the man's face. Helmsley staggers and falls into the street. Major Harrison grabs William's arm.

"Lieutenant." There's sharpness in the major's voice. "You are but a step away from the guardhouse."

"Yes sir." William rubs the knuckles of his right hand.

Helmsley rises. He stares at Major Harrison, his face incredulous.

The major says nothing.

Helmsley turns his back and strides toward his horse. He mounts, then glares alternately at me and William. A trickle of blood seeps from his nose. "This isn't over."

"Take your men back to your unit, Silas," Major Harrison calls.

"Come on," Helmsley shouts. He whirls his gray mount in a tight circle and canters noisily down the street.

Major Harrison peers at the paper order William had handed him.

"Not good judgment, William." He sighs and walks off the same direction as Helmsley.

"Thank you." I approach my friend and extend a hand. William grasps it. He seems so… tired.

"Jackson's on his way out of the city with your family."

I nod.

"Should be past the Neck already."

William helps me retrieve my sickly mount. Together, we ride toward the city's border.

I stare at my friend, scrambling furiously for something to say. But just as last night, we part, both disappointed we could not sway the other. Late May 1775. Near Roxbury Massachusetts.

# Chapter 59

I inhale deeply, but something seems to constrict my chest, leaving me out of breath. I try, but I can't make out any rooftops from the village of Roxbury, well behind me. The militia company, the *entire* company, lies along the edges of a green clearing. They recline with grass stems hanging from their mouths, talking to one another. Some sleep or at least appear to.

Underneath though, is a jitteriness and apprehension that finds no outlet.

Someone anticipates a British raid. Right here, in this spot. I don't know how they know these things; when the British are coming. But they, whoever they are, were right about the raid at the barn. They could be right this time as well.

I search the length of the long, narrow, and empty glade. Lieutenant Braswell is in command and he is inexplicably absent.

I pace close to the center of the open space. Right and left. End to end. I turn and walk slowly back.

I'm startled as Destiny and Jackson come up behind me, returning from Roxbury.

"No Braswell," Jackson reports.

"*Lieutenant* Braswell," I correct, with little conviction.

Jackson scowls at my correction. He hates military rules.

"We're better off without him," he says as he takes his turn gazing across the grassy field.

"I'm not."

"Relax brother. It'll be like the barn. You might take Braswell's place. Be an officer."

"*Lieuten*—." I just wave my hand. It's no use.

Well. Decisions need to be made. Someone must lead.

I narrow my eyes and peer at the sun dropping into the western horizon. Jackson must be set loose. He'll be useless here.

A pang of guilt makes me stare at my feet. That judgment is undeserved.

I've been frustrated by those who don't fit the tight molds I've made for them. I've judged the automatons that meet my every expectation as the most valuable.

There's a place for uniformity. But those who don't fit that mold have valuable contributions to make if I allow them.

"If they surprise us, they'll kill us." Glancing at Destiny and my brother I see instant agreement on their faces. Before I can say another word, Jackson disappears into the thickets and small trees that border the meadow.

I pace back to the middle of the clearing, searching both edges.

There's no place for Destiny. Nothing like the loft in the barn that served her so well.

"I don't know where to put you." I twist in all directions looking for an idea.

"How about I be your bodyguard?"

Her comment brings a quick laugh from me. I gaze at her, still smiling. She stands casually leaning on her gun. A smile lifts one corner of her mouth. Her eyes are so soft.

I don't deserve it.

The sun now flirts with the tops of the trees, its light becoming weak and diffused. The blue of the sky has darkened. Just like Destiny's eyes.

"Okay," I say. "Stay with me until we find a better place."

Shadows lengthen and I call to the company's members. With little instruction, men jostle into a formation. The line stretches across the entire width of the glade.

Stars brighten as though lit by someone with a great match. The blue darkens to indigo. Black curtains close, hiding any movement my enemy might make.

I stare through the darkness seeing nothing. I glance behind me.

No Lieutenant Braswell.

Something rattles.

I think so anyway. I'm sure I heard something, something mechanical, man-made. I trot several paces out in front of the men.

The scene doesn't change. Just blackness.

A hundred feet in front of the company's position. I listen.

Only silence.

Returning, I take my place along the left end of the line where Destiny waits patiently.

"The waiting is the hardest part," she says.

I loathe the waiting, but I'm terrified of the professional killing machine that may be about to roll over us.

Imagine a perfectly disciplined regiment of British infantry marching down the length of this meadow. It would be a massacre.

Taking several steps forward, I stare hard at the distant end of the line of men. We still reach over the entire field, right?

Maybe I should send more scouts.

Sending more scouts will weaken the line. Mentally I measure. The line. The distances. The effect of five fewer muskets.

If they don't get back…

I find Alvin and clutch his arm.

"Take four men. Go through the thickets. Find the enemy."

Alvin takes a step. I hold him for one last instruction.

"Just get back before they find us."

Alvin nods. He runs, calling hoarsely to several militia soldiers.

"It's alright, Jake. Just do what you feel is best. No one can ask more of you." Destiny touches my arm.

Really? Those who may fall in a coming battle can't ask for a better commander? One with more experience? A more senior officer?

"This isn't the barn, Destiny. I just— I just don't feel good about this."

Every few minutes I search behind us. No Braswell.

Back to our front an apparition emerges from the darkness. Jackson.

British soldiers are coming.

I press my brother for more information. No, Jackson hasn't seen them. No, he doesn't know how many. But it's a lot.

The old flintlock pistol is stuck it in my waistband. I adjust the angle of the barrel.

One more thing. There were horses.

Officer's horses?

No. More than that. Many horses.

I step back and let my gaze flow across the clearing at the men I've trained.

Horses.

Horses mean cavalry. Or cannon.

It could mean both.

Maybe we should retreat to the village. We could hide in the buildings there.

But those aren't my orders. Or Braswell's orders.

We are to hold the meadow. Keep the British away from Roxbury.

"Get back to Roxbury," I command my brother. "Tell Captain Rawlins Lieutenant Braswell's not here. Tell him the English have cavalry. Or heavy guns."

Jackson spins in the direction of the town.

"Wait! Take Destiny with you."

Destiny's head swivels away from Jackson to stare at me.

"I'm not going."

"It's an order. You have to go."

"I'm staying."

"Please Destiny." I've already envisioned what might lie ahead. Untold numbers of British professionals marching for us at this instant, heavy cannon…

The militia cannot possibly match the oncoming force.

Destiny shakes her head.

Helplessly I peer at Jackson, but Jackson knows her too. She's his friend.

He turns and runs. Within seconds the darkness swallows him completely.

# Chapter 60

Unable to keep still, I pace across the field to the far end of the company. Then I turn and make my way back to the starting point.

Destiny has given up trying to keep up with me. She looks at me sympathetically every time I come near enough to see her face.

My hands. I put them behind my back, at my sides, behind my back again. My breath rattles when I inhale.

It's impossible for the men not to see my nervousness. They will just have to watch me slowly twist inside out.

"It's alright, Mistah Jake," Lucas says as I pass by his position. "We be fine."

I lean close to him to prevent any eavesdropping. "Will we? After this is over, will everyone still be standing?"

"We'll win. Mebbe not with everyone standing. Won't be yo' fault."

"Yes, it will. Unless someone else wants to take command…"

I dreamed of this once. Being an officer. Leading troops like the great Duke of Marlborough at Blenheim.

I don't want to be an officer anymore. I don't want to command.

The medal is in my pocket. I massage it with my fingers. How had my father saved his men? In the midst of battle?

A pale moon appears low in the sky. It spreads a watery glow across the field.

Like ghosts, Alvin and his scouts return. I stop pacing and listen for the enemy's approach. It seems such a foreign, hollow sound. Disembodied. From another world.

Marching feet. I'm sure of it.

Again, I repeat the same warnings I've spoken a dozen times. Running down the front of the line, I tell the soldiers. Fire only upon orders. No independent fire.

I re-arrange the company into a double line.

We may take casualties. I examine the result. Is it better?

If we take casualties, we still need a solid line. No major holes in it. A double line. A double line is what we need.

I stare at the far end of the meadow then return my gaze to the company formation.

If Braswell shows up now, he can still take command. He's not here.

A distant snort. Horses.

I dash down the line again.

I'd placed the returned scouts into the company formation. Now I drag a couple out of the line.

Off they run, back into the overgrown areas to either side. Warn me! Warn me if the British try to flank.

No Jackson.

I shoulder my way through the line of soldiers and stare towards Roxbury.

No one. No reinforcements. No sounds of approaching militia.

We're alone.

Cavalry. How can we face that?

If there's cavalry it will be a small force. It will have to attack the center.

How should we defend against that?

In Europe they would form a square. Tightly compressed men, shoulder to shoulder, with bayonets pointed outward.

The militia carries hunting muskets. We have no bayonets. I've never even rehearsed the moves to make a square formation.

A square is suicide against infantry anyway. The British have lots of infantry. I can hear them.

A well-timed volley might suffice against a small cavalry force.

Cannons.

What if the horses I hear are dragging cannons?

Again, I run down the line, this time in its rear. I grab Alvin by his sleeve and pull him to the far end.

Cannon might appear on this side of our position. Take two men. Find a firing position. Shoot at the gunners manning the field guns.

Alvin nods and with an urgency nearly matching my own, grabs two companions and ducks into the cover on our right. I sprint back to where Destiny waits.

"Let me go now, Jake. I can pick off gunners before they even load their cannons."

I shake my head no.

She repeats the idea. There's an abundance of cover. Even if the enemy comes after her, they could never find her. Surely, I know her well enough to know that's true, she pleads.

No.

Not a good reason Destiny retorts.

I stretch to grab her sleeve. Just out of reach, she slips off into the night before I can catch her.

Damn! I'm glad Mother's not able to hear that.

In one last futile attempt I call in a hoarse whisper, first with an order, then a plea.

Destiny ducks around a clump of greenery, under a cluster of saplings, and… I can't see her. She's gone.

I turn my attention back on our deteriorating position, searching the darkness.

Black apparitions in the underwater glow dance about the field to our front. Skirmishers.

A musket shot. Then another.

Too far away for accuracy. They melt back.

I strain, leaning forward to see through the murky combination of shadow and a fragile moonlit glow. Nothing.

So, now the British know our position. They'll form up for an attack.

Everything seems immobilized. The men stand straight, muskets held with both hands. They wait for me. All has frozen. Time ceases to move. The moon keeps its position in the sky.

Only my own breathing disturbs the tranquil night.

Did they retreat? Decided not to move on Roxbury if they were opposed?

Perhaps they won't proceed unless they gain complete surprise over the patriots.

I take several steps forward, bending at the waist, peering hard into the darkness.

Then the horse snorts. The rattle of wheels rolling across the ground echoes.

Horses trotting, muffled cries issuing orders to man and beast alike.

I almost stumble as all seems to lurch into movement again.

The moon rises. As though it sights me and my predicament, it throws a brighter light across my enemies.

A small battery of field guns splits up. They labor to deploy cannon at each edge of the clearing.

Metal scrapes upon metal as fasteners are loosed. Horses and limbers are unhitched. Ammunition carts are drawn into position.

Voices become louder. A row of infantry appears between the gun positions.

I turn to check my soldiers. I visualize the field in front of me. The length of it, the spot where I'll shout the first order to fire. The enemy infantry and field guns.

My heart sinks as a cluster of horsemen line up behind the infantry.

Infantry, cavalry, artillery. I'm no longer filled with doubt.

I know.

We can never stand.

# Chapter 61

A tapestry weaves itself before my eyes. Misty shades of gray and black drift over the ground before me. Miniature figures of animal and man scuttle about, ghost-like forms in the gloomy distance.

Orange flame spits from the inky darkness.

I stumble back but manage to stay on my feet.

The sky shrieks as the six-pound iron ball punctures the silence, slashing through the air overhead.

I try to follow it with my eyes as though I could possibly see it.

Behind our position, mountains of dirt spew from the ground. Jerking my gaze to the point of impact, I stare at the spectacle.

Grass, bushes, and even a couple of saplings tumble into the air then drop to earth in a heap. I've never seen a cannon fire before.

I pull myself together. The cannon, firing from the right side of the battlefield, aimed too high. I take a breath.

Destiny's rifle barks. It's her. I know it. I've come to recognize that sound.

A shout. Then the same eruption of belching orange and yellow flame. The same *whoosh* arcing overhead.

Into the pale light, far into the positions occupied by our enemy, I stare. Gunners on both British flanks must be re-setting their sights. They can't miss a second time.

Why don't I have an answer for this? The destructive power of the cannons is frightening.

What can I do? Break into skirmish order?

A cavalry charge would cut us to pieces as though we had no defense at all.

Break up and use the thickets for cover?

Enemy skirmishers will engage us as the main body of the British army marches right into Roxbury, unimpeded.

Lay down?

At first, I snort in disgust. No book I've ever read describes an army formation laying on the ground.

My hand though, finds the medal in my pocket. What did my father do to save his men?

I never asked him.

Maybe…

I glance at the line of militia, then back at the attacking enemy.

The crack of Destiny's rifle cuts through the web of sounds beginning to surround me. A yell erupts from the position of the second cannon.

Two yells. A wounded man wails, and another seems to call for some kind of protection.

The second attempt from the first cannon finds the range. The streaking iron ball pulverizes its target.

It rips a man's leg from him with an explosion of blood and shredded human flesh. The burning projectile repeats the performance with the man just behind.

My double line means that every hit from the artillery pieces will take out at least two soldiers.

My skin erupts in goose flesh. The wild screaming of the wounded freezes me. Never has anything like this happened before. My feet are immovable, glued to the ground.

I'm in charge. I have to do something.

I clasp my father's medal and shove it into my pocket.

Down the line I run.

"Lie down! Lie down! Lie down!"

A jumble of militia hovers over the writhing and gasping wounded. I grab someone's arm.

"Take them!" I extend my arm pointing aimlessly toward the rear. "Take them!"

Straining to find a voice, I command the others to return to their places.

The blood. The stench of burning human flesh. My stomach pushes its way into my throat.

Crimson blood gushes from the torn and mutilated bodies where the legs once connected. As from a spring torrent, the spot where the men stood turns red and sticky.

Those I ordered back into ranks lie on its edges, eyeing it with furtive glances.

The lost limbs will kill the wounded men. I know that. The appearance of doing something is important. Anything to isolate the wounded will steady the remaining soldiers and keep them in place.

I cough, hand over my mouth, willing the contents of my gut to stay down.

Clutching my middle, I run back to my original position. Destiny's rifle fires again at the distant enemy position. Her target lets out a screaming reply. Their cannon fires again but is wildly off the mark.

The big guns continue to blast away. They have trouble finding targets.

Screaming cannonballs skim over the heads of the militia.

Like rodents, the men seem to burrow into the earth. They turn their heads sideways, peering upwards, as though to be sure death passes them by.

Destiny continues to wreak havoc upon the left side, leaving the first cannon as the only effective enemy gun.

Listen, watch. I try to judge the adjustments being made by the enemy.

The trajectory drops.

A huge iron bullet ploughs into the earth straight out in front of me. Dirt and uprooted grasses spew high into the air.

The cannonball tunnels several yards, gouging the meadow unmercifully. It bounces back into the air and sails overhead.

That was close. I let loose the breath I was holding.

The men press their faces into the ground and peer sideways at me.

A search of the blackness towards Roxbury finds nothing. If Braswell would just get here.

The opposite end of the field erupts in a flurry of activity.

Dark shadows singly race toward the beleaguered battery. Shadows of muskets jut into the air as though the tiny stick figures carry toothpicks.

They're going after Destiny.

A surreal quiet looms over the land between cannon shots. A quiet that amplifies and quickens sounds from both ends.

Voices call commands. Metal snaps onto metal and I can see the enemy muskets grow in length.

They've fixed bayonets.

Echoes spring from a drum beating a rhythm. The entire enemy line lurches forward.

They angle to their right, covering the ineffective cannon. The movement allows the first big gun to continue to fire.

The cavalry troopers march forward, nimbly directing their horses to march behind the line of infantry.

The remaining cannon releases another payload of death. The belching flame lights up the dark silhouettes advancing to kill me and my friends.

The projectile finds the range and smashes into its target. The six-pound rocket left little more than mangled remains of what was once a human body.

Mercifully, there were no screams of pain. Those on either side look with terror at the mutilated remains beside them.

I glance toward Destiny's position. Her rifle is silent. Her location now infested with enemies searching to kill her.

A spate of musket fire breaks out near the cannon that has proved so accurate. The big gun belches another stream of fire and smoke.

The drum continues beating its cadence. A pair of fifes add a martial tune to the stamping feet.

The marching line nears, as does the little square of cavalry behind it.

Both cannons are blocked now. They can't fire without hitting their own men.

I sprint down the line.

"Up! Get up! Up!"

Men scramble to their feet.

"Hold fire! Hold fire! Hold fire!" I yell on my return trip.

Listen for my commands I tell them.

I count each step of the enemy, measuring the distance as I watch.

Anytime now.

Surely, they'll stop and fire before charging.

Our most effective volley will be the first.

They'll halt to fire and I will bring the muskets of the entire unit to bear. That blast will tear into them before they can do the same to us.

I stare at them as I roll over in my mind what we need to do.

I feel… odd. I lift an arm in front of my face.

I'm trembling.

Gripping both hands together, I wait to give the order to my company.

The effectiveness of that one moment means survival or defeat.

The milky light of the moon freezes everything in a black and white world.

Until now.

Pastel shades appear, then darken. The blood red uniforms massed in front of us grow and enlarge. The stick figures become giants.

I alternate glances between the militia and the enemy.

They aren't going to stop.

The once predictable professionals are going to come straight in to the charge.

My head swivels. What should I do?

Once the enemy breaks into a run they'll come too fast.

I open my mouth to give the order. Before I can speak, a lone voice rolls across the meadow, ordering its men to halt.

That's the signal.

I scream at my men, voice cracking as I search for all the volume I can muster.

Present!

Fire!

Both ranks, front kneeling, rear standing, spew a curtain of flame.

Acrid, sulfuric smoke fills the air. My ears ring from the explosion.

We did it. The men obeyed my order. They stood and fired a devastating volley.

Haltingly, I begin the command sequence to reload.

A mass of lead bullets is about to come screaming through the billowing cloud, smashing into us.

The smoke. It's too thick to see through in the weak light.

I harden the muscles in my throat. I forcefully tame the tremor I can feel there. I can almost see clouds of bullets obliterating my face.

From the other side of the smoke curtain, the explosion sounds. Eyes riveted, mouth open, I stare, hoping for the impossible.

The men look to me for guidance. My friends. My fellow soldiers.

Bodies fold up and drop from the positions where I placed them.

I can't think about that.

I have to get off another volley.

The British infantry will be upon us.

My voice raises an octave. It cracks.

Return your rammers!

Horses.

I stare into the fog of burnt gunpowder. I can hear the thundering.

The infantry isn't charging. The cavalry is.

Faint apparitions turn physical as they leap from the ghostly veil of smoke.

Enemy horsemen crash into the company.

The vapor weaves another tapestry. It covers part of the scene here, then opens to reveal it and cover another portion there.

Sporadic bursts of muskets flash bright through the haze.

Men still try to get their guns into a firing position. They're bowled over and thrown to the ground.

Glinting cavalry sabers hurtle through the darkness, cutting, slashing.

The man nearest me catches a cavalry trooper's stroke. It severs his arm and sends blood splashing through the air.

The line disintegrates. It's like a sand wall that dries and the grains just blow away until there's nothing.

Men race for Roxbury, but the horses run them down and slaughter them.

Others dive into the cover of the thickets and trees and marshes.

No one is left.

Only me.

The horsemen passed me.

I hear the drum beating, the fifes piping. The infantry marches, closing on me.

I take one more look across the meadow where my men stood.

Nothing but broken bodies and pools of red.

Thickets spring from the earth in the direction Destiny ran. I melt into them.

I have to find her.

# Chapter 62

I've sat here listening to silence for how long? At least an hour, probably more.

I move my limbs with an exaggerated slowness. On my feet. In a low crouch.

A slow deliberate rise and I can just see over the top leaves and stems of the thicket that hides me.

The sun, barely up, throws a dirty gray light across all I can see. Billowing leaden clouds mute the colors of the landscape even more.

All night I've hidden here in this little copse, a thicket with a couple of saplings springing from within. Numb. Cold.

Shuffling my feet, I scrutinize my surroundings.

British light infantry scoured this place last night. At the sight of one searching enemy, I leaped into cover. Every time I considered getting out, some disembodied sound in the blackness froze me in place.

There's complete silence out there now.

Thick branches claw at me as I extricate myself from the thicket. Searching all compass points, I try and get my bearings.

This isn't far from where Destiny wreaked such havoc as a sniper against the cannon.

I turn a full circle looking for the slightest movement, anything that appears out of place. There's no sign of her.

A few tentative steps transport me across an open space and to the edge of another tangled mass of bushes.

The enemy marched back through the meadow well over an hour ago. Surely, they're back in Boston by now.

I take a few more steps. My feet sink into the marshy ground.

No movement. No sign of any living thing, man or animal.

If Destiny escaped, she will have gone inland. I skirt several thickets, searching for drier ground.

Bunches of tall grass huddle under a stiffening breeze. I thread my way cautiously, keeping a sharp eye.

Red.

I drop to a low crouch.

I saw red. Just over the bunches of sea grass. But it was low.

I dissect what I saw trying to use logic, not emotion. It was low, on the ground. There's no sound. There was no movement.

I pull my pistol from my waistband and raise myself slowly until I catch another glimpse of the color of the enemy.

Part of a red coat. Unmoving. Not an empty coat though.

I stand taller.

It's a soldier alright. Obviously dead, his body lies motionless at the edge of sea water creeping in from the harbor. The limbs lay distorted, flung into an awkward pose by a sudden death.

The ashen face, a grotesque expression of surprise still frozen in place, stares at me. Part of me wants to turn away, the other part is mesmerized at the scene.

It's an officer. A young ensign. The blondish hair has a marked reddish tinge to it. Still in place, it's pulled neatly into a tight queue at the back of the neck. A strand of the black ribbon that ties it floats in the water.

The eyes, still open, are gray. Just like mine. Or Jackson's.

The face is half submerged. The red coat soaks up the gray water. The tide is in.

The uniform is neat and fitted. The officer's sword has fallen from his hand and rests mere inches from the outstretched fingers.

That's me. That's what I've wanted to be for so long. An officer. An officer in a well-trained, professional military.

The eyes keep staring at me.

I tear my gaze from the corpse and search around me. Who killed him?

A British 'Brown Bess' musket lies on the ground a few yards away. I approach it, scrutinizing the ground for another body.

Nothing.

I pick up the British gun. There's no bayonet. No cartridge pouch to carry needed ammunition. Certainly, it hadn't belonged to the ensign.

I retrace my steps and look at the body again. It stares back at me, lifeless, one of the gray eyes underwater.

Suddenly I'm overcome with an urgent need to find those I care about.

"Destiny!"

Nothing.

"Destiny!"

No answer.

I run a few steps. How can I know which way?

I call again. No answer.

The ashen face of the dead redcoat slides into my thoughts.

Is that how I will find her? Unseeing eyes staring at me? Face drained of color?

I run several more yards, then stop and wildly throw my gaze from one direction to another.

"Destiny!"

This is no good. I have to keep calm and search in a logical manner. Wrestling my emotions under control, I move fifty feet or so south then methodically trace a new path back.

If she's much farther away than here, she must have escaped.

"Destiny!" I scream with all the volume I can muster.

Almost a hundred yards away, a solitary figure rises from the ground and waves.

Destiny.

She starts to run. I push into the sodden earth and sprint for her.

Casting the musket aside I slow just enough that the collision as she leaps into my arms doesn't send me sprawling to the ground.

She sobs into my chest.

"Are you okay? Are you hurt?" I hold her shoulders, pull her away, and stare into her face.

She shakes her head. "Lost my nerve, I think." She takes a stuttering breath. "They've been all around looking for me."

Her body trembles. I pull her close, stroke her hair and whisper to her.

We've found each other now. We'll be fine.

Destiny relates how she had hidden but couldn't defend herself. Too many enemy soldiers searched the area, thrusting their bayonets into the best hiding places.

Had she killed the British ensign whose body I found?

No. She hadn't dared make a sound.

"You haven't seen Jackson?"

Destiny shakes her head. "We have to find him."

# Chapter 63

Despite the relief at finding each other safe, Destiny and I say little as we trek towards Roxbury. The closer we get, the heavier my feet feel until at the sight of the village's first buildings, I stop.

"What's wrong?" Destiny asks.

I flash her a quick but disingenuous smile and lay a hand on her shoulder. It makes her think I'm considering an answer, so she gives me a moment of silence.

I can't go there. It's like a sorcerer's spell. Something invisible that blocks me from going further.

Repelled might be the word. I'm repelled by Roxbury. Repelled by the survivors of last night's massacre. Repelled by the recriminating looks of those that somehow managed to survive.

Look at me. Alive. Uninjured. Perfectly healthy as far as anyone can see.

In a way, I wish I were one of the casualties.

Destiny jumps and waves.

The road is two tracks of moist earth with weeds and grasses growing shorter in the middle, taller on the sides. Standing in the middle, hardly near enough to recognize, a figure waves in return. Jackson runs to us.

My brother throws his arms around Destiny. He greets her almost as tenderly as I did out in the salt marsh.

He turns to me and hesitates, then hugs me as well.

"I knew you two would make it." Jackson's eyes glisten as he looks away.

Imitating my brother, I search the ground. Destiny's hand presses on my arm. I look up to see her with a little smile that gently mocks the inability of two brothers to freely express emotion to one another.

Jackson and I stutter a few words. I can't wait though. I press him for news.

Twelve of our company are known to be dead. It's possible the number could grow as a couple are still missing.

It's a staggering revelation and I almost reel backwards at the news. What about…

All ten of our original section are accounted for. I bow my head in a silent prayer for that.

Some have been wounded.

Lucas was stepped on by a horse. It probably saved him though, as flat on the ground, he was out of reach of the rider's saber.

Alvin grazed by a musket ball, but by now, bandaged and released.

"No one really thinks it's your fault." Jackson startles me, as though he could read my mind.

I appreciate his words, but … I feel so down, so responsible, so… at fault.

"Let's go get some food," Jackson suggests. He's still watching me.

"I don't know. I —. Not yet."

"Come with us," Destiny implores. "Get something to eat. See the men."

Emotionally I dig in my heels and shake my head. "Not now."

Destiny and Jackson glance at each other as though I can't see them. Like I'm in need of some kind of special care or something.

"Wait for us here then. We'll bring you something." Destiny has hold of my arm again. She presses till it almost hurts. She stares deep into my eyes not letting go until I promise.

Okay. I can wait.

She glances back to wave as she and Jackson disappear around a nearby farmhouse.

I need a place to sit. Against a fence or tree. To my left a group of three chestnut trees grow between the road and the farmhouse Destiny and Jackson passed as they left.

Perfect. I can sit on the far side, out of sight to anyone passing by on the road. Before I can reach the trees, some movement catches my eye.

Part of me doesn't want to see more, but I'm drawn, like a magnet. Like the sorcerer's spell that blocked me from Roxbury pulls me uncontrollably to a place I can hardly look at.

The surgeon's hut. The place where wounded limbs are sawn off.

It's a house of course. Jackson and Destiny passed it, but the angle was wrong. I don't think they saw it.

There's no sign or mark to distinguish the cottage, but there's no mistaking it.

I drift closer.

Around the corner I can see the back side of the small house. One long row of blanket-covered mounds. The line is very straight. Someone got the military precision right for the dead.

The corner of the nearest blanket flutters in the breeze as though it might flip over, revealing the fallen soldier underneath, giving me a glimpse of one of my casualties.

It wavers, but it doesn't lift.

Who's under that blanket? I shrink from the revelation, afraid to know. Afraid to look upon the face that will be white, not breathing, bereft of life.

With a quick turn, I stride up the road toward Cambridge. Before I can duck out of view, a small group of militia surprises me, trudging the opposite direction.

Do they know?

They say nothing. My furtive glances at their faces reveal no accusing stares.

Do they know who I am?

The walk from Roxbury isn't far, a few miles. Along the way nothing but isolated militia camps.

But it feels long. And lonely.

What have I done?

Books with diagrams, circles and arrows identifying procedures and military theory. That's ink on paper.

The men in last night's battle. Those were real people, not diagrams in a book.

It was so chaotic. I didn't have time to think or even see the faces of my fellow soldiers. It was all a blur.

Today, in memory, the images sharpen.

The baker. James. Was that his name?

Jackson identified him as one of the dead. Not that long ago he brought real baked bread to our section. Right after the skirmish at the barn.

No one in our section knows how to bake over a fire. We dump balls of dough into an open pan to cook.

James brought the real thing. Fluffy bread. Loaves that had risen and baked golden in a Dutch oven.

He sat with us. Cut the bread and passed it out. Talked about home.

He has children. Had children. A son. A son who almost came with him.

His boy was bitter about being ordered to stay home. James promised him in a year they could reconsider, if the war lasted that long.

All would be forgiven James said. All would be forgiven when he returned home again. His son would understand and welcome his father.

Last night changed everything. It was all smoke, fire, blood. Screams.

So, now, how does a person say I did my best, a son's father died, but I don't know why?

Something is missing.

As though I were still a boy, I gathered my friends to play army. Unlike childhood games though, the results lay still and unmoving under blankets behind the surgeon's hut.

I know it. Everybody knows it.

# Chapter 64

I need space. I need air. I need solitude.

A chance to think. A chance to sort through what things really mean. A chance to be protected from the gaze of those who must look at me and see a butcher.

As I make my way to the woods, I pull the medallion from my pocket.

Father was a sergeant. Just like me. In a hopeless situation, he rescued his men from death. Those men recognized that.

They were so grateful they spent good money, something they would have little of, to have a small memorial especially made for him.

Only now do I really comprehend the heroism in it.

I don't think anyone's going to do that for me.

To win a battle would be a momentous event. To save unnecessary sacrifice in the face of sure defeat is better.

I ascend a long sloping hill that leads over two hilltops to a small brook that falls between large and mossy boulders.

Right face, left face, present, volley fire. In real battle, when people's lives were on the line, it didn't work. Why is that?

Over another rise and the brook bubbles away in the fold between the two hills. Chilled, spring water pours through the crevices between the boulders jumbled in the narrow ravine.

Climbing down next to it, I sit on the edge and watch the little currents swirl around the stones blocking the way. As I reflect, my mind makes a few connections I haven't really thought about before.

Destiny has taken Amelia's place. I no longer need to gain social position. Destiny will take me as I am. I can have Destiny's love by just being myself.

Despite the season, a handful of leaves from a large oak tree upstream cart-wheeled to the water's surface and float jauntily on the currents. They dance and careen down the falling brook, making crazy changes in direction as the water eddies around the rocks.

A life with Destiny could- would be a pleasant life. I've scarcely let myself imagine what that might be like.

Would anyone share life's burdens with me more than she? I can picture her, at my side in every trial, helping, supporting.

Lying down at night, bone-tired from work, her compact body lying next to me. Head against my shoulder. Arm draped across my chest. Warm and breathing deep.

In the morning we wake in the same position. She smiles. Destiny always smiles.

A squirrel scrambles part way up a tree trunk, and then clings there, peering at me. The black glass eyes shine in the low light.

It shifts position and stares the other direction then scrambles once again to look at me. It twitches its tail and scampers up the tree to safety.

Staring past the tree as the squirrel disappears, movement catches my eye. Over the top of the hill, searching the lower slopes, slinks a red-coated soldier gripping a musket.

# Chapter 65

"Tell Jake, c'mon back. C'mon back home." Lucas' deep baritone voice is soothing. If he weren't limping so bad, Destiny would ask him to come with her. Convince Jake not to take the defeat so personally.

Abandoning Jackson, Lucas and the rest of the men, Destiny returns to where she left Jake.

He's not here. She searches several steps from the road. Calls his name softly.

She starts for a group of three chestnut trees between the road and the little farmhouse over—.

A man steps out. He limps, half his leg wrapped in bandages. The man hobbles toward Roxbury. A closer look and Destiny sees a straight line of blanket-covered mounds.

The dead from last night.

She stares.

All men she served with. All real people that had breathed, talked, slept, eaten… only yesterday. They had families, friends, loved ones. People that will mourn their loss. How steep a price has been paid.

If Jake saw that, and surely, he did…

Destiny moves in a slow circle, studying the ground. The moist earth reveals tracks easily. At the same time, the road is a busy thoroughfare.

But there. Those are Jake's prints, she knows it.

Destiny follows. Away from Roxbury. Sporadically, she finds a few tracks here, a few there. He's going all the way back to camp.

But he's not in camp. There. The tracks angle off into the woods. Destiny draws a mental map. Where would he go? Maybe the brook?

After topping a couple of swells in the ground, she's sure. She leaves the track and angles to find the little creek. Once there she'll simply head upstream until she finds him.

The brook tumbles peaceful and calming. Destiny begins the slow climb upstream. She's tired. Yesterday. Last night. No need to search out individual footprints. Surely. Just head upstream and —.

She freezes mid-step, realizing how careless she's been. Tired and sure of her destination she just…

From here the enemy soldier appears as a tiny figure. He picks his way down the slope, only a short distance from the crest of the hill behind him.

From his gait she can tell he's no woodsman. And he hasn't seen her.

Destiny crouches into her stalking stance. She selects a path and utilizes every obstruction as cover.

One man. One enemy. He has no chance against her here. The woods are hers.

As silently as the permanent residents, Destiny proceeds up the stream. Jake is still ahead of her, she's sure. Has he seen the intruder?

Several minutes and Destiny closes the gap on the British soldier by at least a hundred feet.

He's still a good hundred yards away. The slope is gentler now and he keeps his gaze to his front.

Negotiating the slope in angles his descent isn't rapid. Still, he keeps his head up. He turns as he searches the wooded incline, his musket gripped firmly in both hands.

Destiny's vision sweeps right to left, near to far.

There's Jake.

Lying on the ground, his face is plastered against the trunk of a large oak tree. So, he knows danger is out there.

Destiny lowers herself into the small ravine cut by the water, low enough that she can't be seen. Pebbles have washed into a slack water area as the current swirls around a boulder. She reaches into the cold water and grasps several.

Picking a small brown stone, she flings it toward the oak. It arcs through the air and lands on Jake's back.

In an overreaction Destiny should have anticipated, Jake springs from his position in a burst of rustling of leaves. He stares at her.

Destiny throws a finger to her lips to silence him. He rolls back behind the tree and stares at its base.

The redcoat continues searching for patriots to shoot.

With painstaking slowness, Jake shifts. Watching Destiny, the two communicate with hand signals. He's getting almost as good with the non-verbal communication as Jackson.

Jake slithers straight back from the tree.

Keeping the trunk between him and the enemy soldier, progress is painstakingly slow. Finally, he extends a foot over the embankment.

Destiny grabs him and he slides over the edge to hide in the streambed. She smiles and mouths a greeting to him without sound. As she does, another British soldier creeps silently over the top of the hill.

# Chapter 66

Catching my breath, I crouch low in the streambed, hovering over stones and swirling water. Looking up at Destiny, I stare silently at her hoping she'll know what to do.

How hard would it be to slither our way downstream to safety? Destiny seems to be reading my mind and shakes her head no.

Another look. We'd never make it without being seen. The gully that direction becomes ever shallower as the land flattens.

Up on the slope of the hill, the two British soldiers still creep toward us. They can't be more than a hundred yards off. Way too close for comfort.

Lowering my gaze, I search the brook dancing down the slope, sluicing through the dark boulders. At the outside edge of a bend in the creek, a shallow cut has been created under the bank.

I point. Destiny follows my gaze and nods.

Hands and feet both clutching at river stones, she crawls like a turtle upstream and stops at the scooped-out bank.

Someone whistles. Destiny stares at me, a terrified look on her face. Frozen in place, we wait.

Nothing else.

No words. No sound of feet rushing towards us. No orders being shouted.

Just the whistle.

Destiny tilts her head, listening. We squat over the boulders of the stream as still as the rocks.

Nothing.

Watching my feet and placing them with the greatest care, I push forward the last couple of steps. My shoulders barely squeeze into the hollow space. I shove back until I'm tightly wedged under the low overhang.

Destiny drops to her side. She pushes her way in until she has nestled into me.

The silence grows long and drawn out. I don't know whether the enemy soldiers are searching the streambed or not. It's impossible to keep my nerves at a fever-pitch intensity indefinitely.

I let my muscles relax. I smell Destiny's hair.

I loved Amelia. So much, I did. I'm not sure I want to let that go entirely. Especially after what she went through. Especially with Helmsley still out there getting promotions instead of hanging.

But Destiny. This is the girl I know. The one who accompanies me everywhere. Everywhere I let her.

She supports me, encourages me. Saved my life when I was knifed by the Maryland woodsman. Shot one attacker so I didn't have to try and fight both.

The girl marksman.

As though she reads my thoughts, she stretches a hand back, barely reaching my shoulder. I pull a little tighter.

Silence.

We must remain silent.

#

I wake with a start.

I hear… water. It's black as pitch.

Destiny still lies on her side in front of me. Her breathing is long and slow.

The scrap of sky I can see is black. White pinpricks cluster so tightly together it almost seems like a blur of starlight splashed across the heavens.

I tug lightly on Destiny's shoulder and she stirs.

"I fell asleep," she mutters with an air of amazement.

"Both of us," I say. "Last night was long. Today wasn't much better."

Destiny unfolds herself from the small enclosure. She stands motionless in the streambed, staring in all directions, still in a half-crouched stance.

I tap her on her shin, trying to gain enough space to crawl out myself.

We both survey the emptiness. Destiny shrugs.

Well. If Destiny can't see anything threatening, I'm pretty sure we're safe.

For an hour, we creep down the creek-bed, keeping low and out of sight. My back aches. Leg muscles protest the awkward gait.

Surely, we're safe now. I straighten. Destiny also as I search our surroundings.

Facing the direction of camp, we leave the streambed and trek for home. If we had any food, I could be tempted to stay longer. It's been nice having her company, and no one else's.

"Do you think losing the battle was your fault?" Destiny asks.

I'm uncomfortable with the topic. It wasn't even a battle. Not even a retreat. It was a rout. A slaughter. Worse than Braddock's, the one my father experienced.

"Who else?" I finally say, still searching for words.

"Does it have to be someone's fault?"

That's a rhetorical question, but I answer anyway.

"Usually." I shrug to add a bit of ambiguity to my answer. When things collapse as completely as they did at Roxbury, someone has overlooked something.

"Jake. No one blames you."

I consider that as we cross a fallen tree trunk and continue.

"I talked to them. Alvin. Lucas. They all say there was nothing more you could have done."

"All of them?" I ask, wanting to believe it, but not sure I should.

"Even the ones that grumble. Like Caleb. Alvin asked him what he would have done different."

I look at her anxious to hear what answer my greatest critic might have shared.

"Nothing. That shut him up."

Destiny grabs my arm. I reflect back on Amelia, how married I was to my plans to lift myself into a higher societal class.

The position of Amelia's family would have made that possible. Deep down, I always knew that.

What Destiny wants is for that world to be gone. In the world Destiny envisions, I alone hold the key to my future. I don't have to break into a tight-knit social club in order to have opportunities.

I take another look at my partner as we near the edge of the woods. I can already catch the glimmer of campfires that must belong to the militia.

I recognize Destiny more now than I ever have.

She's Amelia. Amelia in a new world.

"It's still hard," I say referring back to her question. "I don't think I can do it without you."

"You don't have to."

# Chapter 67

"Ain't nothin' happened your fault." Alvin walks slow, the loose ends of a bandage trailing from his head and onto his shoulders. I bet he still has a bear of a headache.

I accept his assurance with a nod.

There's a bend in the road and we lose sight of the bay. We're all on the march. All of us. Brasswell has been sacked, or at least that's the word. Mercifully, I'm back in the small ten-man section, not trying to prove something with the whole company.

Jackson comes dashing back from the head of the column as militia units string out ever further along the road.

"We're headin' for Charlestown," he blurts as he passes us. He's been somewhere up front. Having gathered the hearsay, he now dashes towards the rear, looking to see if the stories match.

Destiny shrugs when I look at her. I was hoping she might have some intuition about Jackson's chances of being right.

Charlestown.

Charlestown clings to the end of a little peninsula extending towards Boston from the north. The expanse of water between the village and Boston is tiny. You could row across it in no time.

"Almost like a challenge if the boy's right," Lucas says, limping along behind me.

It does. Hard to see how occupying Charlestown will push the British out of -.

"He's right!" Why didn't I think of this before? Everyone looks at me, trying to decipher my outburst.

"A few big guns on one of those hills north of Charlestown will control much of the harbor. British ships will be sitting ducks."

Faces illuminate as the realization sinks in. That has to be it. We'll free the harbor of the British Navy. That will make it impossible for the British Army to stay in Boston. It makes perfect sense.

Dusk becomes dark and as the road turns south, we all know. It's Charlestown. Or the scrap of land the village sits on anyway.

The air turns moist as we trudge over Bunker Hill and on to the south slope of Breed's Hill. A halt is called and I stare, almost gaping, in every direction.

Hundreds of militia swarm about the top of the low mount, digging and dragging timbers into place.

"What are they doing?" Destiny asks.

"Pretty sure they're building a redoubt on the crest there." Destiny looks at me with this questioning look. "It's like a small fort."

In an eerie scene, I can see Boston to the south. Lamps in windows and fires in army bivouacs shimmer across the surface of the narrow span of water.

Just to the left is the harbor. Shadowy silhouettes of British warships rock sleepily at anchor, almost invisible. Frigates, sloops, and other ships of war hide in the darkness, immense, pent-up fire power on their gun decks. We are well within their range.

"They don't know we're here, do they?" Destiny watches the shadowy enemy. I sense how new this is to her. Her marksmanship is useless against the mighty warships.

"What's going to happen, Jake?"

"I don't know." It's not a very satisfying answer but I won't lie to her. I'm nervous about our exposed position myself. What will happen if - when the British wake up and realize we are here?

"It'll be alright. We just need to dig deep trenches."

Officers scurry about in continual movement. We are shuffled partway down the slope on the east side of the hill. Rawlins huddles with Sergeant McGregor, gesturing to various points across the hillside.

Ruskin stakes out the location of trenches we are to build. Alvin steps off the size and placement. I grab a shovel for each of us and Destiny and I start digging like everyone else.

I'm motivated. We all are. I keep glancing at those ships, veritable platforms of cannons, wondering how long we have until they wake up and start shooting. We're through the green layer of grass. Into the moist earth beneath. Feverishly, we heap dirt on the front side of the trench as we dig.

Two feet. Not enough, but we're making progress.

A thunderous clap like a great lightning storm rolls in off the water. On my way down I grab Destiny's arm and drag her with me.

We burrow into the dirt like rodents. Destiny's blue eyes, usually so in control, are wide with fright.

I peek over the front edge just in time to see dirt and grass explode into the air. The hillside is alive. A desperate swarm of men, hurl picks and shovels in all directions and dive for cover.

More blasts reverberate across the fields.

A British warship lights up the night in a flash of blinding light. Several of its cannons ignite spewing orange flame from the side of the frigate. Clouds of smoke expand in eerie billowing color.

The flash illuminates the ship so completely that for a split second, I glimpse the scurrying sailors on board. Cannonballs shriek through the night and bury themselves in the side of the hill. The tremors jolt through me all the way to my teeth.

Destiny clambers over next to me, clinging to my side.

"My rifle's no good," she says, staring past the hillside to the warships beyond.

"I don't know how to fight this."

# Chapter 68

A sleepless night, filled with digging, has left me drowsy and fatigued. Standing in the trench we dug, I stare at a no longer slumbering city, and all my weariness is swept away.

Across the slope in front of us are the catastrophic scars left by the deadly cannonade of last night. Across the water, in weak morning light, Boston comes alive.

British soldiers file to the water's edge. Less than a mile from where we stand, longboats fill. They launch from the slip of ground that holds the city. Oars on either side of the boats lift rhythmically then splash into the water.

"They're coming," Destiny says. As though frozen in some kind of framed painting, hundreds of militia stare in awe at the onslaught coming for us.

I can't swallow my mouth is so dry. I remind myself why I'm here. Maybe Amelia will get her revenge. Her family may not have the guts to do it. I do. I hope I do.

"I'm going to place some markers." Jackson leaps the front edge of the trench and begins counting steps as he paces down the hill.

"How many do you think?" Destiny asks. The transports find the sandy beach below us. Redcoats spill over the sides.

"I don't know, Destiny. Several thousand for sure. They'll make more than one trip with the boats."

The number seems to startle her. Even the most boisterous of our group, those most filled with false bravado are quiet.

The enemy assembles into rigid rectangular shapes. They march to other groups. The formations melt into each other, growing ever larger.

The boats turn back to pick up another load.

"Why don't our cannons fire at them?"

"Too far."

Destiny looks at me doubtfully.

"Too far to cause much damage," I elaborate. "There's only so much gunpowder up there." I nod my head toward the crest of Breed's hill where many militia units labored all night digging a great redoubt complete with firing steps inside, gun emplacements, the works.

Down on the beach the boats return. More and more men feed into the red rectangles making them balloon in size. They stretch all across the shoreline.

Cannons wheeled from boats are pushed into position. Mounted officers dash from place to place.

The crimson forms move and wheel as one great ominous machine. They turn to face our position, a sea of musket barrels.

As our attention is riveted to our enemy forming below us, we are surprised by the thunderous explosion from the enemy warships in the harbor. The ground shakes. The roar deafens me.

On my way down I reach for Destiny's arm but miss as she is faster than me at hitting the bottom of the trench. As my head lowers into the cover of our dugout, I catch a glimpse of thousands of militia diving for cover.

Destiny and I stare at each other. The ground shakes. She grabs me. I think she says something, but the thunderous claps and shrieking cannonballs make sure nothing else can be heard. Even when we're right next to each other.

One or more iron balls land nearby as the ground shakes so thoroughly, I'm afraid the giant bullets are tunneling through the earth to kill us right here in our trench.

Then, as suddenly as it started, the cannonade stops, and the air is as still as a new spring morning.

Clear, lone voices roll up the incline to us.

Up and down the line of trenches, heads peek over the embankments, riveted to the spectacle of those preparing to slaughter us.

The initial voices fade and other, more numerous voices yell the same or similar commands. Drums beat a rhythm. Fifes play that odd martial tune that armies seem to like so much.

The great crimson blocks lurch into motion.

I'm mesmerized by the precision. It's what I've explained to the militia dozens of times, but I've never really seen it. Not at this scale.

The red mass breaks into two. One marches on a direct path to the fort at the top of the hill, to our right. The other marches straight down the beach to our left.

I'll never admit it, but I'm relieved. They aren't marching towards me or my friends.

"I wonder if Helmsley is with them," Jackson says as he too seems entranced by the marching enemy.

I shake my head.

"Those are flank companies."

"Flank?"

"Light and grenadier companies stripped from the regiments. That's their best troops. Helmsley's with the regulars."

I can't help but feel some satisfaction in that. The fact that Helmsley is not among the enemy's best soldiers.

The rhythm of the constant drumbeats drives the marching soldiers before them. Thousands of footfalls tramp on the green earth.

The scarlet machine creeps inexorably forward. I feel like a spectator and point out the British formations.

"That attack is headed for the redoubt at the top of the hill." I point my finger and several of my fellow soldiers follow my descriptions along with Destiny.

The other British formation makes a line straight up the beach to the extreme left of our line. There are thousands of them.

"Can the militia hold?" Destiny asks.

"We'll be alright," I say, but I don't really believe it. Those are professional soldiers. The best they have. Destiny deserves the truth. They all do.

"If they break through, they'll turn and start coming up the hill." I point to the attack down near the water's edge. I have the rapt attention of most of my militia section. Or, maybe the British attack has their attention and I'm just adding commentary.

"Once through the colonial line, they attack us from the fl— the side and rear. Our defenses become useless."

I put a hand on Destiny's shoulder. "We stick together. Whatever happens, we stick together."

I get a subdued nod from her. She clings to me almost like we were physically joined somehow. That's good, but…

What if the British do break through? It's surely a possibility. A bunch of farmer's, fishermen, and shopkeepers against the world's greatest army?

Mentally. I begin to sort out what I'll do if red-coated solders overrun the colonial positions and start scrambling up the hill to kill us.

I hear something… out of place. Jackson nudges me. Down at the tip of the peninsula, Charlestown erupts in fire. Great angry flames greedily lick the hapless wood houses. Black smoke billows into what had been a blue sky.

I'm mesmerized by that until a deafening explosion makes me jump and collide with Destiny. We both re-position ourselves to search down at the water's edge where the British attack was headed before I became entranced by the conflagration consuming Charlestown.

The red enemy formation fires a volley of hundreds of bullets at the patriots. So disciplined. The ranks so straight. The guns leveled in such perfect form. For a moment, I wonder how much of the colonial line can be left.

Within seconds though, the militia responds, and a vicious firing explodes from the entrenchments.

The firestorm in Charlestown plays with the sun. Daylight becomes eerie, ever-shifting hues of charcoal, brown, and blue. In the other direction, clouds of sulfuric smoke from thousands of muskets drifts between the two armies.

The British in their fine red coats… the impeccable, uniformed professionals crumple and fall. The perfect, geometric shapes are ruined. The ground becomes littered with soldiers.

The red line falters. The New England militia continues a withering fire.

It only takes minutes before the unstoppable force scatters and retreats to their starting position far out of range. I'm stunned with surprise.

The men behind the fence and in the shallow diggings near the beach celebrate. The whoops of triumph cut clearly through the air.

The vaunted red line, far out of range rejoin their comrades, but mill about in disarray.

Jackson whoops, already declaring victory. Destiny stares at me quizzically.

I shake my head. "It won't be that easy."

A flurry of activity.

Crimson lines and columns re-form. Thick black smoke continues to billow from the flaming buildings of Charlestown. Ink-colored clouds swell into the sky.

Drums roll. Fifes pipe a marching tune. The giant scarlet rectangles wheel, coordinate, and climb the slope. How do they do that?

Down on our extreme left, where the British attacked the militia line, the green slope is littered with bodies.

The new formations marching up the hill are just as large as before. If we can shoot that many of them and yet still the enemy force is not even diminished…

The flank companies, the ones I told Destiny were the best, they're still there. Marching up the hill. This time though, they aim straight for us.

Their rhythm can be felt as much as heard. Countless feet keep time with beating drums.

Bayonets glint in the sun, thousands of knife-like steel points thrust vertically into the sky.

As though waking myself from a trance, I bolt into action.

Does everyone have enough cartridges? Spread out. Don't leave gaps. Fire to your front and only on command.

No firing 'til the enemy reaches Jackson's markers.

I glance up and down, left and right. Back to the front and I'm alarmed at how the red machine has advanced.

This is absurd. Those marching up the hill to slay us are professionals. This is what they do. They train to kill.

I throw the Brown Bess musket I picked up near Roxbury over the dirt to our front.

A quick glance left. Right.

Everyone in the same stance.

We wait, already sighting down the barrels of our guns.

The red line reaches the marker. The order shrieks through the air.

Fire!

A blaze of flame and smoke bursts from the patriot line.

Dozens of the professional British soldiers fall.

Chaos.

In the tight quarters of the trench, we all bump into each other and fumble with our guns to reload. All knowing we need to load faster than we ever have before. Fast enough we have some way to defend ourselves when our enemy charges those last few yards.

Enemy commanders can be heard shouting above the din of militia and British wounded.

Present!

Fire!

Dozens of bullets strike the dirt mound only inches in front of me. I hear them burrow into the dirt we dug last night and put there to catch the enemy bullets before they could find us.

The New Englanders throw their muskets atop the embankment. The red-coated soldiers rapidly work through their own re-loading routine.

Fire!

Dense, acrid smoke bursts from the line of leveled guns.

Dozens more of the enemy soldiers double over and fall to the ground.

"Don't wait for orders," I yell. "Just shoot!"

A non-stop peppering fire commences from our side.

Enemy soldiers continue to drop.

The redcoats stumble.

At first only a sprinkling break from the formation. Then more.

Then the machine collapses and rushes down the hill to safety.

I grab Destiny.

"Are you alright?"

She nods. Yes. Yes, she's alright.

I let out a deep breath I feel I've been holding since the enemy first marched. I lean against the back of the trench relieved. We did it.

"Don't look now boys…"

Alvin's warning jerks my attention back to what a moment before, was a disintegrating mob.

With amazing rapidity, the chaotic mass of red uniforms begins to take form. The professional, crimson clad enemy transforms.

A retreating mob becomes solid units, ready to attack again.

# Chapter 69

Hours ago, the hillside in front of me was a sloping green lawn. Like one of the aristocratic playing fields where they ride fine horses chasing white balls. All the way to the far end of the peninsula.

Now.

Now strewn across those fields, lie crumpled young men. Young men the same age as me, as Jackson, as Destiny.

Red coats, crossed with white belts, and filled with the sons of far-away parents litter the earth. Innumerable mounds of red and white spread across a canvas of spring green.

So fearsome in their ranks. Now they lie helpless and bleeding.

Desperate moans of agony rise from the ground. The pathetic groans of the dying clamber back to where I watch, speechless.

Weeping. Sobbing. Coughing from blood filled lungs desperately trying to breathe. Occasional shrieks from young men in their final anguished moments of life.

Someone calls for his mother. As though she could hear him, he can't give up. A rattling, cough-punctuated gasp for air. Another call for his mum.

Some of the bodies lay still. Others twist into and out of tight bundles desperately trying to find relief from their suffering.

Some twitch a leg, an arm.

They push themselves half erect as though to escape to safety, then collapse. Or reach up as though to gain the helping hand of a friend or loved one, invisible to the living.

I tear my eyes from the scene.

Destiny's face twists in horror. She buries her head in my chest and weeps.

Jackson catches my gaze with a look of disbelief and wonder at the devastation in front of us.

How is this much suffering even possible? How can so many people, suffer so much in one place? At one moment in time?

Overcome with the enormity of the scene, we all look at one another as though to be sure we're still with our same companions. In the same place. Not in some hellish nightmare existing only in tragic dreams.

Still. We need to protect ourselves.

"Check your powder," I order quietly. "They're reforming."

"Ain't they had enough?" Alvin mutters.

Militia officers scurry up and down behind the lines. They shuffle men here and move a unit there.

Captain Rawlins shouts to be prepared to move closer to the redoubt should that be the focal point of the next assault.

Alvin nods. He looks at me. I motion, yes, I understand.

Jackson bumps into me and brings his head near.

"We're short on powder. This may get very close." My brother looks up then lowers his head again.

"Helmsley's with the regulars. I saw him across the field."

I lean against the wall of the trench. How much can be asked of us?

What if the fighting turns into a brutal melee?

Are we to wield hunting muskets like clubs and defend ourselves against the skewering British bayonets?

I close my eyes looking for an escape. To Blackham.

The moans of the dying fall away. The din of soldiers preparing to kill each other fades. My responsibilities drain and in my mind's eye, I'm back home.

It's spring. I cross the little rock fence into Thornby's apple orchard.

As I do, Amelia steps from behind an apple tree, foliage dancing in the morning light. The breeze tosses her auburn hair, pulling stray strands into her face.

She smiles. At me. A wide smile that speaks of love, and the joy of seeing me.

She throws her arms about my neck and presses her warm lips to mine. Sunlight sparkles in her eyes as she gazes at me. We walk through the spring grass, hand in hand.

Until we find Helmsley.

I open my eyes. I push myself from the back of the trench.

The men stand waiting for the next assault.

"Come on!" I shout. "We're moving."

Destiny looks up in surprise. Our little ten-man unit stares at me but seems prepared to follow.

Up the hill. That's where the attack will come. I know it. The British will attack the crest. The battle will be there. Helmsley will be there.

I spring from the fortifications and wave my arm, hurrying my men out into the open. Up the slope we run.

A small knoll lies off to the right. I point. Lay on the back side, I command Destiny. Shoot over it.

As Destiny breaks for the knoll, I drop my musket and grab her shirt. Her eyes fill with concern, then apprehension, then tears.

"Don't let them close to you! If the redcoats charge, run. Run!"

Tears glisten in the light of the late afternoon sun. She looks as if she will refuse, her head starting to swing in a negative response.

I give her a ferocious look.

She cannot be caught in hand to hand fighting. She can't.

Destiny breaks the stare and dives for the bit of cover I've indicated.

Drums sound the cadence far down the slope. I glance towards the British. One great wave of red rolls for the hilltop.

"Into the trench!"

Again, I glance at the red machine, then back at the redoubt. I grab Jackson's arm. "Help me find Helmsley."

Jackson nods.

Minus Destiny, we all leap into the prepared fortification and jostle among other units to find space for ourselves. Every head I can see, from here down to the beaches on the east where the enemy first attacked this morning, stare at the enemy force, all of it this time, advancing as one.

"Jake, we won't get more than two or three shots."

"Got your tomahawk?"

Jackson nods. "Let's stick together."

I slip my own knife in its sheath, verifying it will not stick if I need it.

The redcoats, in tight formation, bristle with vertically held muskets, like tightly bundled matchsticks. The bayonets catch the western sun, and shimmer like gigantic knife blades waiting to plunge into the soft flesh of their enemies.

The redoubt and trenches become a long row of gun barrels.

Like a giant scarlet wave, the British formations steamroll by the markers set by the militia officers and halt.

Before they can even level their muskets, a clap of mighty thunder explodes from the colonial position. Scores of enemy soldiers fold and drop to the earth.

I duck to reload. The answering cloud of lead, fired from hundreds of British guns, thumps into the dirt inches from me or flies overhead.

I jump and look back to Destiny's position. She's invisible.

Then, her rifle peeks over the mound. She sights down its length, and fires.

The men around me shoot as fast as they can reload. Several answer the British volley. We all duck again as officers shout from the enemy line.

Pre - sent!

Fire!

# Chapter 70

Ker-thwak. The sound is amplified, repeated dozens of times as the bullets from the precise British fire smash into the jumbled earth, stone, and wood hiding me.

I search my haversack. No hidden cartridges. I have nothing left to load. Jackson just shrugs.

Sinking deeper behind the earthen mound, I shudder at the picture of what's coming.

Charge!

I jump and peer over the battlement in front of me.

The red British line springs into motion. A thousand sharp points of steel extend to its front.

Waiting here is suicide. The colonials have nothing to ward off the stabbing thrusts of those bayonets.

I glance back at Destiny. Her head and shoulders lie on the mound of dirt, rifle extended, looking for a target. Smoke explodes from the barrel as she fires.

Another look at the charging enemy. A glance at Jackson.

We have to leave. We can't stay here.

I have no authority to call a retreat. Rawlins will be livid.

My heart hammers in my chest. The red-coated soldiers pound up the incline. Their yells drown every other sound. They sprint against a backdrop of swirling smoke and leaping flames from Charlestown. Drums beat a rapid, staccato rhythm.

A smattering of fire continues, especially from the redoubt, but it's not enough.

Enemy soldiers drop from the intricate formations. Those that follow skirt by them or trip.

Then I see the gap. What appears a solid charging line is made up of many units. Some advance faster than others. Spaces between the different companies begin to appear.

The solid steel curtain loses its unbroken front. The formation becomes more ragged.

A violent explosion and my ears ring. A quick turn toward the redoubt at the crest of the hill.

What was left of their gunpowder must have ignited. Several colonial fighters are thrown out of the little fort, bodies flying like ragdolls. The ground shakes, but the British keep coming.

Seconds now. I grab Jackson. Get my brother, get Destiny, and flee what seems to be sure death.

Then in the gap between two enemy units lurches a panicked gray mare.

The rider, a bold officer with an impeccable red uniform, hurls blasphemous oaths at the terrified horse.

I turn to find Jackson staring into my eyes.

"Follow me," my brother orders.

I yell for Destiny behind us. "Retreat!" I scream at her. "Retreat!"

Then I spring from the diggings. Up and over the mound of earth on the front side.

"Now!" Jackson yells as he leaps into the fray.

He drives a shoulder into one British regular bowling the man over on his side. As my brother passes the next, he clips the back of his leg with the tomahawk. Then he spins and drives his hunting knife into the man's throat.

Jackson yanks back and swings his tomahawk to his left, catching another enemy soldier in the side of the neck.

A bayonet drives towards him. Jackson spins, turns a somersault past his attacker's feet then puts his tomahawk into the man from behind.

I'm frozen. This is madness.

Firing muskets at each other from fifty yards apart is one thing. But this.

It can't be my brother. It can't.

Voices climb in volume and pitch. Men cry. Men shout. Officers scream unheard commands.

The militia fire slows to erratic popping of hunting muskets as ammunition dwindles.

I take a deep breath and launch into the melee.

An enemy aims to skewer me with steel. I manage to parry the thrust with my gun barrel then swing the musket, breaking the wood stock over the soldiers back.

Searching the confusion for my brother, I find him standing, staring at Helmsley.

Jackson's shirt sticks to him, grotesque with the stains of other men's blood. His face and hands are spattered. He turns to stare at me then hands me the tomahawk.

"Make it quick. We're starting to retreat."

Up the hill, militia troops spill out the back of the redoubt. Pushed before the unstoppable flood of British, they careen down the north side of the hill.

I take the tomahawk, the handle slippery in my hands. Helmsley has fought his unruly mount into a stalemate. The horse prances, desperate to get away. Helmsley holds it, forcing it into a miniature dance of despair with no destination.

He doesn't even see me coming.

Yelling and ordering others into the fray he doesn't see Amelia's revenge mere steps away.

Then attracted to the speeding object heading for him, he turns to stare at me.

Instant recognition.

Helmsley pulls his hand from the other side of his body.

It holds a pistol. He smiles.

I push myself. There will be no other chance.

I strain to accelerate the last two steps. I leap up and into the captain.

No pistol shot.

We tumble from the horse, arms and legs tangling with one another.

A grunt as the captain lands hard.

A mad scramble to find my feet.

Where's the gun?

Helmsley springs upright. His hands are extended, but empty.

With frenzied twists of his head, he too searches for the weapon.

There it is. Nearer to Helmsley.

He stretches for it. I jump to within striking distance, menacing with the tomahawk.

Helmsley returns to an upright stance. In a blur of movement, he pulls his saber from its scabbard.

Surprise is gone. The advantage I'd seen for myself evaporates. Now my enemy has the upper hand.

I feel the fear. And the doubt.

Helmsley smiles.

"Well boy. Your chance at revenge. Not what you thought?"

With a quick stroke, he stabs the sword towards my middle.

I fling my arm with the tomahawk.

More instinct than anything, but the tomahawk catches the blade and sends it harmlessly off to the side.

"Very good," Helmsley taunts. "Take another try." He whirls his arm to the air and slashes down towards my neck.

Heart in my throat, I dive and wave my weapon in the general direction of Helmsley's blow.

A clang rings in my ears as the sword hits the tomahawk. I fall to the ground, looking up.

The saber blade breaks in two. The broken piece flies and sticks in the ground beside my face.

"Kill him!" Helmsley yells, staring past me.

A soldier approaches, ready to thrust a bayonet into me. From the corner of my eye, a blur flies into view and puts a knife into the soldier's throat.

Jackson.

Destiny screams. I jerk my head and find her.

She stares at me, face filled with horror. Her rifle must be empty.

Destiny drops it butt first to the ground and grabs the barrel as though to swing it like a club.

I spring to my feet. Helmsley turns, the pistol staring into my face.

I stop and retreat a step.

"No revenge for you, I guess."

His foot shifts.

His hand swings mere inches, pointing the pistol at Destiny.

I shout at him. His war is with me, not Destiny.

The pistol fires.

Not again. This can't happen again. I've been unable to handle life after Amelia's death. What will I do without Destiny?

I stare at her. She stands as though unhurt.

Back at Helmsley. Jackson's knife protrudes from the man's arm as the captain's other hand clutches at it.

Blood pours from the wound, dripping from his fingers.

The captain straightens. He spreads his arms, the one with the knife embedded in it trembling.

"You wouldn't murder a gentleman."

"You never were a gentleman."

In a surreal dream, I gather all the injustice suffered into one blow. Amelia's face shines so bright in front of me, I can see nothing else. She seems to reach for me, talk to me as though I could hear. She gazes into my eyes.

I plunge the tomahawk into the captain's chest with all the force I can muster.

Helmsley's eyes become distant, but still stare at me. His arms move as though to reach for something they can't find.

He drops to his knees.

His mouth moves as though he would speak.

No sound comes out.

Helmsley falls to the earth and lies, motionless.

# Chapter 71

I'm here. But I'm not.

Like a disembodied spirit, I stare at a motionless and very dead Helmsley.

I've done it. I've killed him.

A vigorously yanking on my arm makes me stumble.

"We've got to go!" Jackson pleads.

Destiny grabs my other arm.

"Are you alright?"

"We've got to go!" Jackson yells. He leans in the direction of the retreating militia.

My brother jerks his knife free of Helmsley's arm, but the tomahawk is too deep. It can't be retrieved.

More soldiers pour up the hill. A second wave it seems.

Jackson feints and stabs an enemy threatening us. I grab the musket from the dead soldier.

Together we sprint back toward the militia lines.

Enemy formations approach the hilltop from different angles. They threaten to converge, to cut off all escape.

A bayonet thrusts toward Destiny. Jackson tumbles, somersaults and knifes the attacker.

I lose myself as I club and thrust at nameless, faceless enemies.

Uphill the opening threatens to disappear.

Escape or die. The battle rages too hot to surrender.

A great leap. Over the earthen mound, the timbers, the stones.

The converging redcoat soldiers spill into the trench just behind us. Their forward movement stops as they close left and right to fill the dug-in defenses.

Destiny's hand finds mine.

Muskets still fire. The screams of men still fill the air. The battle still rages.

Gaining some distance from the enemy, I stop and search the colonial positions.

Where's the rest of Captain Rawlins' company?

The redoubt at the apex of the hill now swarms with British red.

Militia retreats in disparate groups. Some in disarray. Some orderly.

Scattered across the green slopes, clusters of men viciously try to kill one another. What rages is a lopsided contest out of the reach of the New England amateurs. All semblance of order breaks down. Pockets of red struggle in a lethal clash with pockets of drab brown and gray.

A sprinkling of men on horseback dash about. They call to anyone who will listen.

Riderless horses race madly through the tumult, reins streaming wildly beside them.

Smoke drifts. Muskets fire singly or in small groups. A cacophony of men's voices, scream, order, beg.

I search the position we dug last night.

The remainder of Rawlins' company only now begins to tumble out of it and run for safety.

In my mind, my studies alert me to the danger.

The British have forced the main company out of the trenches and is attempting to drive uphill. Their success will encircle those patriots only now beginning to flee their posts.

The company, my company, becomes a disorganized rabble. They don't walk, they don't trot. They flee.

Rawlins gallops around them. He dashes to the front of the throng of terrified militiamen.

He reins in and waves his arms. He screams commands. He throws insults to their honor.

A handful of men slow. Still, they continue their way toward the rear and perceived safety. Rawlins pleads and threatens.

His arms fly into the air, high above his head.

As from an invisible hand, a ragged hole tears into the captain's coat. Then another.

Blood spreads across his chest. He clasps both hands to the wounds. Leaning to his right, Rawlins topples from his horse.

The shock moves even the racing company. The men pause, realizing the captain is now a casualty of war.

Captain Rawlins. The one who backed Destiny at every step. He'd been loyal, not only to the cause for which he fought, but to those under his command as well. Ever-present on the field of battle.

Destiny leans into me, her hands over her mouth.

In a burst of inspiration, I race to the group milling about the body of their officer.

Sergeant McGregor stares at Rawlins. The disorganized men look alternately at their dead leader and the still advancing red line. They shift uneasily.

"Do your men have powder!" I yell. I sprint the last few strides, stopping to face McGregor.

"Aye!"

The encircling British have crossed the trench. Over the thunderous struggle, I can hear their officer shouting at them, reforming them.

A quick glance back up the hill confirms my fears. Those New Englanders, the ones late to leave their defenses, they will never escape if this British unit is not stopped.

I shout at the company of confused militia.

"Company! Form line!"

I throw out my arm to indicate a position.

No one moves.

"Company! Form line!" My voice cracks as I search for volume.

Jackson appears, and Destiny. They push and cajole, and within seconds, I have a firing line facing the British.

I open my mouth to give orders then freeze. How do you order a firing retreat?

What commands? We've never trained for such an exercise. I've never even seen the maneuver.

Someone crashes into my side. Destiny. She looks up at me.

"Make it work. You can do it."

"Jake?" Jackson's voice calls.

I glance again at the closing enemy.

The red-coated English march shoulder to shoulder. Their muskets slant forward, bayonets positioned to drive into any opposition.

From behind the bright crimson line, drum rolls beat out a steady cadence. The soldiers march in perfect time.

The beats of the drum. The stamping feet.

I return my stare to the men I ordered into a line. I'm committed.

Double line. A double line is what we need.

The orders spill from my mouth too quiet. I catch my breath, re-animate myself.

I push the doubts from my mind. It's too late to give in to them.

I yell the orders again and men shuffle into new positions.

More commands.

The first line kneels.

"First rank!"

"Pre-sent!"

# Chapter 72

"Fire!"

A torrent of angry flame and acrid smoke erupts from the kneeling soldiers.

My gaze burns through the boiling, sulfur fog as it rises. The Atlantic breeze pushes it from my front.

Redcoats crumple and fall. It spoils the precision of their formation.

Officers shout orders. A handful of the enemy scurries faster and the gaps fill in.

They appear untouched.

What should the command be now?

I stutter.

*Just tell the men what they need to do.*

"First rank! Retreat ten paces!" I yell the order, bending forward in an effort to somehow extend my voice all the way down the line.

The kneeling rank stands. They dive between the gaps in the standing men behind them and dash to the rear.

From the corner of my eye, I can see several of the retreating men pulling the ramrods that will allow them to reload.

It's what I wanted. But I didn't know how to issue the command.

Will they actually stop at ten paces? I say a quick prayer and make ready to beg if necessary.

"Second rank!"

"Pre-sent!"

"Fire!"

While the British units had regained momentum, the second volley causes them to stutter.

I can see their faces now.

Some experienced, grizzled, hardened soldiers. Others soft and not yet old enough to shave, fresh from home.

The details of their uniforms sharpen into focus. Pins and clasps hold the imperious costumes in place. Brass buckles. Small haversacks over the shoulders.

Several redcoats trip over their fellow soldiers who have fallen.

I throw a nervous glance behind me. The men I sent back ten paces stand. Their line is straight. They're reloading.

Jackson springs about them communicating something. Jackson, who doesn't believe in military formations, who doesn't know proper commands.

Again, I yell the orders to move back. The rank of soldiers who just fired the second volley turn. The retreating men file through the gaps, reforming behind the line that's now loaded and ready.

"Front rank! Kneel!"

Surely that's all wrong, but each man drops to one knee.

"Fire!"

Bullets find their mark. Enemy soldiers fall. Lines grow ragged.

The British continue to close the distance.

Another ten-pace retreat.

The enemy officer flashes his sword in the air. He's given constant orders and instructions during their advance, all unintelligible from across the field.

This order though. This one I hear.

The English soldiers lower their muskets, pointing their bayonets at us.

"Charge!"

Now there are seconds.

"Present!"

"Fire!"

"Retreat ten paces!"

I don't try to command the reloading sequence. I'll never get it all out in time.

Men stumble as they fall back, reloading the cumbersome weapons as they run.

I fly to the rear rank, now ready to fire.

"Kneel! Kneel!" I wave my arm for emphasis.

The running men dash through the openings.

The red block, bristling with knife-like extensions looms close.

Twenty-five yards.

Most in the rear rank continue to reload.

Those finishing point their guns at the coming enemy, not waiting for the order.

Twenty yards.

We can't wait longer. Already the British are too close.

A few more in my rear rank finish. Their muskets fly to their shoulders as they aim.

Fifteen yards.

"Both ranks!" I scream so hard my voice cracks.

"Fire!"

A thunderous explosion shakes the air. Smoke billows between the two armies.

I'm blind. My lungs revolt at the sulfurous air.

I run, trying to find an edge to the smoke.

Atlantic air pushes at the black cloud.

The veil of spent powder drifts up and inward.

Dozens of the enemy lie upon the ground.

The reverberations of the musket explosions fade away. Moans and screams of wounded men pierce the air.

They lay heaped upon the earth in front of the British formation. Those still standing have been brought to a halt. They appear uncertain. Unable or unwilling to clamber over the dead and wounded in order to continue.

"Reload! Reload! Reload!" I'm screaming. If that British officer gets his men moving again we're dead.

In a frantic run, I regain my position, urging the militia to prepare. We don't have bayonets. With empty guns, we stand here defenseless.

As the drifting air clears, the enemy remains.

They stumble and fall over the mass of their fallen comrades.

They've lost all momentum, all drive. Haplessly, they search around, questioning.

"Retreat."

It isn't screamed like the order to charge. Even so, at this distance the voice is clear and unmistakable. A subdued British officer calls the order to his men.

I watch them to be certain.

Enemy soldiers back away.

It seems they'll retreat without firing a shot. We'll let them.

The adrenaline fades and I sink to my knees.

The men celebrate with a cheer. I peer up the hillside at the still retreating colonials.

The company, my company, stopped the encirclement.

The colonists failed to hold Breed's Hill, and my company will have to retreat with them.

New England may have lost this battle, but I've won mine.

# Chapter 73

A raging fire has been quenched. That's what it feels like.

The British seem content to hold the position at the top of the hill. They control all the works we constructed and then defended.

Even the enormous blaze that consumed Charlestown has quelled. Black smoke still fills the sky, but only occasional flashes of orange flames are visible through it. Those poor people that lived there.

Thousands of militia stream toward the head of the peninsula. The battle's over. The enemy won.

The doubts, the shame of ending so any lives, even if they are the enemy, try to find place in my thoughts. Not now though. I push them away.

My arm encircles Destiny's shoulders. Jackson keeps pace on my other side. Focus on that. The two people who have supported me more than all others. And they have. Especially today.

It stings though, the fact we lost the first battle.

"What will happen now?" Destiny asks.

"We lost a position, Destiny, not the war." I throw my mind back into its military persona. In the end, all that work I did to teach myself military tactics really worked. Roxbury was the exception; it doesn't invalidate all my studies.

"Will everyone keep fighting though? Or will they think it's lost?"

"Wars are long. It takes many battles to win a war. No one's going anywhere."

"We'll get them next time," Jackson adds, still enthusiastic despite the defeat.

Jackson. His shirt is still bloody. Looking at him — he would scare me to death if he were my enemy.

Shadows are long as the sun droops towards the western horizon. We drift along the road, tired, the adrenaline waning.

Jackson freezes in a sudden stop and I turn to stare at him.

"We need muskets," he says as though he just noticed.

Destiny clutches hers in her hand. "Not me."

"Jacob and me lost ours. Should be easy to pick up a couple. I'll catch up with you later."

"Jackson, no!" Destiny warns her friend, my brother, as though she could stop him once his mind is made up. "It could be dangerous out there. They're picking up their wounded."

"She's right Jackson," I add with little conviction. He never listens to me.

Already a couple of steps closer to the battlefield, Jackson spreads his arms as if to ask, 'what can they do to me?'

"I'll be careful," he says, then he's gone.

As Destiny and I both watch him, I waver between concern and resignation.

"Think he'll be alright?" Destiny asks.

"Any small group of redcoats out there will have met their match if they tangle with Jackson."

It's more serious than that of course, but what are we going to do?

We near the head of the peninsula. Groups of militia congregate along the way. They start fires, scrounge and share to find a meal.

A tired and bent man with a grizzled face shuffles through the disorganized masses. There's something about him, his posture, his gait. I stop and watch as he leaves one small camp and enters the one only steps away. I'm captivated by the mournful sound of his entreaty.

"Who you with?" he asks the group gathered around the fire. "You seen a James from Newtown? James from Newtown?"

His head swivels as he tries to peer into the eyes of every man within earshot.

Who is James I wonder? A son? A brother?

The old man looks at Destiny and me. "Find your people. Might be lookin' just like me."

He shuffles off, repeating his questions to others who listen, then shake their heads no.

Before I can get myself started again, another, younger man, makes his way into the same camp.

John. John from Worcester. Anyone seen him? Anyone know John from Worcester?

No. No one's seen him.

The scene threatens to bring back the dread, the sorrow this day will bring to mind for months, years maybe. I turn away and continue up the road with Destiny.

The militia thins out and falls behind. A narrow road twists and dips through the countryside.

The lighted windows of a farmhouse spill warm yellow light out onto the dark silhouettes of towering trees.

I don't know why. Fatigue. Overwhelming emotions. I stop and stare at the scene, wondering who's inside the house. What are they having for supper? Are all members of the family there and accounted for? Do they know how precious their time together is?

Destiny clutches my arm and smiles up at me.

"You really did save those men who were trying to retreat. In the end, all your training and ideas about formations worked."

"Not my ideas, but thank you."

"Do you feel vindicated?"

I think about that for a minute.

"That doesn't really seem very important."

"Really? What about your dreams of a military career?"

"I don't know what I want."

"Then why are you here Jake?"

"Because you're here." The answer came so quick it startles even me. I haven't really thought about it. One thing's kind of led to another and here I am. Not sure I would be if Destiny were back in her cabin in Blackham though.

"And, all the ideas you've been trying to teach me," I add. "Freedom. No titles or social classes."

I seem to have caught Destiny off-guard as she is quiet now. I know she's glad. I always felt these things; it just took her example to make me think they might be worth fighting for. That there was even a hint of a chance that fighting might do some good.

"You avenged Amelia."

That makes me nod with satisfaction. "I think she knows, do you?"

Another pause.

"Yes. I think so." Destiny gives my arm a squeeze. "You deserved her. And somewhere she is pleased with the loyalty you showed. So am I."

I fumble as I withdraw my arm from the crook of Destiny's. I wrap both arms about her shoulders and pull her close.

She fits, warm and safe, right next to me.

"I love you, Jacob Greyson."

I sigh, but I don't hesitate with my reply.

"And I love you Destiny Morris."

*If this moment could last forever...*

"If we didn't have a war to win…" Destiny doesn't finish the thought and I wonder about it. How would I finish it? What would I wish for if we were free from all obligation? Where would we go? What would we do?

"Well, at least we're a team."

"Mmm. What are my orders, Officer Greyson?"

"Stay alive. And stay with me."

Made in the USA
Middletown, DE
21 April 2024

53296841R00213